LION HEART

Hearts of the Highlands
Book Four

Paula Quinn

DRAGONBLADE
PUBLISHING, INC.

ARE YOU SIGNED UP FOR DRAGONBLADE'S BLOG?

You'll get the latest news and information on exclusive giveaways, exclusive excerpts, coming releases, sales, free books, cover reveals and more.

Check out our complete list of authors, too!

No spam, no junk. That's a promise!

Sign Up Here

www.dragonbladepublishing.com

Dearest Reader;

Thank you for your support of a small press. At Dragonblade Publishing, we strive to bring you the highest quality Historical Romance from the some of the best authors in the business. Without your support, there is no 'us', so we sincerely hope you adore these stories and find some new favorite authors along the way.

Happy Reading!

CEO, Dragonblade Publishing

CHAPTER ONE

The village of Sevenoaks, England
Late summer
The Year of Our Lord 1348

ELIAS MOVED SLOWLY around the vine-covered wall of a small shed and looked toward the apothecary shop at the end of the market village of Sevenoaks. He set his steady gaze on the beautiful lass inside the shop, busy with a customer. The sight of her made him want to smile. He didn't know her. He'd never met her before, but just looking at her made him feel good, refreshed, hopeful.

"Let us just go inside and speak to her, Eli!" his closest friend, Brother Simon of the Carmelite order, urged quietly. "I'm weary and the sun is hot on my head. I want to go to the inn and eat and rest. You did not say anything about visiting here, or about this lass when you asked me to come on this pilgrimage with you."

Elias had stopped listening soon after the brother started speaking. Which was often.

"She is not divine, Eli."

"How can ye be so sure, Simon?" Elias whispered without taking his eyes off her. "Does she not remind ye of an angel? Look at the kindness in her eyes, the genuine concern she shows to that woman. Look at her elegant hands, her graceful movements."

Instead of going in and asking her for what he needed, Elias watched her from outside like a fool, *Eli the Lion Heart* afraid to go talk to a lass. But she was unlike any woman he'd ever seen before.

In the midst of a forest of plants hanging all around her, she was slight of frame, not terribly tall, and a bit too thin. Her bosom was humble and her flaxen hair was straight, falling around her heart-shaped face. He wasn't sure if it was her sapphire blue eyes, kind and compassionate toward her customer, or her smile, genuine and beguiling, tempting him to join her from his hiding place.

His eyes followed the course of her fingers to the customer's shoulder where she gave a little squeeze.

"Can I help you, my lord?" A male's voice shattered his thoughts of her. Elias looked toward the doorway of the shed and faced an old man carrying an armful of plants in their pots. His dark brown eyes looked around Elias to Simon. "Father?"

"Brother," the bald brother corrected with a friendly smile on his scarred face. The longest scar went from his right ear to the top of his mouth and turned a bit pink when he smiled. Another, on the other side, was a bit deeper from his left temple to under the middle of his left eye. The last was smaller beneath his lower lip. "My companion here is—"

"I..." Elias stepped forward, finishing for himself. "I was just...ehm...d'ye need aid with those plants?" He reached for the pots and the old man let him take them.

"What is it you need?"

Many things. Elias wasn't truly sure. When he had returned home from fighting in King David II's army two years ago, he sought peace and quiet and became one of the seven shepherds of the MacPherson's sheep. Each herded their flock and kept to themselves. Which was exactly what he wanted. His days were good but, in the night, he'd suffered many afflictions of war: nightmares, battles replaying over and over in his head, darkness, and gloom. Terrible things that he had faced head on and without fear now made him tremble and cry out in the night. Many mornings found him sprawled out on the floor because he couldn't fit under the bed.

"I have trouble sleepin'," Elias told him.

"Terrible trouble," Simon added.

Elias shrugged one shoulder and turned to give Simon a little glare. He didn't need all of England knowing that darkness and his dreams stripped him of his courage, and starved him of sleep.

"Go on, then." The man pointed toward the apothecary shop. "Lily will get you what you need."

Lily. Elias almost repeated it out loud. It sounded beautiful in his head. He gritted his teeth. He didn't want to go in yet. But he needed help. And this was the only village for fifty leagues with a market with an apothecary shop.

Presently though, he'd prefer fighting rather than walking into *this* shop, to talk to *this* lass. What the hell was the matter with him? He'd spoken to lasses before. Many of them were more beautiful than this one. But Lily appeared as a soothing balm for his troubled, weary soul.

She'd stopped his heart when he first saw her just a little while ago. He'd been mesmerized by her grace and beauty. And the more he looked, the more stricken he became. He had seen much in the wars with France and England; violent, ugly things he tried to forget.

But he hadn't seen much compassion, or any genuinely kind gazes. Not like hers. It drew him.

He stepped inside the shop behind Simon and looked around...at everything but her. It was a cozy place with hundreds of different sized, variously painted clay jars set up on dozens of shelves. Candles hung from chains and sat bunched together on small tables. Boxes and sacks were pushed up against walls and plants grew everywhere.

"Set the pots down at your feet," the man directed from outside, busy with something else. "I will be there in a moment." Was he her father?

Elias did as instructed, and then straightened once again. He was ready to leave. He would go and never look back—if he could just go now. His eyes found her standing behind a long table staring back at him.

"What can I do for you today?"

It felt as if he were swallowing his heart when she smiled up at him. Her voice was like satin against his ears. Looking into her eyes close up made him a little lightheaded. He counted three different shades of blue when the candlelight hit at a certain angle.

"I…" he cleared his throat and began again. "I am havin' trouble sleepin'."

"You are a Scot," she said softly and glanced at the old man as he entered the shop.

Hell. He'd forgotten to use his King's English. He rarely used it anymore, and only in certain circumstances that would aid his Highland endeavors. "Aye. D'ye not serve Scots here?"

"Do not take offense at her words, kind sir," the old man hurried forward. "Of course, we serve Scots. We serve whoever needs us. Pardon me, I am Richard Bennett, the village apothecary, and this is my wife, Lily. Lily, some chamomile tea for the stranger."

Elias stared at him for one more moment then closed his mouth. His wife? Had he heard right? Did the old man say *his wife*?

He wondered why her true father would sentence her to this life. His gaze found her again, reaching for a blue jar high up on one of the shelves.

He went to her and reached over her to pluck the jar from the shelf. He handed it to her over her shoulder and looked into her eyes as she turned to thank him. He didn't want her to be married. He was supposed to respect her vows—and he did. He was supposed to forget her and walk away—but he didn't.

She turned, almost in his arms. He stepped away. What the hell was wrong with him? He turned to Simon and almost asked for help. Was he having a breakdown? He'd heard of such things happening to men of battle. Sleepless nights was one of the symptoms. That's what he had come here for. Medicine. Not a woman. Especially not another man's wife.

She weighed some of the herb on a scale and then folded the amount in a sheet of parchment.

He nodded when she instructed him on how to prepare the tea then pulled out his pouch of coins to pay and leave, but the man—her husband, stopped him.

"Are you staying in Sevenoaks or just passing through?"

"Both," Elias answered. "We are passin' through, but we are stayin' fer a few days."

"Where are you and your priest—"

"Brother," Simon corrected again with a sigh. "Notice the brown robes, the bald head."

The apothecary shrugged his sagging shoulders. "Where are you staying?"

"The Pheasant Inn."

"Pah!" the old man breathed out emphatically. "The place is not fit for pigs. We have a bed in our home. You will stay there."

"Nae." Elias backed away. He couldn't stay and ignore the apothecary's wife. And what if he awoke tonight from one of his night terrors and she saw him? "We have already made—"

"Do you need me to speak to Estrid, the owner of the inn?" Richard the apothecary offered.

"Nae." Elias laughed softly. "Dinna speak to anyone on my account." He looked at Mrs. Lily Bennett and shook his head. She was forbidden. He needed to leave.

"Look," said the old man. "You are strong and able bodied. I could use your help around here, stranger. Both of you. Stay for as many days as you have planned, free of charge."

"God is good," Simon said with a smile. "What do you need us to do?"

"Nae," Elias interrupted, glaring at his friend. "We truly canna stay. I dinna mean to be rude, but I will—"

"You can start by telling us where you are from and your names."

"Brother Simon," Simon said pointing at himself, and then at Elias, completely ignoring his friend's scowl. "Elias MacPherson of Invergarry, a commander in—"

"We arena stayin' long." Elias glanced at the apothecary's wife and found her sizing him up.

She creased her delicate brow at him and turned away, looking rather disappointed.

Elias wanted to defend his curtness and his stubborn refusal to stay, but he remained quiet.

"We have supper three hours after sunset," Richard told them. "My wife will not serve you if you are late. Please come inside before midnight so we know the door to our home is locked.

"Now, please go with Lily so she can show you where we live. After that, you can return here and move those sacks against the wall out to the back shed."

Go with Lily. His wife.

Elias hated that she was married. He didn't care what she thought of him, whether she disapproved of his behavior or not. How was he being led into this? How was Simon helping? He would ask his friend when they were alone.

For now, he watched the shape of her, the rhythm of her movements as she walked ahead of them and led them outside.

"'Tis the house there, beyond the church. The one with the red roof." She pointed to a small two-story house nestled within a vale about a half-mile off the road. "Come, I will show you the easiest route to it."

Elias reluctantly followed her, quietly swearing at Simon's back. The brother was supposed to be protecting him from dangers such as another man's wife!

He never considered taking a wife of his own. He'd had no time for love. He wasn't always sure he would live to see the next day. Why make a woman a widow? But *now*, now that he was drawn to a lass, she had to be married?

They passed a large mill to the right of the road and then the church to the left. They walked through the shallow vale and approached the house. Elias noted that it was a longhouse, a certain type of construction some merchants used to keep their shops and their homes attached.

Simon seemed to read his mind—which, irritatingly, he did often—and asked the question. "Why did your husband not build your shop into the house?"

"He owns both properties," she replied. "He wanted the house to be a bit more private. His workshop is within and he needs quiet most times."

Aye, the house was private, tucked away in the trees and ferns, he thought, as they came upon one of the tall, triangular frames of the house, made of oak. This frame was one of three pairs. There was a large, open-shuttered window and a smaller window above it built into walls made of stone and wattle and daub. He could tell this was the side of the house. He couldn't see the front from here, for lavender and herbs, vines and plants grew as high as the first window, bursting in colors of purple, white, and green on either side of him. They followed a narrow dirt path surrounded by flora and herbs to the side door, where Lily let them inside.

Her home. The door opened into a kitchen. The room was neat and stocked with fruit and various leaves hanging from the high oak frames and rafters to dry. Some leaves dried above a heavy oak table set in the center with two chairs around it.

For her and her husband. Elias grimaced at the arrow it shot at him.

Like the shop, there were plants everywhere. A lean, gray cat sat on the floor and meowed when they entered.

"Ehm…" Simon leaped back into the doorway. "I do not like cats."

Lily smiled as she passed him. "You need not worry, Brother. Pip does not like people. She will stay out of your way."

Elias grinned when he, too, passed him and followed his hostess out of the kitchen and into a sitting room bathed in sunlight from the large open windows. There were chairs and stools, and even a small place for books. Plants hung from the rafters and from two long, separate, wooden railings across the second landing. The floors were made of cobblestone and clay.

So much greenery in the house felt warm and fresh to Elias. The way she made him feel.

"That archway leads to Richard's workshop." She pointed the opposite way, to a small, open doorway. She didn't move toward it. "If you wish to look inside, you will have to ask my husband."

Another dart, though this one was cushioned by the loyalty she showed toward the man to whom she was married. A good trait to have, that.

A narrow stairway led to the second landing, where two bedrooms sat side by side. The only wall between them was a colorfully painted curtain that was draped open so the inhabitants of the beds could see each other. He thought of lying in bed looking at her. He would rather have her *in* his bed. More hanging plants. Was one her bed, and one her husband's?

Elias liked the house. It was warm. Like her.

She ascended the stairs and showed them to one of the bedrooms. Hers. He could smell her scent more on this side of the partition. He and Simon would have to sleep together. Elias didn't care. He cared about the other bed. The bed where she would have to sleep with her husband.

"This is where you will sleep."

Elias smiled at the sound of her dulcet voice and angled his head to look at her. "I..." He couldn't stay here. Seeing her all the time would be difficult. Did he want to put himself through it? "We dinna mean to put ye oot."

"You are not putting me out," she reassured with a delicate smile that hit him like a kick to the guts, knocking the breath out of him. "And please call me Lily. We are like a family here."

"Lily." It fell from his lips on a soft whisper. He moved without thinking and bumped his calves into her bed. He smiled again, feeling like a peach-faced babe for the first time in years.

"Lily," Simon's voice broke through the spell he was falling under. "I am curious—"

"About my marriage?" she asked, interrupting, her smile intact.

No! Elias' smile vanished. It would make her feel uncomfortable in her own home. They were strangers. It wasn't their place to know.

"Aye," Simon answered mercilessly. "What is your age, my dear?"

"Brother Simon," Elias tried to stop him. "I think we should be gettin' back to the shop. Richard needs us."

"Aye," his soon-to-be friend-no-more said, "but I'm sure another moment or two will not hurt."

It would hurt Elias!

"I do not mind answering," Lily told Simon, dipping her chin to her chest while her gaze fell back to Elias. "I am a score and one."

"And your husband?" Simon pushed.

Elias wanted to strike him. Did one go to hell for striking a man of God?

"He is sixty and eight."

Simon cringed and Elias sat back onto the bed, more stunned than he thought he would be.

"Why were you bound to an old man?"

Elias closed his eyes and ran his hand down his face. "Simon, must ye—"

"I once belonged to a man named Bertram Chisholm, a relative on his Scot's mother's side, or was it his English father's side?" She threw up her hands, not sure which it was. "To the Bishop of Oxford, Louis Edmundson."

Elias stopped her by putting the tips of his fingers to her arm. "What do ye mean ye belonged to him? Ye were his wife?"

She shook her head no. "He took me from my father while we visited the market in Hastings. I was ten and two."

Elias listened with a dark scowl and fury twisting his belly.

"Did he do the worst to you, lass?" Simon asked.

Elias buried his head in his hands.

"No," she answered coolly and on the barest whisper.

Elias almost didn't hear her and lifted his head.

"By God's divine grace, Bertram suffered a terrible wound to his nethers. It did not kill him, but it made him angry…very angry at me."

Elias wanted to sink even lower or bound up off the bed and gather her in his arms and comfort her, though she didn't seem to need comforting.

"Lily" Simon said, "I was once a slave, beaten often by my master until Eli's father saved me. I truly understand some of your horrors. How did you escape him?"

"We came here two years ago and the people of the village saw that I was a mistreated slave. They tried to help me but he wounded many of them.

"My father was an apothecary like Richard. It made Richard and me friends, for he reminded me of my father. Against Bertram's orders not to, I escaped his overseeing eyes at night and helped Richard tend to the people Bertram had hurt. I pleaded with them not to test Bertram further. But Richard did not give up. He brought Father

Benedict to my door in the dead of night and married me there and then. Then he threatened to get the church and the bishop after Bertram if he harassed us any further. The beast finally left me alone. He soon became bored of being here, and left without a word."

"And ye stayed with Richard," Elias said, not realizing he'd spoken aloud until she looked at him.

"What would you have done, Mr. MacPherson?"

"Elias, please," he insisted with a swallow. "In truth, I dinna know what I would have done. I could only hope that I would remain, but I have never had to make such a decision, so I dinna know fer certain. But I will tell ye this, lass, ye are more worthy of heaven than anyone I know." As if he'd just realized how utterly pitiful he sounded, he coughed into his hand. He caught Simon staring at him, slack jawed. "What I mean is—"

"Thank you," she said meaningfully. "That is very kind to my ears."

"Aye, to mine, as well," Simon said, still gaping at him. After an instant, he grinned and patted Elias on the back. "We should go see about speaking to Estrid."

"Who?" Elias asked.

"Come on, then," his friend said, pulling him toward the stairs. "I think you need some air."

CHAPTER TWO

LILY STAYED BEHIND, outside her front door, watching the two men make their way on foot to The Pheasant Inn. An odd pair. One was tall, broad, and handsome, but mostly mute and looking as if he'd swallowed something foul. The other was much shorter, slim in his robes, bald and badly scarred on his face. He seemed to be the intelligent one of the two.

She turned away for a moment when the dark-haired Scot turned around to have one last look at her.

She hadn't forgotten what he said. She was worthy of heaven. Her heart raced a little. No one had ever said anything like that to her before. Nothing that made her want to smile like a child going off to play. She wasn't certain what to do about it. She knew she had to stop, but she didn't know how.

She would admit that looking at Elias MacPherson was like lying back in the grass on a clear night and seeing stars light up the sky. His beauty was simply…resplendent. He was tall, with strong, straight legs and wide shoulders. Behind soft waves of dark hair, his startling blue eyes glittered with tiny shards of silver, ringed by long, lush, dark lashes. He was chiseled by the Master's hand from face to foot.

She thought about every part of him, like how the muscles in his thighs had trembled and bulged while lowering Richard's potted herbs. She remembered the heat and hardness of his body when he stood close behind her and reached for the jar of chamomile.

She stepped away from the house and headed back to the shop. To her husband. The man she loved. And she did love Richard. She would always stand by him and help him. She would never leave him for a sweet frame and some pretty words.

Richard deserved more than that. He'd saved her from *The Savage Scot*. That was what everyone had called Bertram Chisholm. For he had killed poor John Fenley, the tanner, for tripping over the beast's long claymore while he ate supper in the tavern. He had forced his desires on Deirdre one of the tavern's serving girls and then insisted she was a deceitful harlot who should be banished from the village. When Lily stood up to him about Deirdre's fate, she was struck in the face and put to the ground. When his orders to banish Deirdre were not carried out, he killed Roger the reeve, the senior official under the crown to oversee the peasants, and announced himself the new reeve, then banished Deirdre himself.

When Lily stood up to him for the villagers, they'd grown fond of her and took care of her when her beatings were severe.

She reached the shop now and saw her dear husband gathering sage and comfrey and smiled. Where would her life be now if he hadn't stepped into it?

"I showed them the house, my dear," she called to him merrily. "They have gone to speak to Estrid and will return later."

He nodded and smiled at her then continued mashing leaves.

They had no children, as their marriage was never consummated. With all his knowledge of roots and leaves, Richard could never find a cure for his inability to become physically aroused. And even if he could, Lily could not. She felt no physical attraction to him, but loved him more the way she might have loved her father.

She smiled in greeting as Joan, the miller's wife and Deirdre's mother, stepped inside the shop and pushed down her summer hood. Her bun was the same as Lily remembered it being for the last two years, but now it was silver instead of brown. "Good day to you, Joan. How is Deirdre?"

"Larger than a house," the serving girl's mother huffed. "When will this babe ever arrive?"

"She has a month, at least. Tell her not to forget to take the ginger for bloating." Lily smiled. "How are your ankles?"

Joan lifted her skirts and grinned. "Oh, much better, Sweeting! The cardinalwort...no, what did you call it?"

"Bishopwort," Lily supplied with a slight giggle when she heard Richard snort.

"Oh, aye! Look! No swelling for two days! I have come for more."

Lily nodded and went to a small shelf on the wall behind her table. It was where she kept the most frequently used remedies. As she reached for the bishopwort, she remembered her Scottish guest reaching for the chamomile over her head and felt a little lightheaded.

"We have two guests staying with us, Joan." Better to tell her neighbor now instead of after they terrified Joan when she saw them. "They are Scots. One of them is a priest."

"A brother," Richard called out, correcting her.

"Oh? Where are they coming from?" Joan asked with sudden worry creasing her brow.

"Dearest, what is it?" Lily asked as her neighbor twisted her skirts in her hands.

"Now, I do not know if 'tis true, but Agnes told me, who was told by Ivett that a deadly sickness has ravaged Italy and now parts of France. Many are dead. Some fear 'twill spread."

"Our guests are from Scotland," Lily hastened to let her know. She didn't always listen to rumors and gossip, but this could be important—and sickness was Richard's specialty. "What else do you know about this deadly sickness? Did Ivett tell you anything more?"

Joan shook her head.

Ivett was Osbert, the new reeve's wife. Osbert had contact with men close to the crown. He heard rumors first, told his wife, and she always spread them.

Lily turned to her husband untying his leather apron and setting it aside. "I will go speak to Osbert about this and see what else I can find out."

Lily nodded and watched him leave the shop.

"Lily, these Scots you spoke of are not like Bertram Chisholm, are they?" Joan asked, looking even more worried.

"No, dear. They do not seem to be anything like him. In fact, the brother doesn't even speak like a Scot."

They spoke a little more, mostly about the chill in the air and how it was causing Joan's husband, Martin's bones to ache.

Lily gave her a small pouch of rue and told her to soak the herb in vinegar and water and have her husband drink it.

They talked for a little while longer and then Joan left and Lily finished preparing Richard's herbal mixture.

She continued her work, refilling her jars and going back and forth from the shop to the shed. Colder weather was on its way and they wanted to prepare as much for remedies as they could before the first frost.

"Let me take that," came his deep, melodious voice, and the heavy sack she was struggling to carry to the shed was lifted easily from her arms.

She turned to Elias MacPherson's beautiful face and couldn't help but smile. He could have easily been a vain, arrogant, silver-tongued devil, for the sight of him was mesmerizing. But he was quiet and polite with a bit of a boyishness to his smile.

"Thank you," she said. "'Tis the sixth one I have carried out. My arms are weary."

She looked to the left and saw Brother Simon watching them from the shop doorway.

Elias tossed the heavy sack over his shoulder and reached for her arm with his free hand. "There is nothin' to ye, lass," he said and gave her upper arm a tender squeeze. "I will do the rest."

She liked how he touched her, with boldness and respect—and the way the setting sunlight danced across the chiseled angle of his jaw and made his lightning-splashed eyes dazzle her senseless.

"You are very kind," she offered and smiled with him again when he accepted her compliment. "'Tis a noble characteristic to possess."

"I agree," he replied and turned his face toward the shop and the direct sun. "And I have found that not too many people possess it."

"Uh-hum." She blinked away from his masterfully carved profile "Do you know many people?"

"Aye, we traveled often with the king's army in France and in England—"

"France?" She stepped away from him, remembering what Joan had told her. "You were in France? When?"

"A bit over two years ago? Aye." He looked toward Brother Simon, just a few steps away now and his companion nodded, apparently listening to their conversation. "Why do ye suddenly look afraid of me?"

"There is word of a terrible sickness there. Many have died." She paused and waited for Brother Simon to reach them when he pushed off the archway. "It has gone through Italy and parts of France."

"What? We have heard nothing of this!" the brother exclaimed. "What parts of France? What do you know?"

"Not much," she told him. "Richard went to see the reeve and find out more."

"This is sad news," the brother lamented softly and looked at Elias. "I wonder if our friends at Sénanque Abbey in Provence have been affected."

"We should pray for them, Brother Simon," Lily offered and led them toward the village church.

"'Tis verra kind of ye, Miss."

"Lily," she corrected with a smile. She could feel Elias' gaze on her, warm, hooded, and curious. Her eyes found him before she could stop them. Her smile deepened before she looked away.

Inside the church, hundreds of candles burned and cast shadows on the stone walls and benches. Lily sat first, with Brother Simon scooting in next to sit beside her. Elias sat last, closest to the aisle. She and Elias remained silent while the brother prayed in a soft whisper for a little while. Then they all prayed silently.

Lily was surprised that the people the brother was so worried about were not the priests of the abbey, but the French soldiers who'd fought on the side of the Scots against England. Most of the men had been great warriors, but after the loss of a limb or more, there was no longer any place for them, so they lived at the abbey with the priests. They were their friends.

She prayed earnestly for them for some time before she heard someone else enter the sanctuary. She opened her eyes to see a priest walking toward their bench.

She stood up and smiled at the priest's curious and cautious expression. "Father Benedict, good day."

He nodded and looked to her for an explanation for what she was doing here with two strangers.

"These men are Richard and my guests for as long as they need to stay. We came inside because we wanted to pray. I hope you are not displeased by it."

"Of course I do not mind, Lily." He smiled at her and her guests. "Why would I? Church is for the sick, not those who are already well."

"None of us are well," Brother Simon grinned. "That is why…" He turned and presented them to the altar where a sculpted cross rose out of the ground. "I am Brother Simon of the Carmelite order and this is

Elias MacPherson of Invergarry."

Father Benedict balked and turned his stern dark gaze on her.

"We are no friends of Bertram Chisholm," Elias was quick to reassure him, "and if he were here, I would kill him."

Everyone, including Lily, turned to Elias. Father Benedict looked stunned and appalled that such talk left Elias' lips in the house of God.

"I think our prayers are over." She offered them all a smile and left the bench on the other side of Brother Simon. "Come please, let us continue speaking outside."

All the men followed her out into the brisk air.

"Father, Richard has asked them to stay at the house and help him move all the pots and sacks. You know how difficult 'tis for him, especially this time of year."

"Aye," the priest began, "but where is—"

"My husband went to speak with Osbert about a matter of grave concern."

"What is this matter you speak of?" Father Benedict asked curiously, and then became more authoritative when he asked again.

"We heard rumors of a terrible sickness overtaking France. Richard thought to ask Osbert if he had heard anything more on the matter, and these two men fought beside soldiers in Sénanque Abbey in Provence. When they heard this rumor, they wished to pray for their brothers."

Father Benedict wanted more facts. When Lily told him she didn't have anymore yet, he insisted on going back to the shop with her to wait for word.

They all walked back and on the way, Lily thought to ask why her guests had no horses.

"We do," Elias answered her, coming a bit closer while Brother Simon asked Father Benedict a host of questions. "They are at a stable near The Pheasant Inn. After we spoke to Estrid, we decided to leave the horses there. 'Twas a good day fer walkin'. A bit warm though."

She angled her face at him and smiled. "Aye, Scotland is colder, is it not?"

He nodded. "I almost grew overheated walkin' back."

She laughed softly then covered her mouth with her hand and threw Father Benedict a guilty look. But he was too busy arguing doctrine with the younger brother and hadn't taken notice of them.

"The Highlands are even colder."

"Is that where you live?" she asked. "In the Highlands? It sounds very far away."

"'Tis, and the journey can be taxin' at times." His smile deepened. "But 'tis worth the effort. Our land is breathtakin' and majestic, with jagged mountain ranges that go on fer what seems like forever. It can be dauntin' to look upon if ye are lost."

She lifted her hand to her chest and drew in a breath of air, then smiled. "Just hearing of it robs me of breath."

His gaze went soft on her, as did his smile. "Once ye grow familiar with yer surroundin's the landscape becomes even more wildly breathtakin'."

She let out a small laugh. She wasn't expecting him to pull even more air from her. "You make me regret that I will never see it."

She was glad and relieved that he didn't ask her foolish questions like how she knew she would never see it. He knew she was correct, and he knew why. She liked him all the more for not pushing.

"What aboot ye," he asked while the two men of God began to find some common ground behind her. "How do ye like livin' here fer the past…"

"Two years," she supplied. "I love it here. These people are my family. I do not know where I would be without them. I will likely live and die here."

As grateful as she was to Richard—as much as she loved him for saving her, she felt a bit sad that she would die here. She loved everyone in the village and would miss them and likely finally cry herself to sleep for a month over them if she left, but some innate sense within her wanted to fly away from everything.

And Elias MacPherson had awoken it.

Whatever it was had to end. Not only because of Richard, but because of her vows before God.

"Will you pardon me? I forgot to ask Father Benedict something."

She broke away from him before he could answer. She hated being rude or unkind but he was too dangerous. He tempted her to stare at his lips and wonder what it would be like to kiss him—at his hands and long, broad fingers and think about his callused palms running down her back.

She needed to get back to the shop and to work.

She needed to put Elias MacPherson out of her thoughts.

She needed a distraction until he left.

CHAPTER THREE

"**A**YE, BROTHER," SAID Richard the apothecary to Simon from his place at the long trestle table where he sat with eight other men, including Father Benedict and Osbert the reeve. After Osbert had spoken to Richard, he requested all the men in the village to meet at his home.

Richard invited his guests. No one complained.

"Marseille in Provence was the first place in France to be hit. They are calling it the Black Death."

Elias closed his eyes and said another silent prayer for his French brothers.

Ivett, the reeve's wife, tapped him on the shoulder, interrupting his prayers. "More wine, sir?"

He shook his head and let his gaze settle on Lily standing beside her husband's chair.

"If word of this spreads," Osbert warned, "people will grow terrified and everything will be worse. You men tell your wives the virus has been contained."

"The truth of it is," the reeve continued, passing them all a grave look. "Losses in Italy, France, and even Spain are too numerous to count. There is word that the sickness set down in the port cities, Genoa, Messina, and Marseille. Just to name a few. So no one knows where it came from. There is no sign, so far, that it has come to England."

"But it most likely will," said Norman, a baker and one of Osbert's appointed officials, as he brought his shaking hands to his lips. "I have two little girls."

Lily rested her hand on his shoulder and cast her husband a somber gaze.

"Is there a way to stop it?" Elias asked, thinking of his kin in Invergarry. How long until it reached the Highlands? "If there is a way, I will help."

As always, Elias was the first to volunteer to take down any enemy. If there were no enemies in the Highlands, he'd find some in England.

Everyone turned to him and Richard smiled and nodded. "Kind of you, Elias."

Richard looked around the room. "No one knows how 'tis spread," the apothecary continued, taking over, knowing more about this part of the sickness. "But so far, we have learned that symptoms are fever, expulsion of stomach matter, bleeding from the eyes, nose, or mouth, in some cases, blackening of flesh to the limbs and fingers, and in most cases, death. Once affected, death is usually very swift. One to three days."

Lily followed Father Benedict and Simon when they made the sign of the cross.

"Ye say most cases," Elias said. "What d'ye know aboot the ones who live?"

"Nothing," Richard told him. "'Tis happening too quickly. But I will do my best to find what we need to destroy this unseen enemy."

Elias nodded and raised his cup with the others to Richard Bennett and all his endeavors. They all prayed silently for protection.

"London is a port city," Martin Miller said. "Will the king not stop trade until this pestilence is gone?"

Osbert gave the miller a cynical look. "There is too much coin to be had in trade. Even if he does stop it, there are merchants here who would take bribes. If the pestilence is coming to England, nothing will stop it."

"Thankfully, we are a small village in comparison to the other towns and cities," Osbert told them. "We must not allow anyone in from the south, east, or west." He eyed Elias and Simon. "You say you came from the north?"

"From the Highlands," Simon informed. "We have been nowhere east, west, or south of here."

"Very well," Osbert announced. "I will take you at your word because Father Benedict assures me you are a man of God. But no one else is to enter the village. If someone has a family anywhere below us, near any of the cities, they may not enter. Our neighbor may leave and go with them, but they shall not return. The messengers are due here tonight, so I suggest if any of you have letters you wish to send, begin writing them now. After tonight there will be no contact."

Elias heard a small, slight sound and turned to find Lily sniffling. He longed to get up and go to her, but he stayed where he was.

"We must find a remedy for this, Richard," she told her husband on a shaky voice.

Aye, Elias agreed. Richard Bennett seemed like an intelligent man. Hell, he was an apothecary! If anyone could find a remedy, it was he. "Richard," he said, turning to him. "How long d'ye think 'twould take the Black Death to get here?"

The apothecary shook his head. "Who can say? We will hear of it if it hits London, then it could be a matter of days. It depends on many, many things."

Elias wouldn't back down from it. "Whatever ye need from me or Simon, simply give the word and we are yers."

He looked to Simon sitting across the table. His friend nodded in agreement. Elias knew he would or he wouldn't have volunteered him. If this thing hits London, he will no doubt demand that they leave and return home to Invergarry where Elias would be safe behind the walls of the MacPherson stronghold.

But Simon would never leave him. He had faced death rather than leave Elias' side plenty of times before. This would be no different. It wasn't that the brother was fearless, though more times than not Elias believed he was. Simon simply would not leave him in any situation he deemed dangerous. It seemed the annoying habit began when Elias was two and Simon, recently rescued from his torturous English master by Elias' father, had been asked to keep an eye on Elias for a few moments. Elias had found him at his side often after that, either when fighting a lad who was bigger than he or on a battlefield.

Elias smiled at him and then turned back to Richard.

"All right then, lad," the apothecary said and patted Elias on the back. "I will put you both to work when we get back home and await our supper."

"There is nothing more to be discussed here," said Osbert, pushing his high-backed chair away from the table. "If I hear another word, you can rest assured that I will let you all know."

They bid one another good eve and left the reeve's large manor house. Elias turned back when he saw that Lily wasn't with them. He found her sharing a few last words with Osbert's wife.

When he turned forward once again, he found Simon watching him, and with him, Richard the apothecary.

Elias didn't know what to do. He wanted to hang his head. He liked Richard. He didn't want to do this. He didn't want to be here. He would help the apothecary move everything, anywhere he wanted it and back again, and then Elias would go home.

"Martin," Lily called out, catching up with the men. "Did you drink the tea Joan made for you yet?"

"Aye, Lily," Martin told her. "'Twas foul, indeed."

She waited a moment, then asked, "How do your bones feel?"

He blinked then twirled his ankle and bent both knees. He smiled and nodded. "Better. They pained me when I left to come here and I forgot all about them until now. My bones feel better."

Elias couldn't help but watch her when her husband asked her what she gave him and her wide smile when he nodded and told her she was correct. "You told him to drink it with—"

"—vinegar and water, aye."

"Aye," the apothecary smiled proudly at her. She beamed in response.

"Stop smiling, Eli," Simon said quietly beside him. "We spoke about this on the way to the inn. Have you forgotten already? She is married, little brother. She is bound to someone else whether you like it or not. You will not tease or tempt her to betrayal. That is not the man you are. Aye?"

"She is enchantin'," Elias whispered, his gaze fastened to her while she offered Martin a handful of dried mint leaves for his next dose of tea.

"Do not put the mint in the tea, Martin. Put some in your mouth and chew it after drinking the tea."

"Eli." Simon elbowed him in the ribs. "We shouldn't stay. If you want to help a village, let us go to the next one."

Elias swallowed his heart. Would the Black Death come here? Was there still time to go? Mayhap they could outrun this thing and make it back to Invergarry before the pestilence. Mayhap he could take Lily and Richard Bennett home with him. "I need to help them first, and then we will go home, old friend."

"You want to save her," Simon said in an accusatory tone.

"I *will* save her if the Black Death comes here. I will—"

He wasn't prepared for Simon, older than Elias by eighteen years, to grasp him by the collar of his léine beneath his plaid and drag him away from the others. "You will what? What will you do against a sickness that is killing everyone?"

Elias stared into his friend's dark green eyes. "I will pray."

Simon nodded. He said nothing as he let go of Elias' plaid and stepped back.

The next three hours went by swiftly with Elias and Simon carrying heavy sacks and potted plants, chopping wood for the hearth and carrying it to the Bennetts' house with the red roof.

During his first stop there, Elias commented on the delicious aroma of Lily's cooking, and then remembered Simon's words and said nothing else while they worked.

Supper was vegetable stew made with turnips, onions, carrots, radishes, and an array of herbs, including sage, rosemary, thyme, and cumin to add to the delicious flavor. There was fresh baked bread, sweet butter and Lily's very own homemade ale. Talk at the table was light, with Elias and Lily looking at everything but each other.

When supper was over, Richard put him and Simon back to work. This time, crushing leaves and boiling roots. Elias watched how Richard measured out everything precisely on his scales. He drained the liquid and dredged it for any bits, then added other mixtures of things like vinegar and honey or oils. But they had no idea if it would work against the Black Death.

Lily was present, working with them, trying to find a cure for something they knew nothing about.

When the futility of what they were doing hit them, they went to bed, exhausted and achy.

Elias slept well for one hour and then awoke to men screaming in agony all around him. Some men were screaming from things he'd done to them, slicing off their heads or their arms, or cutting through their bodies and then looking into their soulless eyes. Some men were his comrades, crying out for help or for God, clutching their fatal wounds.

Elias told himself it was a nightmare and that it was not happening now. But it felt like it was. It sounded like it was, and smelled like it was. He wanted to get away from it and clutched his head between his bent knees.

His heart was beating furiously, booming in his ears like a war drum. He had to move. He walked back and forth, crossing the boundary line into Scotland. He wanted to go home.

Someone was speaking to him in a soothing voice.

He reached home and found his family all dead, hanging from the rafters of the MacPherson stronghold. No!

"Elias." Her soft voice tugged at him. "Elias, come and sit."

He wanted to go with her wherever she was going. But no. His kin—

"There now. All is well. All is well."

He let her lead him and stepped up onto something soft...the bed.

"Poor man," she cooed close by. "Whatever have you been through?"

Wars. He wanted to tell her.

Somewhere in the back of his thoughts, he heard Simon's voice, but hers took precedence. "I will go make you some chamomile tea. You stay here with Richard and Brother Simon."

"Dinna go!" He clasped her wrist when she rose to leave.

"I will see to the tea," said Richard the apothecary.

Elias didn't want tea. He wanted her. He closed his eyes and went to a place where he could have her. His dreams.

CHAPTER FOUR

THE NEXT MORNING, Elias rose with the roosters and the aroma of warm bread with butter and apple mead. Simon was already up, likely to get the best portions of food.

Elias dressed quickly in his hose and a léine, dyed as blue as his eyes and belted around his waist. He pulled on his boots and a dark blue quilted doublet that flared at the hips. He tossed a thoughtful glance at his thick belt. Since Lily requested that his sheathed claymore and other various weapons remain in the kitchen with his plaid, there wasn't any need for the belt. He headed down the stairway, feeling light.

He walked through the cozy sitting room and looked into the kitchen.

Sitting at the table were Lily and Simon, laughing softly.

Simon looked up and motioned for him to grab a stool from the sitting room and join them.

How kind of him, Elias ground his jaw and plucked a stool up in his hand. He didn't want to feel envious of his best friend, but he did. He wanted what Simon had right now—just this innocent time with her, laughing, forgetting the world outside and the plague most likely on its way. Best portions, indeed.

"Good morn, Elias," Lily greeted him with a smile. "Would you like some mead while I prepare your meal?"

She rose from her chair as Elias set down his stool. He nodded and swallowed, looking at her. She wore a white chemise beneath a violet, long-sleeved kirtle. Her pale tresses were plaited behind her head, but many wispy strands fell free around her face.

"Good morn, Eli," Simon said after a sip from his cup. "Sleep well?"

"Despite ye kickin' me half the night," Elias told him with a murderous look. "Aye, I did."

"I know." His friend grinned at him, stretching the small scar under his bottom lip. "And after crying out and walking the floors only once!"

Elias' foul mood was shattered and replaced with mortification. He had night terrors last eve? He paled as memories returned, memories of blood and hellish odors, and a beautiful angel calling for him to come away and follow her. It had been Lily. Her voice, her touch, stealing him away from the horror, and bringing him into a different kind of radiant light.

She had seen him trembling. Afraid. "Lass, I..." Hell. He didn't know what to say. He was lost. He had been a commander in King David's army and now he trembled and tried to hide in the night. "I am not...forgive me fer..."

Her sapphire eyes grew rounder with compassionate for him. "What are you asking me to forgive, sir? That you witnessed things God never intended a man to see and it scarred you? It affected you because you are human just like the rest of us." She smiled and made him ache to say more to her. "There is nothing to forgive, I assure you, Elias."

Her voice sounded as it had last night; calm, sincere, and patient in her light, musical tone. He couldn't help but smile. "I slept quite well after yer soothin' ministrations."

"I made you tea you did not even drink!" she told him happily.

It was being here. With her. She cared about people in the world. She was genuine. Being with her felt right. Better than anything else that he could remember since going off to fight. She made him want to stay here. Should he tell Simon later and take whatever penance came?

"Well," she said bringing him his mead. "I am happy you finally slept well."

"Better than all the rest of us, 'twould seem," Simon laughed then explained when Elias gave him a questioning look. "You are the last one up."

Elias hadn't overslept in years.

"Richard was the first one up. He left for the shop."

Elias turned to have a look out the window. He would eat quickly. "Forgive me at least fer sleepin' late."

"No." She turned only enough to grace him with her profile. It seemed she was unable or unwilling to look him straight in the eyes. "I'm happy you slept well. I want nothing more than to see you..." She stopped, shook her head and corrected herself. "...folks well. You do not like your mead?"

Oh, how he wanted to smile at her yet again. "'Tis apple, aye?"

She turned around fully to toss him a pleasantly surprised look at him. "Aye, how did you know? You recognize the fragrance?"

He nodded then drank from his cup. "'Tis perfect, Lily."

He could feel Simon's eyes on him, his own muscles trembling beneath his léine, his heart pounding like an alarm in his chest.

"I grew bored of honey and lemon," she told him merrily while she prepared his bowl—and he tried to take his eyes off her. "I also use mint."

"I would be curious to taste mint," he chuckled. Hell, he chuckled. He hadn't done the like in years.

"Tomorrow then," she promised.

Was he staying until tomorrow?

She set before him a bowl of poached eggs and wilted, season greens. She also pushed forward another larger bowl of bread, along with cups of butter and honey.

He ate, and the food alone made him never want to leave Sevenoaks again. He didn't ask for any more eggs, as she had done enough for them, but helped himself to the remainder of the bread after she insisted he finish it.

He and Simon helped her clean up, though she fretted about them doing so. Simon explained that they'd learned to clean up after themselves in the army. If they didn't do it, no one would.

When the house was to her liking, they left together.

They saw two of Lily's female neighbors. They wore wimples covering their hair, ears, and necks, along with dyed kirtles. They soon hurried over.

"Good day, Lily." The ladies said in unison. One was Estrid, the owner of The Pheasant Inn. "I was just telling Agnes about *your* guests."

The shift of her eyes caught sight of Simon's scars, and though this was now the third time she had seen him and Elias, she was still taken back by the marks. Most people were. Most grimaced straight at him the way Estrid did now. Elias was used to seeing it. He never stopped hating it.

Agnes, the one with brown eyes and who was a bit plumper, introduced herself to Elias and then blushed three different shades of red when he looked her way and she stumbled over her feet.

He caught her before she hit the ground. "Let me help ye. Where are ye off to? I will help ye get there."

"Where are *you* off to?" she countered with a smile and a dimple in her pudgy cheek.

"The apothecary shop," Elias replied, smiling back.

"Well, so am I!" Agnes feigned a gasp, which caused Estrid to roll her eyes heavenward.

Lily covered her mouth with her hand and smiled at Elias as he pulled Agnes' arm gently through his.

"Why, thank you," Agnes giggled. "But, I must tell you, finding out that you are a Scot is a bit alarming. Though we have been assured that you and your companion are nothing like the Savage Scot, Bertram Chisholm."

"That is because no one is like me."

Lily spun around and went pale upon seeing a large brute of a man standing at the entrance of the shop with Richard's neck secured within the circle of his arm.

"I was just askin' yer husband how he was enjoyin' my whore."

Elias handed Agnes off to Simon and moved toward Lily.

"I was never your whore," Lily said, keeping her steady glare on Bertram. "One day, when I kill you, I will prove it to everyone."

Elias wanted to smile at her and the determined tilt of her chin. He hadn't expected to see such fire in her. He found it as alluring as her compassion. But he wasn't here to admire her.

This was Bertram. No one had to tell him. Elias wanted to kill him but he had to free Richard first.

"Lily, I see yer tongue is still sharper than a blade of grass. I should have cut it oot of yer mouth when I first snatched ye from yer father."

"God help us!" Agnes cried out.

"Ah, Agnes," Bertram sneered at her. "I see ye're still enjoyin' yer food."

"Ah, Estrid, ye sour faced crow," Bertram continued, his gaze slipping to her. "'Tis nice to see that I still make ye shiver in yer wrinkled skin. Where is Clare? Now that one I wouldna mind leavin' with." He laughed and then stopped when he noticed Elias.

"Who is this, Lily?" Bertram antagonized, glaring at him. "Yer lover?"

"These two brought the Savage back here!" Estrid accused.

"He just asked Lily who we are, Woman," Simon said sourly. "Why would we bring him here if—"

"Priest!" Bertram bellowed. "Keep yer mouth shut!"

Simon turned to him slowly and said through tight lips, "'Tis Brother."

"Good," Bertram sneered. "Then God willna be so angry with me for killing such an ugly, lowly—"

"Ye arrogant windbag," Elias growled, boiling in his boots. "Let the old man go and prove ye have the balls to come against me, Elias MacPherson."

"Lion Heart," Simon said for all to hear.

Bertram burst into laughter and let Richard go, pushing him away.

"Well, Lion Heart," Bertram snarled. "I have come for what is mine."

"And ye shall get it," Elias promised. He reached for his dagger as Bertram reached for his sword with his *right arm*, Elias noted, and his small blade flew and struck the oaf between his right arm and his shoulder. The pain was intense enough for Bertram to writhe and drop his sword. Enough time for Elias to march forward, yank his dagger free, and hold the bloody tip to Bertram' hairy throat. "Call off yer men or I will cut yer throat."

"Halt and retreat!" Bertram shouted at the mounted men beginning to come forward from the forest.

Elias heard Estrid and Agnes crying. The men retreated.

"If I see ye again," Elias promised on a low warning growl, "my aim will be fer yer heart and then yer head. Open yer mouth and I will cut oot yer tongue. Nod yer head if ye understand."

Bertram nodded. His body shook with anger at his humiliation.

"Now go." Elias wanted to kick him all the way out of Sevenoaks. If the bastard hesitated, he would.

There was no hesitation when Bertram Chisholm ran away. He ran for his life and to tend to his arm. He would likely return and Elias would have to kill him. He would prefer not to do it in front of innocent women and an old man.

He turned around to look behind him and make certain everyone was unharmed. Agnes and Estrid wept in Richard's arms. Simon was shaking his head at him. But it was Lily who smiled at him as if he were the answer to her prayers, at least the ones she used to pray before she was married.

"You have our thanks, Elias," she said in her siren's voice.

"Aye." Richard broke free of Estrid and Agnes and went to him. When he grew closer, he leaned in to speak quietly by Elias' ear. "She could have used you two years ago."

Elias felt ill with guilt. Guilt he deserved. "Thank God she had *ye*, Richard," he whispered back.

The apothecary nodded and clapped Elias on the shoulder then turned to gather his wife.

CHAPTER FIVE

I T WAS A busy morning after they ate. Osbert called a meeting outside the shop, where Richard was asked to confirm the story they had heard about Bertram's return and expulsion thanks to Elias the Lion Heart. (Estrid left nothing out of the telling.) The villagers gathered around Lily's guest and filled his ears with questions. He answered each with patience and kind words, looking at home with so many people gathered around him.

Lily turned her gaze away from him and tried to pay attention to her work. She thought about going to him last night. She had heard him from her bed and got up to peek around the curtain between their rooms. He was sitting up in bed, looking around, calling out.

She'd hurried to him and nearly lost her strength when she looked into his eyes. He was terrified, seeing things she couldn't see, hearing things she couldn't hear. She'd tried to soothe him. He'd looked at her with wide, glassy eyes. Had he seen her? He'd risen from the bed and paced the room, haunted, so very haunted by demons. Brother Simon had awoken and tried talking to him, but Elias had kept his eyes on her, as if he didn't hear his friend, or see Richard when her husband rose from bed.

Brother Simon had told her nothing this morning. He and Elias were friends. She respected his loyalty and hadn't asked.

"He is extraordinarily handsome," Agnes whispered, coming toward her with a furtive smile. "And quite brave."

"Aye." Lily didn't realize she'd spoken out loud until Richard looked up at her from his work and smiled at her.

"Do you know if he is looking for a wife?" Agnes asked, smoothing her skirts, and then her long, golden locks. Agnes was six-yer-old Annabelle's mother. She'd had her daughter a bit later in her life, at the age of twenty-six. The child's father was a smith named Heath in a nearby village. He'd left her soon after she began growing fat with his child.

"The topic has not arisen," Lily told her calmly, though her heart skipped every other beat. Elias and Agnes? It made her belly knot. She had no right.

Agnes finally left, after trying to strike up a conversation with Elias and not having any luck. They were able to get back to work and do whatever Richard needed.

They had let hopelessness fill them last eve but no more. They needed to keep pressing forward, jar every concoction and mark what it was.

Thankfully, Elias and Simon could read and write. Richard could also but she had never learned. She didn't mind it. She knew the purpose for every herb, every root, every thing that grew. Her father had taught her some things and Richard had taught her the rest.

She hated seeing Richard so helpless today against Bertram. It broke her heart to think of anyone hurting such a frail old man. She was afraid of the savage but she was tired of his crushing dominance. She wasn't his anymore.

She'd been foolish to anger him with Richard in his hands though. Bertram was dangerous and capable of anything.

But then Elias stepped in and stopped him...

Lily's hands shook, making the clay mortar and pestle scape instead of smash.

She tried not to think of Elias but it seemed the more she tried, the more he filled her head. He'd stepped in and, with one fluid movement, sent his dagger into Bertram's shoulder. He saved Richard's life and then he thoroughly humiliated Bertram by rendering him helpless! Oh! She'd wanted to jump with joy at the time. She wanted to start leaping now.

No. She had to gain control over herself. She imagined her body was in shock from seeing Bertram Chisholm again. She seethed with fury. How dare he come back into her life and threaten her husband! A part of her wished Elias had killed him. She confessed to Father Benedict when he came for the meeting. But she didn't feel any better. She guessed it was the other sin of lusting after a man who was not her husband that she needed to confess to. She couldn't tell Father Benedict. She sighed. Perhaps she would confess to Brother Simon. He had special privileges with God, didn't he?

Lily was so busy, she almost forgot to feed her husband and their two guests their supper. She hurried out the door and headed toward the house. When she walked past Elias, he put down the armful of hyssop he had gathered and cast a questioning look to Richard.

"My dear," her husband called out.

"Aye," she answered.

"Bring Elias with you, please."

"Pardon, Richard?" she and Elias both asked.

Her husband stopped what he was doing and looked up. "Bring Elias with you. Bertram could be roaming around here—"

"Bertram canna hurt her with his injured arm," Elias countered with a worried expression.

"No, but his companions could," Richard argued. "Lily needs protection, lad. There is no one else here who can protect her from Bertram but you. And now that I think of it, she should learn how to protect herself for when you leave."

Elias avoided everyone's gaze. When was he leaving? Now Richard wanted him to teach her how to fight? That would take time.

"Will you do it, Elias?" Richard asked. "For Lily."

Lily hated to admit it, but Richard was correct. She did need protection against Bertram and his cronies and she was beginning to take offense to Elias' refusal to help her.

She folded her arms across her chest and stared at him until he looked at her. "Are you coming?"

"Aye," he relented and went to her.

They walked together toward the road with Elias looking back once at Simon.

"Why do you hate me?" she finally asked him.

He looked up from his boots. "I dinna hate ye."

"You dislike me then."

"Nae," he bit out, avoiding her gaze once again.

"Then what is it?" she pressed. She hated herself for caring what a stranger thought of her. But he'd saved Richard. He'd saved her. "You smile and offer your arm to Agnes but you do not wish to be anywhere near me. You barely even look at me. You often hide behind your lashes and —"

She hadn't meant to mention his lashes. Why couldn't she have just bitten off her tongue instead? But it was the truth! He'd barely looked at her and when he did—she blinked and stopped thinking as her heart hit a high, massive, impenetrable wall.

He fancied her! Was it true? Could it be true? She wanted to ask him. Why? What would he do if it was? He'd have to leave Sevenoaks. Oh, she thought learning of the plague was the single most catastrophic moment in her life. She was wrong. He had to leave, and she didn't want him to go.

"Lily, I…" he began, pulling her up from the depths. "I know my place, and I will keep it. Yer husband is my friend."

She wanted to tell him he had to go, but she agreed with him instead. "Aye," she agreed on a slightly shaky breath.

He'd just confirmed her suspicions. He liked her, but Richard was his friend and he knew his place. He wasn't leaving. She was so glad. So glad. And at the same time, it would be difficult living with him for however long he remained.

A mist washed across her eyes and then was gone.

She had never kissed a man—not with passion. *Stop it!* she admonished herself.

"Lass," he said in his deep, smooth voice. "Would ye prefer I leave?"

What would her reply mean? What should she say? "You should leave. Aye. But Richard needs you and Simon here."

She hoped it was enough for him to stay but she didn't want to encourage him to do what was wrong. "You are both a great help to him and, with that help, we will find something to fight this Black Death."

"Aye," he agreed quietly. They walked a little more and then he turned to her. "Ye are verra brave to stand up to Bertram."

She smiled and shook her head. "Foolish."

"Nae, lass," he insisted with a slight curve of his lips. "Confident."

She blushed a bonny shade of pink. "I have been told I am foolish."

"I have been told I am reckless."

She slanted her gaze at him and then laughed with him.

They walked to the house with Lily smiling all the way. They stopped to greet Eleanor and her husband, Walter, the butcher. Eleanor and Walter had been at the meeting and invited Elias to their home for supper one night before he left.

For saving Richard, Walter promised him a thick, juicy cut of his finest beef, and Eleanor vowed to make him her delicious fig tarts.

"They like you, Lion Heart," Lily said on a quiet voice as she and Elias finally reached the shop. She didn't want things to be awkward between them. He wasn't leaving. The Black Death might be on its way here. If she were going to die, she would prefer her last days not to be miserable.

"They love Richard," he answered, knowing it was true.

She smiled at him as they stepped inside. "Aye, they do love Richard. As do I."

"I'm glad he is a good husband to ye, Lily. What he did fer ye was valiant."

Her smile remained. When they entered the kitchen, she bid him to sit at the table while she heated up the leftover stew over the fire. "You seem to be familiar with knightly, more courtly ways," she asked. "Did you learn about them in France?"

"Nae. I learned them from my Uncle Torin," he told her with a little light flickering behind his eyes. "He knows the stories of Arthur Pendragon and Avalon, and all sorts of other romantic tales."

"Do you know any of them?"

He nodded when she looked over her shoulder at him. "I know many of them."

"My father used to tell me stories of knights. Perhaps you will tell them to me sometime."

He nodded again and looked a bit muddleheaded. She felt the same way and looked away...still smiling.

"I could teach ye to defend yerself."

"Oh?"

"Aye. Ye dinna even need to know how to swing a blade. There are places on a man's body where cuttin' the muscles renders yer opponent almost completely helpless."

"Like where you threw the knife at Bertram?" she asked, her interest piqued. She knew of one place on a man's body to cause him injury, but that was all she knew.

Elias asked her to stand up so he could show her the most vulnerable places on any body.

"Try to aim between the limb and the body. Cuttin' these muscles and vessels and whatever connects it all together will stop yer enemy instantly. Sometimes, 'twill even kill him. Cut here." He walked around her and bent down to touch his finger to the back of her ankle. "Yer opponent will go down and likely never stand on his legs again."

Elias continued his explanations. "Here is where my knife landed in Bertram. Instantly, the use of his arm was lost." From behind her, he held up her arm and poked his finger in the socket between her shoulder and her chest.

She giggled and stepped forward.

"We can practice some strikes later," he suggested, smiling at her.

"Aye," she said softly, smiling and liking how his hands felt near her.

Someone knocked on the front door, startling them both. It was Brother Simon.

"Did Richard send ye?" Elias asked him as they sat upon stools at the table.

"No, he did not send me. He does not know I came here. I have reason to believe he would be angry with me if he knew, for he wants the two of you to be alone."

Lily laughed, but she felt a little ill. "Why on earth would you say such a thing?"

"Because, lass, he told me so."

She felt her face drain of color and then fill with blood and make her blush. She felt a bit lightheaded from the change. "I do not understand. Why would my husband want me to be alone with another man?"

The brother shrugged his scrawny shoulders. "He wants you to be happy."

"I am happy!" she shouted then stormed out the door.

How dare Richard suggest that she was not happy! Had she not done everything to please him? To be a good, caring, loyal wife? Why did he think she was not happy? Because of sexual relations? She didn't care about that. Had she not told him so these two years? How dare he make such a decision without her! This was her life!

She'd lost her right to make her own decisions from birth and being born a girl. But Bertram had stripped her of *every* right. In the seven years she lived with him, there were days when she prayed to die. She wasn't allowed to interact with anyone. No friends, no fellowship, no comfort. His men were just as bad. They weren't allowed to touch her and their fear of Bertram sealed their obedience. But they harassed her. They spit on her. They were allowed to slap her and pull her hair while she served them in Bertram's company, so they did. It made her wise and not meek. She knew when to stand up to them, even Bertram, and she knew when to keep her mouth shut. There was no place for pride. Just the most frustrating, deep-rooted instinct to survive.

But Richard had changed her life. He gave it back to her and now he thought to just hand her over to the first young stallion that came along?

She reached the shop and pushed open the door.

Her husband looked up from his work and smiled. "Ah, dear, where is Eli? I have work—"

"Aye, I know all about your work, Richard. What do you mean by wanting Elias and me to be alone? What are you hoping will come of this?"

"My dear, child—"

"Do not call me a child!" she cried.

"You are one to me," he said. "You have been a wonderful companion—"

"Richard." She went to him. "Why are you speaking this way? Have I displeased you in some way?"

His eyes filled with tears as he reached out to touch her cheek. "Lily, you could never displease me, but death is coming, my joy." He nodded. "'Tis coming. I want to free you from your obligation to me while there is time for you to enjoy your life."

"'Tis no obligation, Richard. I love you."

"And I love you. But I cannot give you what you deserve. A life of passion and desire. I wish I was forty years younger, but I am not. I—"

"Richard, I do not need passion and desire. I am happy the way things are."

He shook his head. "'Tis not natural. You are young and vibrant. Who knows how long your life will last. You deserve passion and, hell, Lily, if Elias MacPherson is not the most handsome man I have ever clapped eyes on in my sixty-eight years, I do not know who is. More importantly, he's a good, hard-working man. He likes you. Spend more time with him."

"No."

"Enjoy your time with him. Let him kiss—"

"No!"

"Lily, our marriage is not consummated. We are not bound to it by God and it can be easily annulled by the church while I live."

"Absolutely not, Richard," she insisted vehemently, "and I will not hear another word from you about this. This is my life you are tossing around. You always told me to stand up for my decisions. Well, this is one of them. I will not abandon you for some silly physical desire. I only need you. So no more talk of this, aye?"

He looked as if he wanted to say more, but didn't. He smiled, nodded and kissed her on the forehead.

Lily remembered her stew and ran for the door. She pulled it open and ran straight into the wall of Elias' chest. She was grateful that Brother Simon was carrying the stew, but it left Elias' arms free to close around her. She looked up into his stormy blue eyes, became startlingly aware of his rock-hard curves and angles, and doubted everything she had just told her husband.

CHAPTER SIX

ELIAS CHOPPED WOOD behind the house early the next morning. He felt well rested having almost a full night's sleep without any terrors two nights in a row now.

Simon worked close by drawing water from the well.

He thought for certain that his friend was out here to speak to him about Lily, but it was Bertram whom Simon wanted to discuss.

"You know I do not approve of you rushing in the way you did, lad."

"'Twas the best way to gain control, old friend," Elias told him as he brought down his axe into the thick log. "I went to him because he couldna hurt me. I cut his muscles as my father and my uncles taught us. Bertram was helpless." He yanked his axe free and reached for another log. "I showed him mercy and gave him a warnin'. If he returns, I will kill him."

"I have no trouble with that, Eli. I just worry over you. I cannot help it. My old habits are difficult to change."

"I wouldna have those habits change, Simon. I like havin' my own guardian angel." Elias winked at him and lifted his axe high over his head.

Simon put down his bucket and threw up his hands. "What does it matter? The Black Death is coming. We will all likely perish."

"Mayhap," Elias smashed his axe into the wood, splitting it down the center.

Simon took up his bucket, along with another that was waiting for him in the grass. He started back, his legs a bit shaky.

Elias left his axe and ran to help his friend. "Mayhap not."

They exchanged a smile and Simon confessed that he was glad to see Elias happy again. The ravages of war would take time to forget, and mayhap they would never forget all of it, but the good Lord and a beautiful woman would help.

"I willna do as Richard wishes when it comes to his wife," Elias told him. "I believe he would regret it and come to hate me. Not to mention, I'm not an uncontrolled beast."

Simon agreed. "I knew that would be your answer. I respect it. You are a good man, Eli."

"So is Richard Bennett," Elias replied as they came to the kitchen door of the shop. "He wants Lily to be happy."

Simon could do nothing but agree as they entered the kitchen. Richard was a hardworking, patient soul, at the beck and call of the sick. The warm days were giving way to cooler mornings and many of the villagers visited the shop in the day or the red-roofed house at night to stock up on remedies for ailments of their bones and aching limbs. Richard saw to them all with the help of his companion. No one was turned away. If they could not pay Richard for his services, they didn't.

Agnes had offered a freshly-baked apple pie as payment for a small pouch of dried Mugwort leaves to ease her lady issues. Alfred, one of the merchants, had stopped by last night for a little St. John's wort for a burn he received from splattering oil. He had no coin but paid Richard with a freshly-killed chicken. Everyone was a friend, a brother.

It made Elias want to serve him, a truly good man. It made him hate himself because he couldn't quit thinking about the man's wife.

"Good morning."

He heard her voice and slanted his gaze to her. She stood at the table, bending over it to set down a third bowl of porridge. His task wouldn't be easy. His belly churned. "Good morn," he croaked out then cleared his throat. He didn't dare look at Simon.

"Ah, good friends," came Richard's steady voice as he joined them from the other side of the house. "Thank you for the wood and water. You have both far exceeded payment to me of any kind."

He sat down and smiled at his wife as she set down his, the last bowl, before him on the table.

"We want to do more," Elias told him, taking a seat next to him.

"No. *He* wants to do more," Simon corrected, looking down appreciatively at their bowls of porridge dashed with cinnamon and topped in lemon rinds. "I want to do less. My body feels as if it might cease working altogether." He looked up at Lily and his smile widened. "It smells heavenly."

"And it tastes even better," Richard promised with confidence.

"Eat the rinds," Lily told them. "They are very beneficial for almost every ailment, and possibly for what is to come."

"Aye, today we begin adding lemon rinds to our remedies," Richard told them after they prayed and ate. "I will begin tending to my lemon trees around the hill and bringing the lemons to the shop where Lily...and Brother Simon—" he gave Simon a wink, "—will begin the peeling and drying process."

"Leave the lemons to me, Richard," Elias offered. "We need ye well, not so battered down with takin' care of *everythin'* that ye can no longer do what ye are here to do. Keep workin' and mixin' and readin' and leave the heavy work to me."

Richard stopped eating, as did Lily. "I do not know how to thank you, Eli. This work means everything to me," Richard confessed as if they didn't already know.

"I will see it done," Elias vowed.

He could feel Lily's gaze on him and prepared to look at her, to smile at her, just as he would Agnes, or Estrid, or anyone. But when his gaze fell on the soft grace of her grateful smile, he felt his practiced smile fade, replaced by something warmer and more intimate.

"Let us not forget," said Simon, "that you let us sit at your table and partake of your wife's delicious food everyday."

Elias agreed, bringing a spoonful of porridge to his mouth. Richard was correct. It was heavenly. "Did ye add cream to this, lass?"

She nodded and grinned happily. "It adds richness."

He nodded. With her along, they would surely find a cure for this monster.

"'Tis warmin' to my bones," he supplied, liking her reactions to compliments on her cooking.

"Besides tasting so good, the cinnamon has hundreds of uses in cooking and in medicine."

"Sadly, 'tis extremely difficult to get," Richard told them. "'Tis costly because it comes from so far away. We use it sparingly."

Elias listened and took everything in. He also didn't leave a drop of porridge in the bowl.

"I will bring in the wood," Elias said, standing up from his stool. "I willna take long and then I will begin workin' in the orchard."

Richard smiled and agreed. Excusing himself, Elias left the table and went back to work bringing in the wood. He carried several of the split logs inside and set them beside the hearth in the sitting room, then carried more in for the kitchen fires. Richard had gone back to his work and Simon had left to use the small outhouse behind the house.

"You are very helpful to have around." Lily's sweet voice fell on his ears as he was getting ready to leave.

He stopped, bending at the door in the kitchen and turned to her. He didn't know why but he laughed a little. It felt good. How long had it been? Why did he feel so happy here when the only lass who had ever stopped his heart was forbidden? When a damned plague could be headed their way.

He let himself feel the humor in it all.

"I'm happy ye think so, my lady."

He fell in awe of her beauty when she dipped her chin and looked at him from beneath long, dark lashes. "I am not a lady, sir."

"And I have never been knighted."

She looked up to find him grinning like a damned fool. She matched it and they both ended up laughing. They weren't sure what they found so humorous. Perhaps it was desperation to cling to hope and to life. He would hold on to it with one hand and her with the other.

"Are you going to pick lemons now?" she asked, wiping her hands on her apron and then removing it.

Elias watched her, nodding. She did nothing to make herself look beautiful. Her hair was not curled and pinned like the ladies he'd seen in some courts. Her cheeks were dusted with a healthy glow, her lips were a natural deep pink, and her eyes were painted with hues of kindness, compassion, and a fierce love for her husband and the people she lived with.

"May I come along?"

"Aye, but I thought ye were to help Simon peel."

"They have to be picked first, do not they not?"

She came closer and his belly ached because he had to turn away and not take her face in his hands and kiss her.

"Ye are welcome to come with me." He held out his arm before him, offering her a path to take.

"Tell me about your life, Elias MacPherson," she asked him on the way to the orchard. "Tell me about your kin."

He smiled at her use of the Scots' word. "My father and his two brothers built the MacPherson stronghold in Invergarry where we live. He and my uncles were separated when my father was two. They all grew up alone, without a family, so when they finally found one another, they wouldna be separated again. My cousins and I all grew up together. 'Twas good even when we fought," he said, smiling at memories of getting into trouble with his cousins. "I miss them." He wondered if he would ever see them again. "When I returned from the war, I became a shepherd of my father's livestock." They spoke a little bit more about his family and his fighting under the Scot's king, who was now imprisoned.

"I have three half-sisters," Lily told him in a quiet voice. The whites of her eyes grew red with unshed tears, making her blue eyes more startling. The tip of her nose also grew red. "I have not seen them or my father in nine years."

"Have ye never tried to find them?" he asked, wishing he could help.

She shook her head. "Not when I was with Bertram, and when I came here, I stopped needing anything else."

He vowed to himself then and there that he would find her half-sisters and her father and bring them to her.

They came to the sunlit orchard and Elias smiled knowing how much all this meant to Richard...and to Lily.

"There are only three trees," he remarked, stepping under one of them. They were heavily-laden with big, yellow fruit.

"After one of Richard's remedies cured a merchant from Genoa of a terrible skin disease, "Lily told him, "Richard was given a sapling of a lemon tree as payment. He grew the sapling for a few weeks and then cut it into eight more saplings. Only three lived. He has tried to grow more," she said and reached up to brush her fingertips over the leaves, "but alas, they die."

Elias watched her with sunlight streaming onto her through the foliage above. His heart ached to know her more, to tell her more about him. "I thought at first there wouldna be enough, but these trees hold a vast amount. I think if I pluck one from its branch, they will all fall."

"Aye!" she agreed and then ran to a much smaller shed than the one near the shop. She hurried inside and came back out with two wooden buckets inside a wheelbarrow. She handed him a bucket and held hers over her head, and then plucked a lemon loose. They were right. At least a dozen lemons dropped around them. A few hit their buckets.

They laughed and hurried about picking up the lemons that fell. Soon though, Elias realized that picking lemons up off the ground was more backbreaking than reaching up for them.

"Are there any children in the village?" he asked, seeing her place her hand to her side as she bent over and over.

"Aye, there are children." She smiled. "Little Eddie and Terrick the Terrible. Cecily and Liz—"

He stood up straight. "Let us go fetch them."

"To do our work?" she asked, wide-eyed.

He nodded. "And to play."

Her eyes opened wider and she straightened. "To play? To play what?"

She sounded utterly shocked that one would consider making work play, so he would show her.

"Come," he beckoned and raced her to the center of the village. There they found Lily's delight, little Eddie, who was but two summers old, being pulled around by Norman the baker's daughters, Ava and Emma. Charlie was the oldest among them all at twelve. His sister Cecily and her friend Lizbeth, daughter of Alan the carpenter and his wife, Helen, volunteered immediately to help. In fact, they all did. Including Terrick the Terrible, a stout eight-year-old boy who, as young Annabelle told it, liked to cause trouble.

"I do not like to cause trouble!" Terrick shouted in his defense.

"Well, there will be no trouble today," Elias called out, quieting them. "Today, Lily and I need yer help in gatherin' lemons to make medicine."

"There are many of them," Lily added as enthusiastically as the children listened, "but for your work you will get sliced apples and honey."

The children, eight in total, cheered.

"But sadly," Elias interjected, holding up a finger and tossing Lily a sad look, "there are only enough apples and honey fer six of ye." He turned to the small faces looking up at him, some stained with dirt, their smiles fading. "So, we shall have a race! The first six of ye who put the most lemons into the wheelbarrow will win. Who wants to play?"

He said the magic word and the children cheered again and squealed with excitement then took off toward the orchard.

Elias and Lily ran with them, laughing under the sun, forgetting everything but this. When they reached the lemon trees, Elias stopped them and found two more buckets in the shed. He picked four children to hold the buckets over their heads and shook the tree. Everyone screamed and laughed as lemons rained down on their friends. The sound of their merriment drew Richard and Simon out of the house to see what was going on.

Simon covered his eyes and Richard laughed when the second batch of children were hit on their shielded heads with lemons.

There were still too many lemons in the trees for the children to pick them from the ground without more falling on their tender heads, so Elias had everyone stand around the trees. He and the other adults pulled branches down so that each child and each adult had a branch in each hand to shake.

The children shook vigorously and squealed with joy over the falling lemons. They laughed even harder when Terrick ran beneath the trees with his bare head, was hit with a lemon, tripped over one on the ground and fell flat on his face, only to be pelted with more lemons as everyone kept shaking the branches.

"They do not even know they are working," Lily laughed, tilting her lips toward his ear so he could hear her over the laughter.

"I had plenty of children to play with when I was a lad. We made games oot of all our work," he told her. "All right then lads and lassies, time to gather the lemons. Everyone get ready. Go!"

They watched Charlie and Lizbeth bringing in the most lemons in the fastest amount of time. Cecily and Terrick were next, with Elias having to warn Terrick twice about pushing. Little Eddie even dropped a few lemons into the wheelbarrow and gave Elias an extra smile for letting him play. Elias praised him for his hard work and mussed the boys golden curls.

"He likes you," Richard pointed out with a smile.

"I like him, as well," Elias replied with a kind smile of his own and patted his older friend on the back.

The children filled two wheelbarrows and were all invited into the apothecary's shop where each and every child was given apples and honey.

A bit later, when Elias headed for the shop with one of the wheelbarrows, all the children followed after him. He didn't mind. In fact, he enjoyed their small, soft voices when they spoke, and their enthusiasm to have fun and make the most of the day. They taught him a song he was sure his uncle, Torin, would approve of and he listened to each of them when they sought his attention.

They made him miss home and his nieces and nephews, and he had many. He stopped questioning *if* he would see them again and believed that he would. Being here was going to take courage, more than it would take to leave. Richard knew it and so did his wife. But they might not have a choice. They might have to leave. There was still time to take them to Invergarry, but would Lily and Richard leave their friends behind? Could he take them all, even these little ones, on such a journey? Were they all free of the illness? When would he know?

He looked around at their happy faces and felt his heart lurch.

He and Simon could leave today. The longer they waited the more dangerous it became of possibly bringing the disease home. Were these people worth possibly dying over?

Was she?

CHAPTER SEVEN

LILY DREW HER fingers to her mouth to conceal her smile and control her laughter. She was in her kitchen with Bother Simon peeling lemons when her cat, Pip, entered and poor Brother Simon hit the floor.

"Oh, my!" he lamented and then leaped up and over a chair to escape little Pip. "I do not like cats."

"Why? What has one done to you?" she asked, trying not to giggle at his antics. "Are you truly this frightened of my cat, or are you pretending?" She hoped he was pretending because, any moment now, she was going to burst into laughter.

"I—" He stopped speaking and his large eyes grew larger as Pip pounced closer to him as if the brother were prey.

He scrambled out of the way, around the kitchen table and went pale when Pip sprang up to the table and continued toward him.

Poor Brother Simon. He looked about to fall faint. Lily guessed this was what mice felt when Pip saw them.

"What is this?" Elias asked, stepping into the shop and reaching for the cat on the table. "How do ye do..." He peeked between Pip's chubby thighs. "...lass?"

Pip purred and rubbed her gray-striped head under Elias' chin.

Lily had held her laughter back too long and hiccupped. The force of it lifted her off her heels and startled Pip out of Elias' arm and Brother Simon out of the kitchen.

Elias laughed softly, drawing Lily's gaze to him. Her heart raced in her chest.

"He fears cats," he told her.

"I gathered that," she said, covering her smile with her hand.

Had Elias stepped closer? He smelled like lemons.

"Lily." He grew serious "Where is Richard? There is a matter of importance I need to discuss with ye and him."

"He is on the other side of the house. What is it?" she asked, her smile fading with his and putting down her lemon.

"There is talk aboot some people in London," he told her. "That they died with symptoms of the Black Death."

"No!" she almost blurted out. "'Tis here then. Oh, Elias!"

"I know 'tis frightenin', lass. Osbert has called a meetin' of the officials. He wants Richard there but I would like to speak to Richard first."

"What about?"

"Aboot leavin' Sevenoaks. The four of us. Me, Simon, ye, and Richard. We will go to Invergarry."

"What? What are you saying?"

"It is time to leave here, Lily."

"Leave everyone here?" she asked, her eyes wide.

He knew it was going to be difficult to get her to go, but they had to, and they had to hurry before it was too late. There were too many people coming and going. If one person showed up sick here, his home would have to be forgotten.

"Lily, I know ye dinna want to leave them. I dinna want to go either, but goin' to Invergarry as soon as we can is the only way to secure our safety."

She shook her head. "No. They have been the only family I have known since I was taken from mine. I will not leave them."

"Lily, hear me, I beg ye—"

"I will not leave them, Elias," she said, trying to conceal her anger. "You may go anytime you wish. You do not owe us a thing. You have done all you can and now 'tis time to for you to leave."

He stared at her as if he were surprised she could say such a thing. She wanted to say more. How could he expect her to leave them all to possibly die while she escaped to safety? She turned away from him, angry and not caring to say another word to him. He would go speak to Richard. He knew that if he could convince Richard to go, as his wife, she would have to follow. She would fight it. And if she were forced to go, she would never speak to Elias again.

He was quiet for a few moments, then said, "Verra well then, Lily."

She closed her eyes, hating that he was going to go. He was so wonderful with the children. He made them all laugh and enjoy the day. He made her laugh and feel young again.

She didn't want him to leave. She didn't want to not have him around. She didn't want to stop looking at him when he wasn't watching, or to feel pretty when he caught her looking and smiled. How was she to resist him when he made her feel like a woman again just by slanting his gaze her way?

"We will take everyone with us. MacPherson stronghold is big enough, but we canna tarry. 'Twill be taxin', but we can do it."

For a moment, she simply stared at him as if he'd grown a third eye between the other two. Did he mean it? Would he do this for her? Could they bring everyone? The pestilence could not likely withstand Highland winters. They might all live! Elias...

She nodded her head and smiled at him.

"How will we pack everything up? We only have two donkeys."

"Pack verra little," he said. "Only what ye canna do without. I need only speak to Richard aboot it and then we will tell everyone else."

Lily's smile grew into a grin and she nodded. "You are a gift from God, Elias. Go. Speak with him. I will wait here."

She watched him move down the long hall.

When Brother Simon returned, she pointed down the hall. "Go. He has news."

Could they all truly go with Elias to Invergarry? Why had he changed his mind? She didn't care what made him do it, she was glad he did. She thought about what she would pack. She only needed her herbs and plants. How were they going to transport it all? Would it all die up north along with the sickness? The lemon trees would never survive.

Her smile began to vanish as she thought about all the reasons she and Richard could not go. They needed to find a cure. Help everyone, not just themselves and their friends.

"You can do your research in Invergarry, Richard," she heard Elias say as he and Richard entered the kitchen and moved toward her.

She frowned, knowing her husband would not agree, knowing she agreed with him.

"'Twould take too long to get to those who need it in London," Richard argued.

Lily lowered her gaze to the lemon she was peeling.

"So ye would risk the people of Sevenoaks—yer friends, fer people ye dinna know?" Elias asked.

Richard did not answer.

Lily turned around to face both of them. "Elias, we wish to help *more* than just our friends. Please do not wrangle my husband any further."

Elias stared at her, his hopes falling around his feet—or were they? She had the feeling he was called Lion Heart because he did not back down.

"Lass," he said, proving her correct a moment later, "there isna much time. We must ootrun this thing. 'Tis how to battle it—by stayin' away from it long enough to create the remedy. Aye?" He didn't wait for her to answer. "People in London are dyin'. Every moment matters because if one person here gets sick, I willna bring anyone home, includin' myself."

Lily swallowed, understanding. Understanding why he was a commander.

"Richard, ye can ride my horse," he continued and then set his eyes on her again. "Ye can ride Simon's. We will use the two other horses we saw in the stable, along with the donkeys, to carry yer work, but we need to go."

Lily nodded and looked at Richard, then took his hand. "Perhaps he is right. You need to live so you can keep trying."

"Aye," her dear husband agreed and then nodded to Elias. "We will have to convince Osbert."

Elias was too happy to care about any other opposition. He threw his arm around Richard's neck and pulled him close. "Thank ye, my friend. I want ye to live."

"As do I," Lily told him when Elias let him go. She slipped her hand into Richard's and gave her husband a nervous smile. He lifted their hands and patted hers with his other hand.

"Let us go to Osbert now," Richard suggested. He let her go and gathered his cloak. "We have much to do."

Elias smiled at her as they reached the door.

As she stepped outside and looked around, she thought she should be happy for other reasons, such as they would all have a better chance of living by following him. But the truth was that she was most happy she was going to see the breathtaking land he had spoken of with its jagged mountain ranges that go on forever. She was happy she wouldn't have to bid him farewell, happy that he cared for her husband, and the people here. And for her. If Richard found a cure, they would find a way to get it to the proper people, who would duplicate it and spread it throughout the world.

She followed them to Osbert's house, walking behind Richard and Simon with Elias at her side. He felt big beside her, like a guardian. She felt safe. She liked it.

"How are we going to bring everything? 'Tis overwhelming to think about. And what about the mothers who are alone with their children, like Clare and Agnes and Alice?" She suffered doubts about their ability to leave and her hands began to shake.

"Lily," Brother Simon stopped her. "Do ye have much influence over the reeve?"

She shook her head no.

"Nor do I. Maybe we would do better by going to pray."

She nodded and promised her husband she would pray for the best decisions to be made.

She walked with the brother to the church.

"Let us sit outside today," Brother Simon suggested and turned toward a single bench behind the church, facing a narrow running stream.

Lily thought it a nice idea and smiled at him as they sat down to pray. A cool wind pulled at her hood, but it was not brisk or overly cold. That was coming, as well.

How long would it take them to reach Invergarry? Would winter find them traveling?

She asked the brother her questions after they prayed. "It should not take longer than a fortnight—with so many walking—"

"A fortnight! How will we all eat?"

"We will hunt and eat from the land."

She wanted to laugh because it sounded so preposterous, but he said it with conviction and made her believe it.

So be it then. The choice was not hers to make and she did, now, see both points of view.

"Tell me about your life, Brother," she said to set her mind on other things. She lifted her fingers to his scars. "I can give you oil to apply every day. 'Twill help keep them from turning red."

"I am already in your debt."

She shook her head. "There is no debt. How did you get them?"

He gave her a surprised look and then a short laugh and she wondered when was the last time anyone showed interest in him.

"Ah, let me think now." He set his fathomless, dark green eyes on the window. "I was eight when my mother died. Nine when I was sold to the Earl of Hampton in Norham."

"Was servitude terrible for you?"

"Aye, most terrible," he replied.

Lily didn't come from a town or a city like London. She wasn't aware of how lords and ladies treated their servants. Country folk, like her, didn't have servants.

"Did your master do this? Why?" she asked when he nodded.

"Someone accused me of trying to gain his daughter's favor."

"And were you trying to gain it?"

"In truth, I was," he confessed. "Rohesia has the face of an angel. I could not help myself from liking her. So to prevent the chance of his daughter returning my affections, he had me whipped once across the face. The three scars are from one strike coming around and getting me from the other side. I have more on my back. He turned me into a hideous monster."

"You are not a hideous monster, Brother Simon," she assured him. "The one who did this to you is."

"He is dead by now," he said, waving away the story and the effects of it. "'Tis a time best forgotten."

"Aye," she agreed. "Tell me how you met Elias. You mentioned his father rescuing you from your lord."

"Aye," he smiled and told her about Nicholas MacPherson and his bonny, beloved Julianna, Elias' stepmother. "Lord Nicky found me when I was sixteen and I have been like an older brother to Eli since."

He laughed. "A much older brother."

"And a wiser one," she pointed out. "Tell me about the MacPherson stronghold, Brother." If she was going to be living there, she wanted to like it. She hoped she did. "Is it like Sevenoaks?"

"In a way," he said. "'Tis more…fortified. Most of the houses are connected by walkways and a wall surrounds all of it. Everyone there is safe. Everyone would die for his or her neighbor. But 'tis growing in size and soon the brothers will have to do away with their wall. Sooner now than later."

"Is it unsafe in Invergarry?" she asked, worried.

"Nowhere in Scotland is safe from the English. If we are caught traveling together, you are to say I am your servant. If not, they will likely kill me and rape you."

She shivered in her spot, never knowing until now what it meant to be a Scot. They were England's servants.

She felt a little ill and rubbed her belly.

"How are you holding up under all this, lass?" he asked, sobering suddenly. "Not just the worry of the pestilence, but the rest of it. With Eli. You care for him?"

His questions were so unexpected that she stumbled over her words, not knowing how to answer or where to begin. She could have pretended ignorance but she was not daft, and she wouldn't pretend to be. "Aye." She lowered her voice. She'd wanted to confess anyway, didn't she? "I have tried to stop it from happening, but being near him, in the same room with him, sets my heart to thumping. I know I am a married woman and I do not care if our marriage is not physical, I love my husband. So, tell me, Brother, how do I stop my heart from wanting Elias?"

He shook his head. "I have had similar conversations with him and I must tell you, lass, I do not know."

"Similar conversations?" she asked, her ears perked up. "About me?"

He squirmed—just a little. "Lass, you must know he cares for you. Even your husband knows."

At this, she closed her eyes and clutched her chest. She didn't want Richard to be aware of her feelings or Elias. "Oh," she cried. "Mayhap 'tis for the best that you and Elias leave here and never return. I cannot bear the thought of hurting Richard."

"Lily," he consoled gently. "If you do not come with us, you will likely die here. You are young so you might have to watch Richard die first."

She stared at him, horrified. Stunned that he would say something so cruel—as the truth. She let out a breath in a sorrowful sigh and turned away. "We will come with you."

"Sweeting," he tried, sounding heartbroken. "There can be no doubts or hesitation about this. We are not very far from London. This thing will come. 'Tis only a matter of time. All we can do is pray and leave while we can."

"I know you are correct, Brother," she said, returning her gaze to his. "If I stay, I will likely die after Richard. But the other option is live with the shame of what I feel for Elias."

Brother Simon rested his hand on her shoulder and hung his head, knowing there was nothing more to say. Whatever she decided, she was doomed.

"I want to think God sent you and Elias to save us, but then why am I tempted by him? Do you think you are both here to bring us away from the pestilence?"

He shook his head. "I do not know why we are here, but I know that once Eli saw you, he changed. I thought him mad for staring at you the way he did, as if you were something he had been looking for and had finally found. Something divine. Nothing will pull you from him now. I know him and I can tell you he will wait for you and he will be yours when you are free—" she looked away "—but until then, you must think of Elias as a friend."

She nodded, but it was easier said than done.

Easily proven when Elias and Richard found them on the bench and her heart pounded hard in her breast, her mouth went dry, and her palms grew sweaty.

Elias' adventurous gaze found her and then he smiled. "We leave at first light."

CHAPTER EIGHT

L ILY PACKED THE last of her clay jars into a large sack. Each jar was secured closed with twine. Some of the older children had helped peel more lemons and the rinds were gathered and set out to dry while the rest of the packing was done. Joan and Agnes and some other women of the village had spent the day cooking and baking their food instead of letting it spoil.

They'd invited everyone to eat together as the sun began to set. The ale and wine were plenty and the delicious food abounded, but their smiles did not reach their eyes.

By now, they all knew the truth. The Black Death was most likely coming. Osbert had informed the men of the perilous conditions in London. The unaffected did all they could to remain that way, leaving even dying loved ones to die alone. Physicians and apothecaries refused to see patients, and priests refused to give last rites to the dying. Vendors left, and shops closed. The pestilence showed no mercy to children and even the farm animals were affected.

The villagers sang and laughed rather than think on it all, or that they were leaving their homes. Everything they knew. Everything that belonged to them because the pestilence *might* come here. No one wanted to leave but they were all afraid to stay.

"We must head to bed soon," Elias said, leaning down to Osbert's ear from behind his chair in the reeve's grand dining hall. "We will be risin' early to leave."

"Aye," Richard agreed and called out for everyone to listen. "We must end this celebration and get some rest, for we will not enjoy many hours of sleep tonight. I know leaving home is difficult, but we will return when the pestilence dies. We will live and return." People cheered. "But we must rest now, my friends. The journey will be tiresome."

The people soon left to return to their beds. Lily promised to help Ivett clean up but there were too many bowls and cups and they decided to let it all soak in buckets until whenever they returned. They gave each other hopeful smiles and parted for the night.

Lily walked home with Richard, Elias and Brother Simon. She wasn't sleepy and found herself still awake an hour after Richard fell asleep. She was ready to jump out of her skin and left the bed without a sound. She dressed quietly, thinking she would go to the shop and gather a few more things, since she was up. She hurried down the stairs and slipped out of the house, unheard by her husband and one of their guests.

What would her life be like if she lived? If they all lived? What if the MacPhersons hated them for intruding on their lives? What if one of the villagers was ill? They would know before they arrived in Invergarry, but what good would it do them? They would all die out in the cold.

"I'm sorry ye have to leave yer home, Lily," she heard Elias' voice behind her, deep, soft, compassionate.

She stopped and looked at him in the moonlight. Her heart skipped and then fell on its arse.

"I will help ye get back here," he promised, staring back at her, looking just as affected.

"What if it comes to Invergarry, Elias?"

"It willna."

"How do you know for certain?"

"Because no one will be allowed inside after us. As long as the sickness isna already with us then there is no way it can enter the stronghold."

She closed her eyes praying he was correct.

"I'm frightened," she confessed.

"I know," he answered, as if he understood. But she was not only speaking of the pestilence. She was speaking of him also. She was afraid of what to do about him.

"Are you afraid, Elias?"

"A little, lass. But I am confident."

She smiled as the wind battered her wispy hair around her face. She was glad he hadn't realized what she was truly talking about, and happy to know that he was certain they would escape the sickness.

"Here, take my cloak as extra—"

"No. I will not take your warmth because I was foolish enough to come outdoors at night."

He stopped untying and held out his arm, inviting her to come under his cloak. "If ye need it."

She did, but she knew she could not accept without wanting more, a kiss mayhap, the scrape of his teeth against her throat. The scruff on his jaw between her breasts. She wouldn't be able to separate his kindness from the thrill of being tucked under his arm, safe from the cold, from the disease, from everything but guilt.

She shook her head and moved away, continuing on.

"Are ye goin' to work?" he asked, following her.

"Aye."

"I will help ye."

She shouldn't be, but she was glad he was coming with her. "Were you having another sleepless night?" she asked him, though the silence between them was not awkward. "Mayhap I could unpack some chamomile and make you some tea."

"I was sleepless, but not over the same things that once haunted me. When I heard ye leave the house, I didna want ye to be alone oot here at night, so I left my bed."

She liked that he took it upon himself to protect her. She liked it too much. "What are the things that once haunted you? Would you tell them to me?" She didn't want to know what had kept him awake tonight. No matter what it was, it wasn't good for her.

"Nae, lass. They arena fit fer yer ears."

She smiled as she reached the shop and stepped inside with him. "My ears and your eyes, and yet you saw them. Besides," she added while she went about the shop lighting several lanterns, "you forget I am the wife of an apothecary. You would be stunned and horrified to learn what I have heard people say."

"I havena forgotten, lass," he told her in voice as deep as the shadows.

She turned to him as he hung his cloak on a peg near the door. In the soft golden glow of the lantern light, he looked more like an angel than a man of war. *She* haunted him now. Brother Simon didn't have to tell her that Elias cared for her for her to know. She wanted to tell him he haunted her as well, but she couldn't. Her heart and her belly ached with the need. She would have to find a way to speak with Brother Simon tomorrow while they traveled.

For now though, all she could do was try to help Elias. "You saw many men die?"

"Aye," he said, nodding, and then saying nothing more.

"And women and children?"

He nodded again and picked an empty jar up off a shelf and looked inside.

"'Tis a difficult thing to forget," she thought out loud.

"There is no forgettin'," he told her quietly while the wind howled outside and light around them flickered and danced with the shadows. "Ye must learn to live with it."

"How do you do that?" she asked and went behind her table and began crushing some coriander.

"I havena figured that oot yet." He dragged a stool to the opposite side of the table and smiled at her as he sat.

"What is the worst thing that haunts you?" she probed. He most likely never spoke of the horrors he'd seen. Mayhap he needed to. She wasn't here to heal him. She was here to help him. "I can tell you the most horrific thing someone once told me about their foot if you prefer. You will discover that you do not always have to see a thing with your eyes to have it affect you."

He laughed with a soft mocking tone. "I already have things I wish to forget and ye wish to burden me with more?"

"What do you want to forget most?"

His laughter subsided into a remorseful smile. "That Richard is yer husband."

She brought the pestle down on the coriander and her finger.

"Owwww!" she squeaked and pulled her finger away to shake it. He took hold of her hand in one of his hands and covered it with the other.

"It could be broken, lass. Dinna shake it. Let me have a look." He leaned over the table and pulled a lantern closer.

Her blood pumped loudly in her ears while she watched him examine her in the light. His much bigger hands were gentle moving her finger, testing the bone. She almost forgot the pain staring at him, breathing in the scent of him. "I dinna think 'tis broken," he said and his breath fell warm on her hand. "Just bruised."

He lingered a moment longer as if he had more to say, but didn't.

Finally, he let her go and straightened again on the stool. He closed his callused hands around the mortar and pestle and took it with him as he went.

"You do not have to—"

"I said I would help."

"I am not usually so ungraceful," she laughed at herself.

"My lady," he said, slowing his work with the mortar and pestle and looking at her across the table, "every single thing aboot ye is graceful."

She was glad he wasn't holding her hand anymore because it was shaking. She lowered both hands under the table. She didn't want him to see how he affected her. She was ashamed that he did.

Seeming to sense her sudden unease, he resumed pulverizing coriander, even adding more leaves to the bowl. "What is this good fer?" he asked, lightening her mood. She loved talking about her herbs.

"Fever." Their eyes met again, knowing fever was one symptom of the pestilence. There were many others.

"And that?" He pointed the pestle to a tied bunch of stalks and leaves on the window.

It broke Lily's heart that she could not take everything.

"'Tis hemlock. When mixed with henbane 'tis applied to aching joints."

He smiled at her. "Is this yer passion?"

"Aye." She felt her mouth smiling, wider. She couldn't stop it. "Though the pestilence is terrifying, I love what we were doing— mixing, testing this herb with that."

"Ye will continue such work in the stronghold. More, everything ye and Richard need will be provided."

She wanted to ask him how when it was difficult enough in Sevenoaks to get herbs from faraway places. Invergarry was far north. But she didn't want to sound or feel hopeless. This likely was the last night she would spend under the cover of a roof. She wanted to enjoy it, with him and with her herbs.

"Why are you called Lion Heart?" she asked, turning the conversation to him. Elias was quickly becoming her other passion. "What have you done to earn such a name?"

He laughed softly and returned the mortar to her. The leaves inside were mashed perfectly. He shrugged his broad shoulders. "I have a habit of fightin' the ones everyone else is afraid to fight."

She raised an eyebrow at him and pulled a stool closer so she could sit, forgetting her shaking hands, her coriander, and everything else. "Oh?" she asked, resting her elbow on the table and putting her chin in her hand. "Tell me who everyone was afraid to fight."

"Hmm, let me see." Light and shadows from his lashes made his eyes dance as he thought about it. "There was King Edward's second in command, Edgar Erickson. He fought the Scots in a different part of France than I. He killed many. Most were afraid of him, nicknamed *Skull Smasher*, he stood almost seven feet tall, with shoulders as wide as the length of a claymore. I was told he was of Vikin' heritage. He had a nasty habit of huntin' oot Scots and smashin' in their skulls with his mace.

"Finally, I was sent into battle at Crécy, where Dunbar John, a friend of mine, had recently been killed by Erickson. I knew he had to die and I wanted to be the one to do it, whether we won the battle or lost.

"I fought him on the field. Both of us were bloody and weary—him, more than me because of his size, which became his disadvantage. I knew where I had to strike him. I had to bring him down as quickly as possible. I blocked his terrible blows a few times and then ducked and ran around him. Quickly, I swiped my blade across the backs of his ankles and then simply waited fer him to go down. When he did, I cracked open his skull with my axe and then retreated with my men."

She stared at him for a moment, shocked by his words and the merciless way he spoke them. He was no innocent beauty. He was deadly, clever, and brave, she spoke out loud and then blinked.

He gave her a crooked smile and shrugged again.

"Who else?"

"A bear."

"You fought a bear?" she asked with skepticism tainting her brow.

"I had no choice," he defended. "It took a swipe at Simon that would have taken Simon's head clean off. We were all in danger."

"No!" She held up her hands to stop him from speaking. "Do not tell me how you did it. I believe you."

She got up to bring them two cups then sat back down and reached under the table to produce a small jug of ale.

"How did you become so courageous?" she asked him, pulling on the cork and pouring the liquid.

"I dinna know. Simon tells me I was afraid of my own father when I was a babe."

"Why would you be afraid of your own father?" she asked.

"He was verra hairy."

They laughed then spoke a little more about Elias' father.

"He was orphaned and sold as a slave from the age of two," Elias told her.

She loved the deep pitch of his voice, the musical inflections. She wanted to listen to it for the rest of her life.

"He fell in love with his lord's daughter, my stepmother. He was nineteen when he finally kissed her and was beaten and tossed out of the city gates of Berwick a few hours before the Scots besieged the castle and massacred everyone. My stepmother also escaped and was brought to safety by my uncle."

Lily had to remember to close her mouth. "How did she become your stepmother? Did she love your father? But he was a servant!" she gasped when Elias nodded.

"They had grown up in the same house, one in the privileged quarters and one in the servants' quarters. After the conquest of Berwick, they became separated."

"But they found each other again," Lily finished breathlessly.

"Aye," he said with a smile, "they did. Even after he wed my mother and she died givin' birth to me, he still longed fer Julianna. They were designed to be together."

She narrowed her eyes on him and cocked her mouth slightly to one side.

"Do you believe that, Elias?"

He nodded without hesitancy. "Sometimes folks are brought together under the most difficult of circumstances. They survive because of each other."

Aye, she thought, mayhap he was correct. Some were designed to be together. But that didn't mean she and Elias were. "I believe it for Richard and me."

"Aye," he said with a sincere smile. "I believe it as well. He saved yer life, lass. I believe it as well."

Lily was surprised and thankful he did. He wouldn't be bold with her because he respected her marriage vows. She straightened before her heart melted all over the table.

She reached for a piece of cloth and scooped the coriander into it. "'Tis always good to carry some herbs with you."

"I will carry some, too," Elias told her while she tied the small pouch with twine. "What shall we crush next?"

"Balm!" she said excitedly. "One can never have enough balm." She laughed at herself and wondered if she was drunk on ale...or on him.

And what was she doing to keep herself from falling for him? Nothing! Her mood quickly changed as she began pulverizing her herbs.

If they were designed to be together, why had he arrived two years too late? She wanted to punch him and then put balm on his wound. Not that she could inflict much pain on him.

"What troubles ye suddenly, lass?

And why, when he called her lass, did her knees shake and almost crumble? It didn't have the same effect when Brother Simon called her lass.

It was because Elias said it with indulgence and tenderness and the deep baritone that resonated through her bones.

She shook her head and was careful not to crush her finger again. "The unknown."

"The unknown could be yer greatest adventure."

Would he be in the unknown? She wanted to ask him. "We should go to bed." Her face went pale, her eyes wide at how what had just come from her mouth sounded. "I mean home. We should go home and go to our separate beds."

His smile turned to soft laughter that drew her from her seat.

He feigned seriousness. "I thought I would teach ye a wee bit of defense."

She came around the narrow table and stood near him. "Aye, then. Teach me."

"All right." He sobered and produced a dagger from his left boot. He crooked his finger at her. She came closer to him. He handed the hilt of the dagger to her and hurried to the back room. He retuned a few moments later with a piece of coal from her small trivet, went to the opposite wall and drew a square within a square on it.

When he was done, he went back to her and stood a little bit behind her. "It doesna matter where ye hold the dagger, by the blade or by the handle. What matters is distance. I will show ye."

He held her wrist and at one point, her waist—until they both realized it and separated. They practiced for another hour, forgetting the time.

When they finally did end their practice, she put her balm in a pouch, tied it, and carried it and the coriander to the door. Elias was there, behind her. His fingers brushed her shoulder as he put his cloak around her, sending fire through her veins.

"Let me keep ye warm."

His fathomless whisper set her hands to shaking.

He wrapped her in the soft wool and, leaning in, inhaled her scent. She hoped she smelled pleasant and not like the dozens of onions she'd chopped for Joan today.

He didn't speak but moved his head an inch or two downward, toward her nape and breathed in again. She felt like a living flame, ready to set everything to ash. She wanted to turn around and stand so close that their bodies touched while they breathed against each other. She wanted to feel those strong, muscular arms she'd seen carrying four heavy sacks at a time close around her. She wanted to stare into his eyes while he prepared to kiss her...

She stepped forward and left the shop instead.

CHAPTER NINE

L ILY WAS UP at dawn, as was everyone else in the house with the red roof. Sitting together at the table, they broke their fast on bread, butter seasoned with rosemary and garlic, two apples each, and ale.

She listened to the men talk about the landscape and how some parts of the journey would be harder than others. But her thoughts were solely on Elias, sitting across from her, and the hours they'd spent in the shop last eve. Talking, laughing, practicing. He made her feel happy and hopeful. And she was able to forget her shame for a little while.

She turned her gaze on Richard while he spoke. She was certain he'd been quite a handsome man in his youth. His eyes were dark sable brown, his nose was straight and his chin, beneath his long gray beard was still strong.

He caught her gaze and smiled at her. She smiled back and felt her eyes begin to burn. Being with him was like having her father back. There was no sexual interaction of any kind between them, just gentleness and patience. She loved him and she hated herself for betraying it.

She tried to think of anything to get her mind off Elias and the touch of his hands when he took hers after she'd smashed her finger. The way his indomitable strength covered her when he stood behind her and helped her toss his dagger and then wrapped her in his cloak and pressed his nose to her hair, and the back of her neck. Fire had crackled her bones and turned to liquid in her blood. It was happening now, just thinking of him. He'd walked her to bed and bid her good sleep.

She hadn't gotten any.

She wanted to fall at Richard's feet and beg his forgiveness for enjoying her time with someone else so much.

One of them said something that made the others smile and look at her.

"I must fetch Pip before we go," she told them and rose from her seat. Brother Simon nearly jumped out of his when she went near him.

She went to him and tried to comfort him. "Dear Brother, I do not have her in my hands. Does even the talk of cats frighten you?"

He nodded sheepishly.

"Will you tell me why sometime?" she asked, genuinely interested.

"Of course, lass," the brother replied. "Mayhap on the way home."

"Aye," she grinned at him and then went off to find her cat.

She found Pip inside the shop. Before she left, she looked around at the bare shelves and the few pots of herbs hanging from the rafters. It made her belly knot and her heart break. She didn't want to leave her life here, but she wiped her nose, grabbed her cat, and left the shop.

It took another hour and a half for everyone to be ready to go with his or her belongings. Most carried sacks. Some laid their sacks and goods on makeshift wooden sleds. They'd gone through everything they had and were forced to choose only the bare basics of what they needed.

"I do not know how my daughter, Deirdre, is going to hold up."

Martin Miller found her and filled her ear with concern over his daughter. "She is due to have her child any time now."

Walter the butcher and his wife, Eleanor, hurried toward her. "Lily, I need to see Richard," Walter pleaded. "I did not sleep last eve and now my head is splitting."

Lily was moved with compassion for him, for she knew what he was feeling. "Forgive me, Walter, but I do hope you will understand how scarce the herbs are going to be. We must endure some things and preserve what we have."

"Aye," he said, looking disappointed, and walked away rubbing his head.

She turned back to Martin. "Where were we? Oh, aye. Deirdre. Fear not, she will ride on Brother Simon's horse."

His face transformed and he offered her a radiant smile. "Bless you, Lily."

She found Clare next. She and Elias helped Clare secure her two sacks to the donkey. "I'm frightened, Lily," Clare confided. "I'm frightened for my child. What if the pestilence follows us?"

"We will keep eyes on it through Osbert's friends and keep moving if we have to. But we will not die."

Clare sniffed and nodded, but she didn't look convinced. She smiled at Elias, though, when he lifted little Eddie over his head and set him down on his shoulders.

A thought flashed across Lily's mind. What if she died? Would Elias marry Clare? What was stopping him from pursuing little Eddie's mother now?

She hated her thoughts and tried to outrun them by going to Richard and helping him mount Elias' horse. The stallion was enormous. It took Lily, Father Benedict, Simon, and Osbert to help.

She didn't want to ride. She wanted to walk, to be among her friends as they set out on this new adventure. She saw Elias and little Eddie and went to them, drawn to him, stirred from some primitive part of her by the sight of him with the two-year-old boy, to have his children.

Before she had time to feel guilty over her thoughts, she heard someone scream and stopped in her tracks just before she reached them. Her heart felt as if it were about to leap from her throat and wither up. What was it? Her mind thought the worst. No! No, not now when they were just about to escape it! Had the pestilence come?

Worse. It was Bertram. He'd returned, a bit slumped over on his horse. His shoulder where Elias' dagger had landed, was wrapped in dirty bandages. He brought with him six mounted men. They surrounded the group of villagers and two of the men expelled the contents of their bellies, spreading their disease they carried to the four winds.

"LILY!" ELIAS SHOUTED to her. He had to think clearly! His thoughts had never been influenced by his heart before. Panic and urgency filled him as he lowered little Eddie to the ground. He had once command-ed five hundred men and, thankfully, his training kicked in. "Get the children and move oot of the way!"

While she moved, he yanked a knife free from his belt and flung it at the man closest to her. The blade landed keenly into the man's throat. He ran for his horse and helped Richard out of the saddle. "Go to Simon," he commanded the apothecary. To Simon, he called out, "Take him and Lily and the children back to the shop!" He leaped into the saddle and rode his horse to the front of the line and set his gaze on Bertram. He would kill him for this.

He heard someone sniffle and looked to his left at Deirdre, just a few feet away on Simon's horse.

She stared at him and tears spilled from her eyes. "You are willing to fight for people you hardly know."

He didn't answer her or look around to see who was watching him. He didn't listen to Bertram ordering Richard to get him and his men something for their sickness. The apothecary hadn't gone to the shop. Had Lily? He didn't turn around to find out but yanked on the reins with one hand and tore his claymore from its scabbard with the other. He rode directly for Bertram but two of his men rode in front of him to stop Elias. They died just as quickly. Another foolish man who was sweating profusely came at him pointing his shaky sword. Elias swung his blade around his shoulders and separated the man's head from his body. A woman screamed. No, several women screamed. Elias chanced a look around. Agnes and Estrid were weeping loudly.

Bertram had moved away from him, leaving in his place two more of his men. These could barely hold themselves up in their saddles. Some parts of their skin had turned black, like their fingers. There appeared to be large boils on their necks beneath their hoods.

"Please," one of them begged. "We just want a cure."

How many of the villagers were affected? How long would it take for the rest of them now? Everything had changed. In an instant. They weren't going to Invergarry. Instead, they had just been sentenced to death. A very unpleasant one.

"Ye shouldna have come here," he told them and killed them within seconds of each other.

"He has Lily!" Osbert's wife, Ivett, screamed, pointing somewhere beyond the evergreens.

Elias' stout heart nearly faltered. *No! Please, no!* He saw Simon trying to hold back Richard but when the old man saw Elias thundering forward on his horse, he managed to break free.

"Elias, do not kill him!" Richard shouted as Elias turned the bend and came to Bertram and Lily standing face to face.

Damn it! Why hadn't she listened to him and gone inside? "Lily…"

he began.

"Do you know what you have done?" she screamed, pointing a dagger at Bertram. "You have killed us all!"

"Lily," Richard commanded. "Put away your dagger! We need him to find a cure! Wife, do you hear me?" he asked with authority. "We need him. How can I know what works if I have no one with whom to try my mixtures?"

"Perform yer experiments on me," Elias offered, moving his horse closer to Bertram's.

Bertram knew he was too weak to fight, especially with one arm. He dropped his sword and held up his hand.

"Get off yer horse," Elias demanded.

Bertram did as he was told and wiped his sweaty brow. "Hell, but 'tis hot."

"I do not want to wait until one of us is stricken," Richard called out as many sobbed and wept bitterly, for they knew they would most likely die now. "I want to have some knowledge of this monster before all my friends are gone. Let me try my remedies on him now."

"Kill him!" someone called out. "As he has killed us!"

"Aye, kill him!" others shouted. "We do not want him alive to infect more of us."

"He will not come near you," Richard shouted to them. "Everyone here will likely become ill by the rest of us. Finding a cure is vital now! You must let me try now that I have a living patient."

Everyone cried the same thing. Kill him! Elias wanted to. He hated Bertram Chisholm for all he'd done to Lily, for what he had just done to Sevenoaks.

Elias slanted his gaze to Lily. He wanted to scream and tear out his hair. No! He wouldn't let her die! He wouldn't let the sickness take her! It was too late for everyone now. Richard needed to start practicing his remedies on someone who was ill now! The choice wasn't his to make. Lily was the one he'd hurt the most. But this was about more than Lily now. This was about the lives in Sevenoaks.

Elias pointed the tip of his blade into Bertram' back and looked to Richard. "Where do ye want him?"

"In the shed."

"Richard," Elias said before they left. "If he gets well, I'm killin' him."

Richard nodded. There wasn't much else he could do. No one would stop Elias from what he meant to do.

"Ye took Lily from her family," he growled, giving Bertram a shove forward. "Someone verra close to me was taken from his family at a young age. I have seen the effects of it firsthand. I will not let ye live."

"Ye are a Scot," Bertram breathed out in front of him. "A Highlander judgin' by yer plaid. Ye know how lonely winter can be."

Elias pushed him through the door and hurled him inside the half-empty shed.

"Ye know ye have been stricken with the pestilence, aye?" Elias asked him, dragging him to a post. "Ye are dyin'."

"I suspect it."

"Ye brought it here," Elias said, tying him to the post. "For that, I might allow the villagers some time alone with ye before ye die."

"The bishop knows I'm here," Bertram warned.

"Good, I will invite him here to examine yer body," Elias promised, then kicked him in the kneecaps to get him to sit on the floor.

"Take a nap or somethin'," Elias told him, leaving him alone. "Enjoy the short time ye still have alive."

"Ye do the same, MacPherson," Bertram called out in a low, guttural voice.

At the door, Elias turned to him and smiled. "I will."

He shut the door and took a long, deep breath. What was he to do now? Come to terms that he would likely be dead within a few days, and Lily a few days after that? No. No, he wouldn't.

He stepped outside and found a dozen villagers, including Lily, Richard and Simon staring back at him. A blink of his long spray of lashes was all it took to get them all talking. It all came at once. Most begged him to take them to Invergarry. Everything was ready to leave. Mayhap none of them were afflicted, but he wouldn't take that chance.

"What will we do now?" Walter called out.

"My girls are just children," Norman lamented.

"Aye, our son, Terrick is only eight summers," cried Walter's wife, Eleanor.

"Richard, are we going to die?" Martin Miller asked, holding on to Joan and his daughter.

The apothecary held up his hands to try to quiet them. "We know very little about this illness. We do not know how 'tis spread only that 'tis moving quickly. That is all we know, so…based on that alone, I would say 'tis likely that many of us have become afflicted."

Horror ensued. Two women fainted. Men cried out and fell to their knees.

Elias understood it. He never really had before. He'd grown up in the sheltering safety of a fortified, mostly self-sustaining village—with no reason to be afraid. Life had been dull and he'd grown curious for more. He'd been trained to master the art of fighting and he'd wanted to use his skill in battle. He left the stronghold at seventeen to fight the English in Dunbar.

It wasn't that he didn't feel fear. He felt it. He liked how alive it made him feel. He'd experienced it often in battle, but something was different with this enemy. This enemy wanted her… his gaze flicked to Lily trying to calm Estrid and Eleanor.

Miserably, he reconciled himself to the fact that he was beginning to care a bit too much for her. He was sorry for it, but that didn't stop it. He'd have to confess the deep, dark things that crossed his mind at times…things about her husband, his friend.

Would the sickness take her? He had the sensation of his heart and belly sinking downward. A different kind of fear, like nothing he'd ever felt before, encased him like a dark cloud. It didn't feel invigorating. It felt as if he were being smothered to death. Slowly. He wanted to take Lily and run. Take her and hide.

But there was no place to go without possibly spreading the sickness to others. He wouldn't do it and he wouldn't let the others do it.

"Everyone!" he shouted once, and then again in a thunderous voice. "There is no sense in cryin' over what canna be changed. The pestilence may be here, but we have the most intelligent apothecary the good Lord has ever created here with us. Let us help him find a remedy. If ye want to be a part of doin' somethin' to help, to give us all hope, then grab some of Richard's bags containin' his herbs and let us help him bring them back to the shop."

He took a step forward and clasped one hand around Richard's thin arm and the other around Lily's even thinner wrist. "Come, there is work to be done." He pulled them gently along, leaving the villagers to follow or not.

There was nothing left to do but find a cure...and pray. Pray hard.

CHAPTER TEN

O N RICHARD'S INSTRUCTION and Osbert's agreement, they burned
the dead bodies of Bertram Chisholm's men. Richard had
requested that everyone tear a cloth and tie it around their face as a
makeshift mask and wash their hands as often as possible. Some
complained about wasting water and what did their hands have to do
with anything? Richard confessed that he didn't know if it would help,
but his reasoning was that it wouldn't hurt.

Now, standing around the shop, waiting for the first batch of tea to
boil on her small trivet in the back, Lily watched her husband. He
mixed and stirred, smelled and tasted three different concoctions. Elias
wrote the ingredients of each on a sheet of parchment then dipped his
finger into different colored dyes and marked each list and a small
bottle with a corresponding color.

She watched them both, thankful for them, thankful for Richard's
knowledge of herbs and roots and his skill at using them, and thankful
that Elias was here to offer so much help, in so many different ways.
He was strong and able to lift and carry many things to bring them
back to the shop. Things were done faster because of him. He was
intelligent and clever in a time of sheer panic, able to protect them

with his sword if needed. And he knew how to read and write, which also made Richard's tasks easier.

Bother Simon, too, made himself available to everyone young and old, praying with them and offering comfort—from the most terrifying, horrific sickness to ever fall upon mankind. The Black Death was here. It had found them.

It seemed as if the wailing never ceased. Someone was always weeping, whether man, woman, or child.

They had almost been away from here. On their way to a new life. Lily had wanted to lament with Joan when she last saw her, but she hadn't. She had never given up her life before. She wouldn't begin now.

She was sorry others were dying, but that didn't mean any of them would.

The tea boiled in the kettle and filled the air with an aromatic scent.

"'Tis ready," she informed them and stepped back when Richard filled a small cup with the mixture.

"Richard, why do you and Elias have to go near him and expose yourselves to the sickness?" What if they both fell ill? What would she do then? What would any of them do?

"I must know if this can cure him, my dear. Imagine how many people we could save. We have already been exposed, Lily. The three of us more than the rest. I must be about my work." Her husband turned and left the shop.

She didn't know if she agreed with Richard and Elias' decision to let Bertram live. Save an evil man in order to try to save everyone else? Or let him die and rot in hell for the things he'd done and would do again if he were given the chance.

If they didn't find the cure before he died, what good was letting the sickness spread from him?

But if they found something...

She caught Elias slanting his gaze at her over his shoulder. Did he wink? Oddly, she felt a little better about everything and leaned back against the doorframe and watched them head toward the shed.

A little while later, she saw Brother Simon coming toward her and smiled, though he couldn't see it behind her mask.

"Are they inside?" he asked, reaching her.

"Aye."

"I have been praying in the church with Father Benedict," the brother told her without moving to go into the shed after them. "We have different views on some things. But we agree that we need the Lord's intervention here."

"Do you think He will let Bertram live?" she asked him.

"God might," Brother Simon guessed, "but Bertram will have Elias to worry about after that."

"Aye," she said with a hint of a smile hovering over her lips. "Richard told me Elias' promise."

Brother Simon looked toward the shed and spoke solemnly. "I have never known him to go back on his word."

She couldn't help but wish Elias had come to Sevenoaks two years ago. But everything happens for a reason. He was here. Now. For a reason. What was it?

Did it have something to do with her...or the Black Death?

She suspected she would soon find out.

"Brother Simon?"

"Aye, lass?"

"There is something I have been meaning to ask. Why did you and Elias stay when you first heard about the pestilence? Why did you both not race back home to the north?"

His cheeks turned red and he swallowed as if he fought to keep his words in his mouth, but they pushed out. "He...he is sometimes reckless, or so 'twould seem. One always comes to realize that he had his victory planned out from the beginning. As in the case of Bertram.

He rushed to your defense and to mine, but not before he rendered Bertram helpless. In your case, he saw you, met you—and everyone here, and once more stood up to the threat of death."

She closed her eyes and tried to slow her heartbeat. He cared for her and for Richard and the villagers. He'd proven it. He was courageous and compassionate. *Lion Heart*. Oh, it was difficult to resist him.

She looked around then leaned in closer to Brother Simon. "I have been dreaming about him," she confessed, knowing she could trust him. Even so, she felt ill speaking it aloud. But if she was going to die, she wouldn't go guilty. "I do not mean to. I pray not to, but then there he is, every night. Tell me what to do."

He pulled down his mask and his luminously large eyes softened on her. "These are dire times—"

"Never mind," she whispered nervously when Elias and Richard left the shed and headed back.

Brother Simon pulled his mask back up and turned to greet them. "Does he still live?"

"Aye," Richard told them. "But he is worse. It progresses swiftly. I must get back to my task. Eli will fill you both in on what happened." He walked away and returned to the back room.

"He is weary," Elias remarked about Richard. "He will not rest."

Aye. She knew it was true. Richard barely sat down and had been awake all night. Now that he had a patient, he would find a cure.

"Did Bertram drink the tea?" she asked Elias, letting her gaze drift over the top half of his features. She loved looking at his eyes, not just looking into them. She loved the silver shards against a background of blue—like a sky lit with stars, or lightning. She wished she could pull down the cloth covering the rest of his face. She wanted to take in the strength of his jaw, the…

She blinked out of her reverie, when she realized he was speaking.

"He complained like a child aboot the taste and was takin' too long to drink. I had to convince him to drink faster with the cold tip of my blade against his throat."

"You enjoy pushing him around," Brother Simon accused Elias with a teasing smile.

"Verra much," Elias confirmed with a sinister snarl that made her catch her breath. "We will give him more tea in two hours. Richard says we will know more after that."

Lily looked toward the shed rather than at Elias. She would like to go in and have a word or two with Bertram while he was still alive to hear her. She knew it wasn't safe, but she had already been exposed. Besides, Richard and Elias had gone into the shed. If they both died, she would prefer to die, as well.

But what was there to say to him? That she hated him for taking so much of her life, and then returning to take the rest of it? Would it make her feel better to tell him that she hoped he lived so that she could watch Elias kill him, or mayhap, she would kill him herself? Was he worth her soul?

No.

But she would speak to him…tonight, when everyone was asleep.

They started back to work, preparing for the next batch, talking about the sickness.

Lily turned to both of them with a pleading look in her eyes. "I do not wish to speak of this thing any further today. We do not know what tomorrow will bring, or whose life the sickness will claim." She spread her eyes over the village. "I do not want to think on it any- more."

Brother Simon lowered his gaze and nodded in silent, somber agreement.

"I dinna want to think on it anymore today either!" Elias pro- claimed across the narrow table. He turned to look down and offer her a bright smile. "Let us gather everyone, includin' Richard fer some hours of drinkin' and mirth. Simon, knock at every door and tell the villagers to meet us ootside the shop in an hour. Lily, gather the children, invite them to come and meet me fer some games. Also, who was that man playin' the lute last eve?"

"Norman the baker."

"Tell him, too! I will convince Richard to rest for a little while."

Lily shook her head. "He will say it needs to be done now more than ever. Even though he will be correct, he has not slept and he has not sat down all day."

"I will ask him fer an hour or two." He winked at her. "Have faith in me. If I say I will do somethin', I will do it. Richard will sit."

She gave him a hopeful smile and left to go about her task. Aye, this was the right thing to do. At least it would get the children away from their wailing parents.

Poor Brother Simon. She didn't envy his task. No one was going to want to drink and laugh with a death sentence over their head.

She wasn't sure she wanted to. But it was better than trying to stop something she couldn't control. In that, the pestilence was like her feelings for Elias.

One would destroy her body. The other, her soul.

She wanted to weep but she saw Charlie and his sister, Cecily, getting water from the well. She smiled instead.

"Elias invites you to meet him for some games."

They looked relieved and more grateful than if she'd just given them a sennight's worth of cookies. They happily agreed to tell the other children and ran off hollering and making quite a fuss—drowning out the sound of crying.

THE SUN BEGAN its slow descent, leaving the world in an odd orange-crimson glow. No one wanted to go indoors yet to eat, for they had unpacked their food and prepared another feast in Osbert the reeve's dining hall.

Some sat on blankets in the cool grass watching and cheering the children while they played foot ball with lemons. Elias had taught them how to play after he taught them and Lily more defensive maneuvers with his dagger. Eventually, some of the parents joined in.

Everyone was there. Even Richard had kicked a lemon around the markers before he took a seat in a cushioned chair—one of three Elias had carried out of Osbert's house and placed in the grass for the elders to sit.

Elias had kept his word.

They cheered when young Annabelle kicked one lemon through Simon's legs and hit a marker. They laughed when little Eddie, who seemed to always miss hitting the lemon when he kicked his short legs at it, finally dropped on all fours, stole the lemon, and ran off with it.

Not everyone participated in the merriment, but they all showed up.

Lily was thankful. She looked over at Elias laughing with the children. How did he do it? How did he manage to remain so strong? Strong enough for them all?

The lemon came her way and she shoved it forward with her foot, gently enough not to hurt any of the children running at her. She looked for a clearing and pushed the lemon to her left. She kicked, but the fruit was intercepted by Norman's daughters, Ava and Emma. The rest of the children reached her and she laughed in the midst of them. She felt better than she had since she was a child. She enjoyed kicking lemons around in the grass and being chased by laughing children.

"You have turned a horrific day into something less horrific," she told Elias on the way back to Osbert's house for supper. Richard walked ahead with Osbert and Father Benedict.

He bowed in his place, leaving her to stare at the soft waves in his dark hair. "I'm pleased ye think so, my lady."

"Elias." Six-year-old Annabelle tugged on his cloak and looked up at him from over her mask, her huge blue eyes shining in the torchlight. "Tomorrow, want to play with my toys?" She was out of breath from running to catch up with him. Her mask sucked in and out. "I have clay poppets and wooden horses, and I have teacups and a kettle. I could make you some tea!"

Lily watched Elias, already bent to the girl. "I would like that verra much, Annabelle."

The little girl giggled and then ran off to her mother.

"How are you so good at this?" Lily asked, marveling at him. No one was crying and everyone was hungry.

"I have a huge family," he explained. "I have two brothers, two sisters, and nine cousins. My brother, Colin, has four bairns. Elysande, my cousin, has six with her husband, Raphael. Her brother, Milo, has five and Robin has five, as well."

"My, that is large!" Her eyes crinkled when she laughed under her mask. "And do you all play?"

"We used to."

"You miss them," she said, knowing he must. "We were so close to going back. I'm sorry you came here."

His warm gaze skipped back to hers. "I'm not sorry."

"Elias," she said stopping. She grabbed hold of his arm to stop him, too. "You could have gone. You could have left yesterday and escaped this. I do not want to think that you gave up your life for me. I do not want to live knowing that." Tears misted her eyes. "Not even for a few days."

He breathed out a gust of breath beneath the cloth tied around his face. "I didna want ye to fall ill, Lily. The thought of it crushes me. All I could think aboot was keepin' ye and Simon and Richard safe. Then, when ye refused to leave, ye forced me to realize why ye wouldna go. So, first, please accept my sincerest apologies fer askin' such a selfish thing from ye. And also, forgive me fer bein' so selfish. I had a lapse in good judgment due to…fear." He looked as if he wanted to say more, but he kept silent for a moment. Then he said with a shrug, "Normally, I dinna run from anythin'."

She crooked her mouth at him, but he couldn't see. "I can see how some would call you reckless."

She wished they didn't have to wear these masks! She liked looking at his mouth while he spoke. If they were all affected, wasn't it too late for masks anyway?

"It all depends on what you believe is reckless."

Now she felt wretched for giving him the impression that she thought risking your life for others was reckless—in the foolish sense. She didn't. She found it noble and admirable. Should she tell him? Would it seem as if she were trying to woo him into something?

The silver shards in his eyes twinkled in the firelight when he smiled at her. "If I hadna stayed, then I wouldna be here today."

He made it sound so simple, as if it should all make perfect sense now.

But why was she trying to make sense of any of it? In the end, and the end was coming, it wouldn't matter. She was happy he was here today.

"Elias?" She wanted to tell him that she was glad he was here. Tell him things she'd already confessed to Brother Simon. She thought about Elias all the time. And when she was asleep, she dreamed of him.

"Come now, both of you," Father Benedict scolded them from where he waited at Osbert's front door. "We do not have all night to wait for you!"

Elias scowled right back at him and then lowered his head when he saw Charlie and Terrick watching him. "Aye, forgive us, Father," he corrected.

"Aye," Lily agreed, and then spoke to the priest in a hushed tone while Elias stepped inside. Father Benedict would not allow them to leave once he had them. "And forgive me but I forgot something at the shop. Start without me, Father." She hurried away. The shed wasn't too far.

By the time Elias realized she had slipped away, she would be on her way back to him. She only wanted a moment with Bertram.

She stepped inside the shed and reached for the burning torch on the wall. The door hadn't shut all the way and almost blew out the light. She hurried to the door and secured it shut. She took four steps to where Bertram sat sleeping on the floor. He wore a mask over half his face and his wrists were tied over his head to the post behind him in a small part of the shed where Richard usually kept his old horse, Peony. Richard had changed the bandages around his shoulder.

"Bertram! Wake up!" she demanded with a soft kick. She waited a moment to see if he would respond before kicking him again. "I cannot wait to finally be free of you. I will—"

"Boy." Bertram whispered and grinned at her.

"I am not a boy. I am Lily. Open your eyes."

He did. They were so bloodshot that they were almost solid red. "Always...the...boy."

She had no idea why he would say anything about a boy. It must be the sickness. He must be dreaming of only God knows what.

"Bertram!" She kicked him harder. "Wake up. I wish to tell you something. Bertram?"

What did it matter? He would be dead soon and face God.

She left and returned to Osbert's home.

She didn't see or hear Elias when he stepped into the torchlight after she'd gone.

CHAPTER ELEVEN

B Y EARLY THE next morn, every herb and plant was back on the shelves and Richard had tried three different mixtures on Bertram. Normally, the apothecary had explained to her and Elias, he would work faster with fewer ingredients. Time was their greatest enemy. Elias spent the morning playing with Annabelle, as he'd promised. When Joan fell ill by mid-afternoon, Richard had his second patient and was able to double his work.

Lily sat by Joan's bedside for long periods during the day. She wiped her friend's head down with vinegar and fed her the teas Richard had prescribed. She prayed for Joan and for everyone in Sevenoaks, in England and beyond. She wondered if her husband would be the one who found a cure for the Black Death.

"Joan, dearest," she said softly to her friend. "Richard is working feverishly. We will fight this. *You* will fight."

"Be away from me, Lily," Joan cried out. "Be away!"

"I will not go away, Joan," Lily let her know. "I will not abandon my closest friend."

"Be away as my husband and daughter are away." Joan cried.

Lily frowned, knowing that Martin hadn't visited his wife at all, nor had Deirdre, though Deirdre was heavy with child. "Your daughter should stay in bed—"

"Aye, that is what I told Martin! But he pulled Deirdre out of bed and onto a horse and left with her."

"What?" Lily sat up, alarmed. What should she do? "They left?"

"Aye," Joan wheezed out, but Lily was gone.

She hurried to the shop and burst inside when she reached it.

Elias was there, crushing herbs and writing things down on a piece of parchment on the table before him.

"Richard!" she shouted to get him out front.

Elias was away from the table instantly. "What is it, lass?"

"There, there now, what is this sound you are making, Wife?" Richard asked hurrying to her side.

"Martin and Deirdre have left Sevenoaks," she labored to tell them.

"No!" Richard said then looked toward Elias.

The Highlander didn't flinch or hesitate. Not once. Not even for an instant. He hurried past Lily and left the shop. He sprinted for his horse. Filling Simon in when his friend saw him and joined him.

Martin might not listen to two strangers. He almost assuredly wouldn't put his cherished daughter into the hands of a Highlander. She had to go with them.

"Richard needs ye here." Elias told her when she ran to the stable.

"I'm coming."

"Nae," he said, sounding as if his mind were made up.

"Elias, they might not listen to you," she insisted. "I cannot sit here do nothing while my friends die!"

"We dinna know what is oot there, Lily," he countered. "Please, my lady, do as I ask and stay."

Oh, she felt herself giving in to him. "Elias—"

He held up his hand. "Please, Lily."

She nodded, biting her lip, and then spun around on her heel and left the stable.

On her way back to Richard, she saw Charlie and Terrick running toward the shop. Something was wrong, She hurried forward and entered the shop at the same time the boys did.

"Richard!" Terrick cried. "My father is ill."

"My mother, also," Charlie tried to sound brave. "She said to tell you she has been feeling ill all day."

Lily turned a terrified look to her husband. "Three people in less than two days," she whispered to him. "I have to do something."

He swallowed and nodded, then wiped his brow and set about collecting what she needed. His formulas of hawthorn, milk thistle, cordyceps, crushed alfalfa leaves, blackberry and hot peppers—among other things.

She wanted to crumble to her knees and weep. These were her friends. People she cared about. But there was no time for crying. She hurried to Richard and he gave her four blends and two extra that would only be given to Walter and Charlie's mother, Alice.

"Take me to them," she told the boys, running with them from the shop.

They went to Alice's cottage first, since the seamstress had no husband. Lily hurried inside and found Alice on the floor with Cecily sitting beside her and crying.

"All right," Lily comforted. "'Tis all right. Charlie, take your sister outside with Terrick, please."

When she was alone with her friend, Lily curled Alice's arm around her shoulders and pulled her to her feet. "Come on, then, dearest. Let me walk you to your bed."

Alice tried, but her legs gave out. Lily couldn't hold her up. She fought to keep Alice up and then her friend grew lighter. Charlie had returned and helped his mother get to her bed. When she was down, Lily poured one of her teas into a cup by the bed and held it to her friend's mouth.

"Drink," she urged and tipped the cup as Alice drank, and then coughed up blood.

How? Lily grieved, how was it attacking so quickly? Alice appeared fine the night before. A chill swept through her thinking about who would be ill tonight, and how many would be dead in the morning?

No. Stop. She admonished herself. She would remain strong as long as she was alive. She would be of help to no one if she fell apart.

But, oh, it was hard to stay together. When she looked at Charlie sitting on the other side of the bed, she felt her heart tear to pieces inside her.

"I must go and see to Terrick's father. I will return to give her another cup of tea in an hour. Why do you not go sit outside your house for now."

He shook his head. "I want to stay here with her. Mayhap Cecily could stay with you."

She nodded and promised to return.

Walter wasn't in as bad a state as Alice but Eleanor was hysterical, making Terrick and Cecily cry. Lily sent them outside and went to Walter with a cup of Richard's tea. "Drink this, Walter. Eleanor. Eleanor!" she shouted at the butcher's wife and finally got her attention. "Your husband and your son need you to control yourself. We are all frightened. But imagine what it would be like for the children if all the adults fell apart."

"But Lily—" she cried.

Lily shook her head at the woman. "Leave the house if you cannot be a comfort to your husband."

Eleanor gasped, but took hold of herself.

Lily went outside and spoke to the children in between her visits to Joan, Alice, and Water. Who would be next?

She smiled at Cecily and took Terrick in her arms when he wept over his father. She returned twice more to her patients, administering more tea and prayers with Father Benedict.

She ate supper with Richard, Charlie, Cecily, and Terrick. She liked having the children with her. They didn't remain morose for long and ended their night in laughter with Lily and Cecily in one bed and Richard and the boys in another—although Richard didn't come in until much later.

Lily stayed awake all night, wondering where Elias and Simon were. Had they found Martin and Deirdre Miller? Were they ill? Was Elias ill? The more she thought about it the more she couldn't sleep.

"Lily?"

She opened her eyes to Cecily's gossamer voice.

"Aye, love?"

"Is mummy going to die?"

What was she to say to such a question, put to her by a ten-year-old child? "I hope not, darling. Richard and I are going to do everything we can to help her live."

"Thank you, Lily," Cecily whispered with her eyes closed and her fingers entwined in Lily's.

Lily thought she would cry herself to sleep but she was still awake at midnight when Elias returned.

Slipping from her bed, she pulled a green woolen kirtle over her chemise and tiptoed quickly down the stairs.

She was so glad to see Elias hanging up his cloak in her kitchen, looking tired and somber, but alive and healthy, she was tempted to run to him and fling her arms around him. "Did you find them?" she asked in a quiet voice instead. "How is Deirdre?"

He looked away and swung his leg over a stool at the table and straddled it.

"Should I sit, as well?" she asked, afraid he would say aye.

He nodded. Her heart pounded. She could feel it reverberate in her blood. Something terrible had happened. Did she want to hear?

She sat in her chair at the table and waited, squeezing her own entwined fingers until they ached.

"We found them on the road to Netherfield." His eyes gleamed with sorrow at what he had to tell her. She had the urge to leap off the stool and run before he said another word. She didn't want to hear—

"They had been robbed," he continued telling her. "Martin was...ehm...dead from a stab wound." He reached across the table to cover one of her hands in his. He remained silent while she closed her eyes and shook her head.

"And Deirdre? Her babe?"

He said nothing but looked away.

"No?" She couldn't take it in. No. She left her chair, grabbed her cloak and left the house. She felt something ready to erupt and she didn't want to wake the whole house.

She heard Elias come out after her. His hand on her shoulder seemed to ignite what was brewing but she held on and did not weep. Deirdre, her baby. Martin, all of them. All of them were dying. She needed comfort from today, from all the horrors, all the sadness and Richard had enough weight on his shoulders.

She turned in Elias' arms and let them come around her, engulfing her in strength and courage. She remained quiet against his hard chest and drew strength from him.

"Walter the butcher and Alice, Charlie and Cecily's mother, are sick. None of the herbs are helping, Elias. I do not know who it will strike next."

"Aye, I have thought of it, as well," he admitted. "'Tis indeed a terrible time right now."

She sniffled against him. "Just a few days ago, my biggest trouble was what to give Joan for her ankles."

"Aye," he consoled, "but let us not live as though we have already been defeated, aye?"

She lifted her head and stared at him and then smiled. He was telling her what she'd forgotten for a moment. "Aye," she agreed.

"Where are the Millers' bodies?" she asked him, hating the words and moving out of his embrace.

"We buried them."

She wanted to thank him for it—and for his comforting arms.

"Where is Brother Simon?"

"He has gone to pray fer Joan." His eyes took her in as if he only had a moment before he was caught.

They returned to the warmth of the kitchen hearth, where Lily prepared lemon tea prepared with some of the herbs Richard was using in his remedies. She told him about the children sleeping above stairs in the beds. He promised he didn't mind sleeping on the floor in the sitting room and she promised to make it more comfortable with many blankets.

Simon entered the kitchen from outside and with him came a gust of wind and a wide smile from Lily.

"Brother Simon," she said in a hushed tone, going to him. "I'm so happy to see you."

"As I am happy to see you. How is Richard?"

"He is well. Asleep. Come." She took the brother's hand and led him to a chair. "How is Joan?"

"Worse than when I left."

"Elias told me about Martin and Deirdre…and the babe. We must not tell Joan about her family," she said quietly. "She will lose all hope to live."

The two men agreed somberly and accepted their cups of tea. She gave Brother Simon hers and made more. She told him about the others who were sick and he promised to see them tomorrow. They broke it to him that there were children in the beds.

"Well, at least we a have roof over our head," the brother said.

Elias smiled at him. "Sleepin' ootdoors isna so bad. Ye have done it many times."

"Aye, and each time I hated it," the small-boned brother retorted. "Bugs everywhere. You do not know what might be crawling on you in the darkness. Moonlight does not help because sometimes seeing what is on you is worse."

He and Lily cringed then shivered.

"That is not to mention," he continued with a sour face, "the things out there that can eat you, or stab you in the heart and steal your coin."

Lily didn't know how anyone did it. Just the thought...and what about bats?

She felt Elias' eyes on her and looked at him. He smiled, watching her reaction to his friend's words. She felt a little giddy. She was so happy that he was well. So happy he'd come back. If she was going to die, let her last days be giddy ones.

They sipped their tea and talked about other things. Elias told her about his family members and Brother Simon told her about some of their adventures in France. She told them about little Eddie being born the night she and Bertram had arrived. "He holds a special place in my heart because I helped bring him into this world. He is very precious. Even Bertram was gentle around him."

They finally laid their heads down, and the sun came up two hours later.

Lily didn't want to get out of bed and face a new day with more of her friends, perhaps even those who meant even more to her, sick.

Someone was tapping her on the arm, rousing her from the last remnants of sleep.

"Lily." It was Charlie, Cecily's brother. He was standing over her, his face ashen gray. "I think my mother is dead."

CHAPTER TWELVE

E LIAS HELD A long stick with a piece of cloth dipped in tar around the tip of it. He dipped the tip into the fire and turned the stick over Alice's body wrapped in linen and placed on a small platform.

He held the flames to her until her linens caught fire, then stepped back.

Father Benedict had prayed over her and over her children. Simon included a prayer for the animals, as well, since a donkey, his and Elias' horses, and three ducks had also died in the last few days.

They all looked on, wondering who would be next.

The good news—if one could find anything good these days—was Bertram was still alive. Richard knew what blends he'd given him, thanks to their color system, and started Joan and Walter on the same blend immediately.

Word arrived from London that King Edward's own daughter had succumbed to the terrible disease. Many were going hungry as merchants were either too sick to travel, or refused to.

Sevenoaks had had a good harvest and the mill was full. There was plenty of food, but how long would it last? How long would anything last?

Elias tried to put on a lighthearted smile but Deirdre Miller's face and body haunted his thoughts. He'd seen much in battle. Terrible things. But Deirdre was heavy with child. He'd searched for the thieves, tracking them to the outskirts of Netherfield. There had been two men appearing to be about the same age as Elias. He found their camp and listened to them talk around the fire about the woman they'd killed with the full belly. One had asked the other if they would go to hell for it.

Elias stepped out of the trees and told them he would help them find out. He took them down in a blur of steel and blood and then returned to the Millers and buried them properly.

He hadn't told Lily about killing the thieves. Her delicate ears didn't need to hear such ugly things. Each hour was difficult enough. He wouldn't add more to it.

When Alice's funeral was over, they walked back to the house and had something to eat. They comforted Charlie and Cecily as best they could and Lily promised to take care of them now that they had no mother.

Elias left her soon after to go with Richard to check on Bertram and feed him more tea. The bastard was getting better. It was cause to celebrate. Richard had found a cure! They would live! Elias would get to kill him.

But he couldn't get Alice...or her orphaned children out of his head. He pushed the tip of his sword closer to Bertram's throat while he drank.

Richard had told him the sword was unnecessary since Bertram was weak and restrained. Elias didn't care. He couldn't wait to kill him. He wanted him to know it.

He left the shed after Richard and shoved his sword into its sheath at his belt as he stepped out into the afternoon sun.

He saw Lily coming across the grass toward them. Her gaze darted away from him and returned to her husband. She looked shaken, pale.

Was she feeling ill?

He moved forward, reaching Richard, and waited for her.

"Joan has died," she informed them with a gentle wind pulling strands of her flaxen hair across her face. She closed her eyes for a moment and just breathed. Elias thought that mayhap she was trying to hold herself together, trying to be strong. It made him want to comfort her and be strong for her. Joan was her friend.

Moved by compassion, he took a step toward her and then stopped, remembering she had a husband and he was standing close by.

"At least she is with her family now," she said, sounding miserably resigned.

"Elias and I will tend to her, Lily," Richard said.

She swiped something from her eye and then began to turn away, to return to Walter and the children, and her plants. Elias wanted to do something for her to take her away from all this—mayhap get Richard to rest for a few hours.

"We will attend to Joan tomorrow," he said. "Let me and Simon be in charge of supper tonight, my lady."

"No, no, I could not let you do that—"

He shooed her along, refusing to take no for an answer. Richard was grateful. Simon most likely wouldn't be. Elias had a plan. He hoped the sun stayed out, and he prayed that no one else turned up sick today.

He was correct. Simon wasn't pleased, but he agreed to help. Elias had learned how to cook some things while he was in France but he wasn't sure Lily had any deer meat, heron, or salt barrel herring sitting around. He wondered if Agnes would help him cook something fitting for Lily and Richard.

He decided to pay Agnes a visit. She didn't live too far from the shop. He picked up Annabelle, Cecily, and Charlie on the way.

Agnes was happy to help. In fact, she smiled at him and blushed often while she oversaw his supper of cooked fish fillets with *Poivre Jaunet.*

Usually the yellow pepper sauce was used for meats. But there were no fresh kills in Sevenoaks. Fish would do. Thankfully, Lily had almost every spice and herb he needed to make the sauce. He would grind ginger, saffron, and long peppers, also cloves if they were on hand. They were. He had everything he needed to make supper for six.

Simon helped, as did the lasses. Charlie fetched whatever Elias needed. Osbert the reeve and Father Benedict helped keep Richard and Lily at the shop and away from the house, the west side of the house to be precise, where the lavender and delicate, white lilies-of-the-valley grew. Elias had seen the garden the day she brought him here. It was the perfect place.

Agnes also agreed to keep Cecily and Charlie with her for supper if he wished it. Elias asked the children what they wished to do. Cecily wanted to stay with Annabelle.

"With you," Charlie told him.

Elias bent to him and smiled, glad to have his company. It would be a pleasant supper. Elias was happy to be a part of it and felt a bit foolish for it in the middle of such a catastrophic time. He should be afraid for what was coming. For what was here. These people he'd begun to care about because of Lily Bennett might all die. He might have to watch. They might have to watch him.

But all he felt was anger at the one who did this. The man who was alive in the shed. He would speak to Richard about it later. They were giving Walter the butcher the same herbal teas they'd given Bertram. What did they need Bertram for?

He hadn't told Lily he'd had, in fact, escaped Father Benedict and followed her to the shed when she'd tried to speak to Bertram. He hadn't wanted to intrude on whatever she had to say to him. He'd simply wanted to make sure she was safe near the bastard.

"Where do you want this chair?" Charlie asked him.

Later. Elias thought. Tonight was for them. He pointed down the narrow path between the colorful bushes. He carried the supper table out of the kitchen and followed Charlie. Simon was behind him with two stools. When he came to the desired spot, where the sunset would cast its crimson glow on the table, he set the table down, steadied it, and covered it with a clean plaid he had packed in his saddlebag. Charlie helped Simon carry out another chair and stool, while Annabelle carried a candle to the table. Agnes and Cecily helped him bring the food and ale out.

They tried to light the candle but it wouldn't stay lit in the wind. Elias finally gave up and shoved a few sprigs of lavender into a cup instead and ran back to the house for another cup. He nearly knocked Lily over in the kitchen.

"Ah, good! Come with me. Wait, where is Richard?"

She pointed to his workshop at the other end of the house.

"Richard!" Elias called out.

"Elias, where is my table? Where are my chairs?"

"Ye will see, lass." He smiled and then stepped around her and called for Richard again.

"I'm coming," the old apothecary called out. "Why all the haste?"

Elias led them out through the kitchen and into the garden painted in rich, warm, golden hues. "Just a few steps more."

When the table and chairs came into view, with Simon sitting on a stool with Charlie beside him waiting for them, Lily paused to walk backwards and looked at Elias. "You brought my kitchen outdoors?"

"Aye," he told her with a grin.

"And cooked this meal for all of you," Agnes told her as she passed Lily with the lasses and returned to her cottage.

Richard lifted his arm and patted Elias on the shoulder. "That was quite thoughtful of you, Eli, my boy. Was it not, Lily?"

She was looking at everything. She appeared a bit restless. It was good that she was smiling. Wasn't it?

He told her about Simon helping, and all that Agnes had done and was still doing by taking care of Cecily for a few hours. She settled her gaze on Charlie then swiped a curl away from his face and smiled.

Richard went to him and covered Charlie's hand with his. "We are happy you chose to sit with us for supper, Charlie."

"This," Lily began and looked at the table and the food set out upon it, and took a shallow breath, "this is one of my favorite places. I love being out here and now..." She looked at Elias and smiled and took a deep, shaky breath "Thank you," she said to him and to Simon and Charlie.

Elias held out Lily's chair first and then Richard's, and then removed his mask. The others did the same. They toasted one another with cups of ale, and included Charlie and his dear departed mother. They did their best to put the sickness out of their thoughts. Lily was first to tell Elias that the supper he'd prepared for them was delicious. The fish was cooked to perfection and the Poivre Jaunet was heavenly.

Richard appreciated the flavors and the herbs Elias had used in the sauce but he didn't care for the ginger. Some didn't. It was an overpowering spice that stung going down. Elias had used a very small amount, but he patted Richard's back and scraped off the sauce on his friend's dish with his knife. Lily and Charlie enjoyed theirs and smiled while they ate.

Richard told Charlie to remember the taste of it and then told him what ginger can do for the body. Elias listened, too, pouring more ale and water for the lad.

They laughed when Simon told them about the time Elias was six years old and ran through the great hall of Lismoor naked. He defended himself by explaining that there were biting ants in his clothes.

They listened with awe when Charlie told them about the summer he was nine and his kin had gone to a nearby lake for refreshment and merriment. The summer his sister had nearly drowned. "There were many of us in the lake and no one had noticed that Cecily was drowning. But I did. I saw her go down and I swam to her as fast as I could and dove into the water to find her."

Lily's eyes widened when she caught Elias' gaze. He could do nothing but agree in amazement as the lad continued his tale of saving Cecily's life.

Elias wanted to stand up and toast him, so he did. Everyone rose with him. They talked about Charlie's father and Elias told him that if he were the lad's father, he would be bursting with pride in him. "As Richard no doubt was."

Richard agreed.

"Well, 'tis getting late." Lily started to rise but the touch of Elias' fingertips stopped her.

"But we have not heard anythin' aboot ye yet."

"I can help there," Richard offered, raising his cup to himself and swigging the contents down his throat. "A week after we married, she tried to roast my supper on a spit over a fire in my kitchen and burned down my house."

Simon and Charlie both held their hands over their mouths. Elias smiled at her. He understood it was the only way she knew how to cook *outdoors*.

She didn't seem to mind the mild teasing but laughed along and swiped at Richard's arm when he said, "The next day, when we were homeless, she cooked my dinner over a makeshift spit and it was delicious."

They admired the lavender and orange sunset and Elias found her looking at him more than once. "I do not usually get a chance to see this anymore."

"Then," he said, feeling ridiculously pleased with himself for making her so happy. "I am glad ye are seein' it now."

When Richard rose, the rest of them followed. "Simon, help Charlie clean up and bring the chairs inside. Elias, you will return my wife's table. Lily, go fetch Cecily."

He left the table with a wobble in his step and walked back to the house. Simon and Charlie left after him, but not before Lily gave them both a kiss on the cheek and thanked them for helping to make this night special in her mind forever.

She turned to Elias. Would it be even more obvious if she didn't kiss his cheek? "I will see you inside when I return."

"Wait fer me," he pleaded and turned to hoist the table onto his back. He returned it to the kitchen, crossing paths with his friends going back for the stools.

Elias placed the table down and begged Simon to change the covering for him. "I dinna want her oot there alone," he told Simon and then ran from the kitchen.

She hadn't waited. He felt a surge of disappointment over it and then took off after her.

He spotted her walking quickly toward the village and Agnes' house. He called her name into the indigo night. She turned and waited with a smile until he caught up. "Ye are fast," he remarked.

"I wanted to hurry and get home."

"Are ye still afraid?"

"A little. But not of being out here, and not of you, Elias. 'Tis hard to explain. I just do not feel safe anymore."

He moved a bit closer and offered her a confident grin. "Do not be afraid, Lily. I will stop at nothin' to keep ye safe."

He didn't want to talk about dying. "Were ye verra pleased with supper, lass?"

She spun around to face him. "Oh, Elias! I loved it! I want to eat there every day and enjoy the beauty of my garden."

He listened and thought of a thousand ways to build her a small table with a chair to match, for her and her alone. Someplace where she could sit in her garden and get away from everything.

They picked up Cecily and took her home, playing a game while they went.

None of them noticed the shed door swinging open in the gentle breeze.

CHAPTER THIRTEEN

L ILY WOKE THE next morning, thinking about the night before. She never wanted to forget it. If life was normal and children hadn't lost their mother, she would have thought supper was one of the most pleasant times of her life that she could remember. All thanks to Elias. He knew she would enjoy sitting in the midst of her flowers and herbs. He'd carried out her kitchen table! He'd helped her forget, even for a little while, that they were saying farewell to Joan today.

She looked over at Cecily sleeping and said a prayer for them all, and for Joan's dear soul.

Before long, her thoughts switched back to Elias. What he did last eve was one of the most thoughtful things anyone had ever done for her. Not to mention, he'd cooked a very elegant supper and provided her and Richard with the most wonderful company in him, Simon, and Charlie. She remembered how his lips pursed when he said the name of the French sauce, Poivre Jaunet. She would like to learn more French words from him.

She hated herself for feeling the way she did about Elias when she was a married woman. She loved Richard. But...had he told her the truth? Were they not truly bound until their marriage was consummated? Wasn't there more to love than helping and cooking and cleaning?

She didn't know. According to women of the village, marriage wasn't any better than slavery. It reminded her that she had to hurry and get to Eleanor's home to give Walter his morning dose of herbs.

Joan, Walter and Bertram had all been given different herbs. She wished she'd given Joan Bertram's blend first, for Richard had told her that Bertram seemed to be improving a little more each day.

A rooster crowed.

She sat up and stretched then quietly left the bed. She washed and dressed without making a sound. She wore a pale blue kirtle with long sleeves and full skirts over a white chemise. She slipped her feet into her boots and crept down the stairs. She didn't know if Elias or Simon was still asleep but she tiptoed past their shadowy blankets so as not to make too much noise.

She prepared her mixture for Walter and left the house, thinking about how the silver shards in Elias' eyes glistened like stars across the midnight sky. The way his dark hair fell over his forehead in thick, dark locks that he often dragged his fingers through. She didn't want to think about those things, but she couldn't stop. Besides, it helped keep her mind off the pestilence.

She found herself smiling on her way out the front door, thinking about sitting in her garden, listening to the birds' delightful calls to one another before the night fell...and the men's voices around her like a favored blanket on a cold night. For a little while, she had forgotten the cruel world she lived in and laughed instead, as if she hadn't a care in the—

"Morning, my lady," Elias said, about to cross her path with a pile of wood under each arm.

Lord, help her, she thought, unable to take her eyes off his handsome, chiseled face. "Sir, were you chopping wood?" Truly? Was that obvious fact truly what she just asked him? "I did not hear your axe."

There.

He gave her an indulgent half-smile that made his eyes appear bluer, his gaze, softer. "I went ootside the village. I didna want to wake everyone."

"Aye," she barely breathed out. "That was very considerate of you."

He shrugged one shoulder and his bundle of wood scraped together.

"That must be heavy." She did her best to sound and look unaffected by his presence. "You should be going."

"'Tis not so heavy," he quickly corrected, and lifted his knee to support the pile for a moment. "Are ye off to see Walter?"

She nodded, wishing everything was normal here. "Aye. I will see you after—when we attend to Joan."

She stepped around him and closed her eyes, trying to keep her emotions inside. She had to be strong. This was likely going to get worse. She took a deep breath and found the strength to keep walking.

She refused to think of him as he hurried toward the house and she climbed the hill and reached the church. But she failed and thought about nothing but him for the next few minutes.

"I thought it best if I accompanied ye."

She turned to Elias, his arms empty, and knew she was in trouble by the way her heart thrashed wildly in her chest. "Why is that? Will you protect me from the sickness, Elias?"

He nodded, his expression, serious. "If I can."

The mad thing about it was that she believed he would, if there was any way he could. She smiled at him. "Walk with me then. 'Twill give me a chance to thank you for last eve."

"I need no thanks, my lady," he said, keeping pace with her.

"It made me forget."

"'Tis what I wished," he said with a smile.

It was what he wished. Why? Why was he so concerned with

her…and with Richard? "Where were you two years ago, sir?" she asked, pulling boldness from within.

"Hmm, let me think." He was quiet for a few moments, giving her time to appreciate his size next to her. She barely reached his neck. He smelled like pine. She wanted to move closer, mayhap tilt her face to his neck and smell him.

"I was returnin' home from Edinburgh."

"Did you have a lover, a wife?" She swallowed, wishing there was a door on her mouth and she could bolt it.

"Nae," he told her, making her want to smile again. "I have been fightin' wars fer a long time. 'Twould be selfish of me to drag someone else there with me."

"You speak of your night terrors?"

"Aye, but they have subsided quite a bit."

They both smiled at each other.

"What do you dream about," she asked him.

"Fightin'. Killin'. Losin' friends. Losin' myself."

Her heart broke for him. Like many soldiers of war, he had been wounded. But his wounds were not visible to the eyes. How could she help him? There were no herbs or roots or anything that she knew of that would take nightmarish thoughts from his head.

"Would you like to talk about it?"

He began to shake his head and then went a little pale. She lifted her fingers to his shoulder and gave him a little pat.

"When we returned from the king's exile in France," he began, "he ordered many futile raids into England, which got most of my friends killed. But we had sworn fealty to him and couldna abandon him. He'd been a young boy when his father died. He was forced onto the throne, leader of volatile men who hated the English king. He thought he had somethin' to prove and kept sendin' us in. I kept fightin' fer my life. We were massacred, time after time…and I…I saw things…"

"I'm sorry that you did," she leaned in and whispered to him.

"As am I," he dipped his head to hers and whispered back. "When David was captured," he continued for her ears only, "and taken prisoner, those of us who were left privately rejoiced."

"Oh, Elias," she said softly, straightening and trying to ignore that part of her that wanted to stay close to him. "I wish you had peace."

"I have it now." He took her hand in both of his and brought it to his chest. He spoke her name and closed his eyes. "From the moment I first saw ye, I knew I would never forget yer face and the way ye smiled at yer patron." He opened his eyes and stared into hers. "Ye were like healin' oil to my soul. Since then, ye have come to mean more to me than I intended. I want ye to know that I respect yer husband so much fer all he is doin' that sometimes my shame overwhelms me."

"As does mine," she told him. She watched him hang his head and she was tempted to lift her fingers to his hair. "But...but I will not leave my husband, in body or in soul."

"I willna ask such a thing of ye," he promised and they picked up their steps again.

They heard crying when they passed the mill. They looked around at the houses. Lily's belly sank, along with her heart. She wanted to call out. She heard it again. It was a child. She looked left where Agnes' cottage was, pulled up her mask, and started running.

Elias got there first. Annabelle was standing outside her door. Tears were streaming down her cheeks. Her golden curls hung limply around her face. "Mummy is feeling poorly. Will she die like Cecily's mother and Joan?"

"No, no, Annabelle," Lily soothed.

"I dinna know," Elias answered truthfully from under his mask and stepped into the cottage.

"Agnes," Lily heard him call out and entered the house behind him.

They found her lying in her bed, curled up and groaning in pain.

She had small boils on her neck and under her arms. Her face with flush with fever and her body and her eyes looked to be bleeding.

"Agnes!" Lily moved to hurry to her but Agnes held up her hand.

"Stay away, Lily!" Agnes cried out. "Keep Annabelle away from me!"

Lily stopped and turned to the child, but she wasn't there. Elias had taken her back outside. "Agnes, my dear, please let me tend to you. I have the herbs Bertram has taken and he is better."

But Agnes shook her head. "No. Leave my house."

"Come, dearest," Lily went to her and tried to lift her head, but Agnes smacked her hands away, knocking the herb mixture from Lily's hands. Everything spilled to the floor.

Lily refused to cry. She hadn't cried a single day while she was a slave to Bertram, not even when he took her from her father. She had almost lost herself to tears a few times since learning of the pestilence and after her friends died, but she would not do it. If she started, she feared she would never stop.

"Lily."

She looked up at Elias standing in the doorway with Annabelle in his arms.

"Come, love," he beckoned calmly. "Bertram is not in the shed."

She took a step toward him and then stopped and looked back at Agnes. Her friend looked worse somehow than she had looked a few moments ago. It wasn't possible. No illness that she'd ever heard of progressed this quickly.

"Lily."

He'd called her love. She wanted to lower her head and never look up again. Why now? Was she going to die in such guilt and shame after everything? "I will not leave her."

"There is nothing ye can do for her."

"You do not know that!" she argued. "I will prepare more tea and—"

"'Tis not workin', lass," he said gently, taking a step closer and speaking quietly so that Agnes didn't hear. "Walter is dead."

She clenched her jaw and then smiled at Annabelle. "How would you like to help me wake up Cecily?"

Annabelle nodded but stared at her mother.

"Go with Lily now, Annabelle," her mother ordered.

The little girl nodded. Lily squeezed her eyes shut and bit her lip. And left Agnes' house.

Outside, Elias picked up their pace and pulled her toward home. "When I get ye home, I want ye to take Annabelle inside and bolt the doors. Tell Richard and Simon that Bertram has escaped."

"Where are you going?" But she knew. Her heart felt as if it were going to burst from her chest and cling to him.

"To find him."

She didn't want him to go. She wanted him to be safe, the same as he wanted for her. They hurried toward home and the closer they came, the harder her heart pounded. What if Bertram killed him?

"Elias," she pleaded as they slowed at the door and he set Annabelle down. "If anything were to happen to you because of us...because of me, I would never forgive myself."

"Nothin' will happen to me, Lily. He willna know what he is fightin' when I find him," Elias replied with a flash of silver in his eyes and an unsheathed sword in his hand. "I will show him no mercy."

"Now is not the time for that," she said, pulling on his sleeve when he started to open the door. "Richard and I need you here. I need you here. Do not go."

Heaven help her, he looked like he wanted to kiss her, or hold her, or both. She could feel it radiating from his gaze. Her body tingled and warmed in response, though he did not touch her.

He opened the door and stepped inside first. He looked around, as did Lily behind him. They both turned to Simon starting for the door to greet them.

He put up his hands to stop them.

Lily put one foot forward. She didn't want to wait to hear.

"Richard and Charlie are sick."

No! She would not believe it. Not Richard. Was she being punished for her adultery? She raced toward the stairs and stopped when she came to Charlie sitting up in one of Richard's most cozy chairs in the sitting room. He didn't appear too sickly, but when she put her knuckles to his cheek, she almost pulled away at how hot he was.

"Do not fear, Charlie," she leaned in and told him. "I will get you something for your fever." She looked longingly up the stairs then moved to turn away from them to make Charlie his tea.

She stopped when she faced Elias behind her, moving toward Charlie.

"Simon," he said to his friend. "Make Charlie whatever she tells ye. Lily, ye go up and see to yer husband. I will see to Charlie."

"You are staying then?" she asked.

"Aye. I'm stayin'."

He'd chosen to remain with her and the sick, rather than to ride off and exact revenge on Bertram. She thanked him and then raced up the stairs and passed her bed to Richard's, beyond the curtain.

He looked small and old in his bed.

"Richard!" she breathed out against his chest. "No! No, you must not have the sickness!"

"I'm afraid I do, my fairest Lily."

"You cannot leave me!" She shook her head against him. "Tell me what I must do to help you? What do you need?"

He told her what herbs to prepare and how often to feed them to him. Also, what ointment to apply to any boils.

She listened to him, thinking that in just a day or two she might never hear his voice again. It made her want to weep. "Oh, my dearest of all, I ask forgiveness from you and from God for the things that I think about."

"There is nothing to forgive," her husband said on a husky whisper. "No adultery has ben committed. I release you, child."

"No!" she told him, leaning up above him and staring into his eyes. "I do not release you! I made promises I intend to keep. 'Tis not about my body, but my heart, Husband. Now, you rest while I prepare your medicine."

She lowered her mask and kissed his forehead then hurried to the stairs.

Elias was sitting on the floor of the sitting room in front of Richard's chair and Charlie's small body in it. They were talking and Charlie was smiling.

Lily felt her heart swell with emotion. She smiled at Elias when he looked at her before she left them alone and entered the kitchen. She saw Cecily sitting with Annabelle at the table eating what the brother must have prepared for them. She went to Cecily and felt her skin.

"How do you feel?" Lily asked her.

"Well," Cecily answered, looking alarmed. "Am I sick, too?"

"No, Sweeting," Lily assured her gently and then turned to Brother Simon. "Is that Charlie's tea you are carrying?"

"Aye," the brother told her. "Elias wants to give it to him."

She looked into the sitting room and let her gaze linger on Elias for just an instant. "Would you bring it to him?" she asked. "I would like to start on tea for my husband."

"Of course," he told her and stepped away.

"Lily, is my brother going to die?"

Both girls began to cry.

Lily didn't know what to say to them, but Elias had been right in being honest—even if it hurt. "I will do everything I can to help them," she promised the girls. "You can help, too. Would you like to?"

They both nodded.

Good. She wanted to show them how to mix the only two concoctions that Richard had given Bertram—just in case no one else was able to prepare it. She pointed to her jars of herbs and showed them how to measure the blends, what herbs to use, and how long to steep the leaves.

"I'm going to add lemon rind to the mixture," she told them, doing so. She allowed the girls to make a pot of the mixture, while she made another. She brought a cup to Richard, and then she went to the door in the kitchen and stood before it.

"He is oot there."

"He might have run away," she countered and refused to turn around and see Elias standing there behind her.

"I willna take a chance of him gettin' to ye," he vowed.

"Then I cannot see or help any of my friends in the village?" She turned to stare at him. "Is that what you are telling me?"

He almost took a step back. "If ye mean to go, I will accompany ye."

She blinked. So then he would—she looked around at the people in the house. Would she leave them with only Brother Simon to look after them?

She exhaled. No. "But I cannot just let them die," she said on a strangled whisper.

His gaze softened on her. "Aye, they need ye, lass. But we all need Richard. Tending to yer husband is first and foremost."

"Aye," she agreed with a smile and rushed up the stairs to tend to him.

CHAPTER FOURTEEN

RICHARD DIED TWO days later, as did Agnes. Other villagers had come down with sickness, and it was these whom Elias and Simon tried to help.

Elias had tried to comfort Lily in her loss but she would not let him. She mourned her husband in the church. With Simon. For a full day, until Cecily got sick.

Much of the time she remained at Cecily's side. When she wasn't there, Elias was, seeing to Cecily and helping Charlie through it.

Elias had never witnessed the grief of losing a beloved spouse, or a dear friend. But if he lost Simon...he understood that kind of pain. Lily didn't expunge her sorrow with tears, or with words. She was keeping all her emotions tied up inside.

"Eli?" said Annabelle, standing behind him, the tips of her toes on his stool where he sat. She'd cried into his shoulder while Father Benedict prayed over her mother's body earlier this morning. She leaned across his back with her chin on his shoulder now. "Are you not going out to search for Bertram this morning?"

"Not today," he told her. He couldn't go when Cecily was so sick. He'd been out searching, tracking. Bertram was gone. For now.

"There you are, Annabelle." Lily's satiny, soothing voice washed over him.

His gaze remained on Cecily in the chair before him.

"Would you like to come help me pick my herbs for supper?"

Elias' blood drained from his head. He forgot to breathe. Was she speaking to him?

"Aye, I want to come!" Annabelle squeaked, moving away from his ear.

He couldn't help but smile. Annabelle was a babe. This was too much for a babe. It was all she was seeing. He'd meant to take her fishing with him but then Richard and the others died and Cecily got sick—and Lily either spent her time doing things, or praying. There had been no time for Annabelle.

Did this mean Lily was feeling a little better?

He reached around and scooped Annabelle up in his arm and saw her gently to her feet. He turned to smile at the gel and caught Lily's eye.

She let her gaze linger on his for a moment and then she looked away shyly.

Elias watched them leave and then felt Charlie tug on his sleeve.

"Why are you staying so close today, Eli?" Charlie asked him, his huge dark eyes wide. He still had dark circles under his eyes from being sick, but he'd grown stronger over the last pair of days. Elias was more thankful than he could express.

"Do you believe Cecily is worse?"

Elias closed his eyes and nodded.

"Bad enough to die today?" the lad asked, his voice crackled with tears that he let roll down his face.

"Aye, lad." Elias didn't want to say it but the sickness seemed to ravage some more quickly than others. Cecily fell ill a day and a half ago and was unresponsive in a matter of hours. Her neck, under her arms, and above her pelvis were covered in boils, as had everyone else's been who died.

Some went more slowly, like Walter. Others, more quickly.

"Charlie, why do ye not go with Lily? Some sun will do ye good."

Charlie shook his head. "I will stay with my sister."

Elias nodded and reached out to pat the lad on the shoulder.

When Cecily left them a few hours later, Elias leaned over his chair and pulled Charlie's head closer. He held the lad's face in his hands and spoke comforting words. But Charlie didn't want them. He wanted to fight and pummel his way through any wall—even one made of hard muscle.

Elias put his arms around the boy and held him while he wept. Charlie responded by coiling his arms around Elias' neck and holding on to him as if his life depended on it.

Elias didn't worry over what to say. There were no words, so he stayed quiet.

His heart broke for Charlie—for everyone. For the first time in his life, he didn't want to go fight. Was he becoming weak over this woman and the people she loved?

There was nothing he could do about it.

Of course, he didn't like it. As a matter of fact, he hated wondering who would die next. Would it be Lily? He wouldn't let himself think in such a way. Doing so bred fear, and if there was one thing no one needed right now, it was panic. He'd learned in times of battle how to spend the days before it appreciating hours, minutes. Time was always precious and it passed one way or the other.

He wanted to use it wisely and win Lily's favor. He ached to take her in his arms. He was afraid. Truly afraid—not of ghosts and shadows of his past. No, he was afraid she would die now that he found her. He was afraid, even for just fleeting moments before he scattered his fears to the winds, of not being able to save her. He wanted to tell her that he loved her. That he'd never loved anyone like this before her, and now he understood why. If their time was running out, he wanted to make certain she knew.

He spoke to Charlie and comforted him as best he could, which wasn't anything like the way Lily soothed a soul.

"Do you think there is a heaven, Elias?" Charlie asked him, wiping his eyes.

"Aye," Elias told him. "I do."

"Do you think Cecily is there with my mum?" The boy sobbed a little and Elias wiped his eyes.

"Aye, they are there with Richard and Joan and the others. Someday, we will be along, but not anytime soon, aye, lad?"

He didn't know Lily had returned and was watching from the kitchen. "Come now, Charlie. Let us go prepare her cover."

He turned and saw Lily. When she took her eyes off Cecily and found his gaze, her eyes filled with tears. But none fell as she went to the girl and pursed her lips behind her mask to kiss Cecily's forehead first, and then Charlie's.

Elias watched her, remembering when, less than a sennight ago, he first saw her in her shop. It felt like ages ago.

"Where is Annabelle?" he asked her when she straightened.

"She is with Norman and his daughters, Ava and Emma. I thought she needed a rest from all the sorrow."

"Aye, I agree," Elias told her and stepped past her with Charlie hot on his heels. "We must see to Cecily's pyre."

"And Osbert's," she added with a sorrowful sigh. "Ivett is not far behind."

"Father Benedict is feeling unwell today," Simon added, coming in from outside.

Elias wanted to fall to his stool and cover his head in his hands. Everyday—every hour there were more. "We have lost Cecily."

Simon's eyes filled with tears as he breathed in a short gasped. "No!" His gaze fell on Charlie and he shook his head then took him in his arms. "My ears are yours, young lad. No matter what time, I will be there to thankfully listen and help if the Lord wills it."

Elias wanted to ask him why some had lived? Why were he and Lily and Simon seemingly unaffected? He prayed it remained that way—and for everyone in Sevenoaks.

"Come, Charlie," Elias said, leaving.

He needed some air. He went to the kitchen and left through the back door. He stepped into Lily's beautiful garden with Charlie and stood there for a moment, taking in the sweet scents and colorful array of flowers.

"How come the herbs that helped me did not help my sister?"

"I dinna know," Elias told him truthfully. "I dinna know if the herbs have anythin' to do with it. Some of us are insusceptible to the pestilence and some are not."

"I'm very sad, Eli," the lad told him.

"I know. I'm verra sad, too," Elias agreed solemnly, reaching the path. "Come. We have much to do. Grab one of those small axes and follow me. I havena cut any wood in days. There is none fer her pyre."

They walked a long way off, beyond the houses and into the forest beyond. There, they found fallen branches and began chopping. They didn't speak. They simply chopped and chopped until they had more than enough. Charlie had stopped more than once to rest but then he continued on though he had just recovered.

Elias let him chop—for a little while. He knew the lad needed to do something. He'd not only lost his sister and his mother, but people he'd known all his life.

"We have enough," Elias told him, tucking his axe into his belt. "After we see to Cecily, I will have Brother Simon bring you back to the house so ye can rest."

"Are you going back to the house?" Charlie asked. "Is Lily?" he added when Elias shook his head.

"She will not likely leave until everyone has been seen to," Elias told him.

Charlie tucked his axe into his belt the same way Elias had. "I have been spared, though I would gladly give my life in exchange for Cecily's if I could. But since I am the one who remains, I will not be a coward who runs when disaster strikes." He swiped at a tear running down his cheek. "I do not want any more rest. I will remain with you and see to the dead."

Elias nodded and began picking up the wood. He let Charlie carry one log under each arm, and no more—despite the lad's protests.

He was fond of Charlie. In fact, he believed he might love the boy. He didn't want to leave him when he returned to Invergarry one day. His parents would like Charlie. Aye. Elias would finish raising him. He felt better just thinking about it.

What about Lily now that she was a widow?

Hell, he still couldn't believe that Richard had succumbed to the sickness. Richard had been his friend and Elias missed him. He missed working with him and learning which plant or root was best for what. He was filled with guilt over the way he felt about Richard's wife. Worse, Richard knew and was glad! When Elias had pleaded his forgiveness, Richard granted it easily and made him promise to take good care of her and not let her die. He'd sounded more like a father than a husband. Elias had promised.

They would live through this and he hoped she would become his wife. She was everything any man could ever want in a woman. Loyal, beautiful, kind, thoughtful, loving. So many things. So many reasons to love her.

She was balm for his aching soul. He'd killed too much, saw too much—and only she had made him forget. Lily was his chamomile. He smiled then laughed at himself.

Even in the midst of preparing to do what he had to do, he laughed because of her.

"What makes you smile, Eli?" Charlie asked with a shred of hope for some happiness, too. "Share it with me."

Elias slanted his gaze at the boy. He should have known the lad was watching him. "I am in love with Lily."

Charlie smiled, glad for him, without any judgment about her being so recently a widow. "Does she love you?"

He thought about it for a moment and his smile deepened. "Aye. I hope so. She was loyal to Richard and never gave me a reason to pursue her. But now her bond is broken."

"Will you marry her?"

"If she will have me."

"But you are a Scot."

"So?" Elias wondered what he meant by that.

"Do Scots not take their wives with or without her consent?"

Elias laughed. "Try to force a Scottish lass into anythin' and ye will be fortunate to escape with yer life. What ye have been taught is incorrect."

"I was not taught it," Charlie reminded it. "I saw it with Bertram and Lily two years ago when I was ten."

Elias saw his point and assured him that neither he nor any man in his family had or would ever do such a terrible thing. His father had been raised a slave to the Governor of Berwick. He told the boy the story of his parents.

"So," Charlie asked as they approached the house. "When you marry Lily, will you have children with her?"

"Aye," Elias told him. "Ye and Annabelle to start."

Charlie dropped his logs and threw his arms around him. "Thank you," he cried.

Elias could not let go or else some of the logs might fall on their feet. He leaned in though and touched his forehead to Charlie's. "Ye are a good lad. 'Tis my honor." He swallowed his heart and the wish that Cecily was here with her brother.

"Now, come. Let us get this done. And dinna spread the news of my heart to anyone."

Charlie promised and picked up his logs.

"I have aboot six or seven more trips," he said. "I dinna want ye comin' along. 'Tis too rigorous."

"Eli, I—"

"Charlie." He said nothing else. The matter was closed. He wouldn't lose Charlie.

He walked to the back of the house and set down the logs then clapped his hands together, wiping the dirt from them, and set out again.

"Oh, Elias, there you are!"

He turned at the sound of Lily's voice and smiled at Charlie on the way around. When his gaze came to her, he felt as if his body was being drained of himself and then filled again, better than before.

She was like daylight piercing the gloom, spreading warmth despite the rain.

"I was gettin' some wood with Charlie."

"Why? We have plenty of wood in the shed," she informed him with a curious scowl.

There was plenty of wood – "In the shed? Who went into the shed?"

"I did," she told him. "I cleaned it up and then Estrid, Clare, and I chopped some wood. 'Tis an excellent way to get rid of some things."

He nodded. He couldn't help but grin at her. She had chopped wood. She and her friends...her sisters. What was better than a wife who would not perish without him? But with Bertram still out there, it was dangerous for her to be so far away, alone.

Cleaning the shed was mayhap even more dangerous.

"Did ye wear yer mask?" he asked.

"Of course," she thankfully replied. "So, now will you sit and eat with me, Annabelle and Simon?"

He hadn't known she'd be preparing any meals today or he would not have been late. "Forgive me."

She graced him with a smile and then turned back to the kitchen from where she came. Elias washed his hands in the well, a habit he'd irritatingly picked up because of Lily, and picked a few splinters from his skin. He hurried back to the kitchen and then slowed at the door and let Charlie enter first.

The room smelled wonderful with mixed herbs and spices, chopped and roasted roots, like carrots, dandelion, and turmeric over rice. He saw that everyone at the table already had their bowls, so he went to the pots and prepared his own bowl. Charlie did the same—after he held his clean hands up to Lily.

There was cooled bread on the table and melting butter.

Elias was starving and helped himself.

"How is everyone feelin'?" he asked, looking them all over.

They agreed that they did not feel sick.

Elias closed his eyes in thanks and then began to eat.

Lily smiled at him then turned to Simon and nodded at something he said.

Should he ask her tonight or wait for a less busy day? Would there be anymore less busy days? Aye, when the pestilence ran its course. Did he want to wait until then?

"This is delicious," he let her know. She returned her attention to him and smiled again. "Ye cook verra well."

Charlie covered his mouth and laughed into his hand. He stopped when Elias glared at him.

She was still smiling. Mayhap harder. Was her mourning over then? What should he do?

He ate. He watched Charlie eat and was happy the boy was well. They complimented Lily a number of times, and laughed when Lily's cat leaped up into Simon's lap and Simon and the cat *and* the chair all fell over backwards. After that, they enjoyed a few stories from Elias about Simon's terrors with various cats throughout his life.

And then it was time to wait no longer and go see to the dead.

CHAPTER FIFTEEN

THE CANDLELIT SERVICE held outside was the same as it was the last time they held one, and the time before that. Today, though, a little girl was among the dead.

Lily did everything she could to comfort Charlie but, in the end, like her, he wanted to be alone.

After Cecily and Osbert's services, Norman was appointed the new reeve of the village and sent everyone home for their supper. What they had would last even longer now that there weren't many of them still able to eat.

On the walk home, Elias invited Charlie to go hunting with him tomorrow. Charlie agreed. Lily wanted to hug Elias for all he was doing for the poor boy. Losing his mother had to be hard enough. Lily knew what Cecily meant to her brother.

Elias was the only one who could lift Charlie from the gloom.

Brother Simon had been such a wonderful help with cooking. He'd also kept the children busy with chores and games while she chopped wood or spent time in church with Father Benedict, all while Elias was busy with Charlie, taking care of him and making sure he smiled at least part of the day.

Elias had done the same for Cecily when Alice had died.

He had tried to do it for her when she lost Richard, but she hadn't let him. She couldn't. Not right away. She didn't understand why God would let Richard die when so many needed him, but more had died or were dying since Richard had left.

There were so few of them remaining, she could take care of the sick by herself, but Elias had promised to help her. What would she have done without him and Brother Simon? What if they hadn't come to Sevenoaks, or hadn't stayed? They could have left and avoided all this. Who would she have left? Clare would be no help.

Poor Clare, she thought, entering the house through the kitchen and getting started on their late meal. Clare spent most of her time in church, even before the Black Death hit. Every day, she looked more terrified. Lily didn't think Clare's large, hollow eyes could get any wider with fear but, each day, they did. She'd had a rough time of it in the past. She had served one of London's prestigious lords, whose name Clare withheld from all. A lord who got her with child and never looked at her again. She'd come to live in Sevenoaks about two and a half years ago and never stepped out again.

Thank God, little Eddie was doing well, with no signs of being sick despite tearing off his mask every ten breaths. Lily loved holding and kissing the babe. She missed doing it in these last, sad days.

Lily smiled and made a mental point of inviting Clare and little Eddie to supper tomorrow.

"What is it that brings a smile to yer bonny face?" Elias came closer to her and asked.

"I was thinking of inviting Clare to supper tomorrow..." Her smile faded. "If tomorrow—"

Elias held up a knife he'd plucked from the table and then began helping her separate leaves and stems for her soup. "That is a good plan. Clare needs to think on other things besides what is happenin' here—just as the rest of us do." His smile radiated from within and

Lily wondered where his boundless confidence and peace came from.

Lion Heart. She remembered what Brother Simon had called him. It was a good name for a shepherd, for he guarded his little flock well.

He cast Charlie a furtive glance, making Lily wonder what they had talked about today.

"After I help ye see to the sick tonight," Elias said, looking a bit anxious, "mayhap, if ye dinna want to be alone, ye will walk with me."

"Of course," she said, brightening his expression. "Who else would I walk with?"

Brother Simon and Charlie laughed. Lily winked at Charlie. She had an idea that Elias likely spoke with the boy, who would be an adult in a few short years, about being fond of her. She would have to be a fool not to know Elias cared for her. He grew breathless when he saw her. Truly, irresistibly breathless. Every time. When they were together, his eyes were always on her, drinking her in. She could feel his gaze and often caught him on the brink of a smile. It had made her want to giggle for some silly reason. But she couldn't. She had been married.

But she wasn't married anymore. For two years, she had done her best to honor the man who'd saved her life. Even toward the closing of his life, she stayed by his side and did not so much as glance in Elias' direction if their paths crossed. She remained devoted, as she'd promised. Until he died.

She caught Elias looking once again and smiled at him before he could look away. She liked basking in the chiseled angles of his face, the mesmerizing beauty of his silver-speckled eyes, the tantalizing contours of his mouth that made her want to delight in them.

She felt her face flush and watched him chop. He was helping her. Good. They would get done faster and go on their walk. She couldn't wait to be alone with him.

What would she say? Brother Simon had told her a little more about Elias, but all she needed to know was that she liked standing close to him, like now, and his arm or leg brushed her and sent fire shooting through her veins. It made her forget everything and think only on his size, the length and thickness of his well-muscled thighs and his broad, deft fingers.

They prepared soup and yesterday's warmed black bread and ate with Simon and the children. When they were done, Lily prepared her remedies and Elias cleaned up, while Simon readied his charges for bedtime.

"I will go to Ivett while you see to Father Benedict," Lily told Elias outside. She handed him a jug of tea, some pouches of ointment, and a torch.

"No," he said, shaking his head and lighting his torch on hers. "Alan the carpenter lives closer to Ivett, so I will see to him first."

"You worry still about Bertram showing up?" she asked in the dim light.

"I should have killed him when I had the chance."

She shook her head in disagreement. "You see that God did not want him dead yet. 'Twas right not to take his life."

"I have taken many lives, my lady," he said disparagingly.

"And now you are saving them—or doing your best to," she countered with a smile, lighting his path.

"I know you were a warrior, one of King David's best—"

"Ye have been speakin' to Simon," he scowled, though it didn't last longer than an instant.

"You are a masterful swordsman and you fear nothing. Is it true? Do you fear nothing?"

"I never had a reason to fear before. What is the worst that can happen?'

"You could die!"

"I was taught from a young age how to save my life and the lives of others. Because of it, I also understood that I could die. That my life could be quick. I'm not afraid of death. Not my own," he added and stared at her between their torches' light.

"Are you afraid of someone else's death? Whose?" she asked and then answered before he could. "Brother Simon."

"Aye. And ye."

"Me?" she asked incredulously and started walking. "No, I will not be the one who weakens Lion Heart's heart."

He laughed and caught up with her. "What do ye mean? Ye willna weaken my heart, lass," he tried to assure her.

"How do you know that, Elias?" she asked him, holding the torch at an angle that helped her see his face. "I sometimes think you would die for me."

He grew serious and gazed into her eyes while they walked. "I would, my lady. Dyin' fer ye isna the trouble. 'Tis *yer* death that I fear."

Her knees almost buckled right there while she was walking. She would have fallen into his arms. It was one way to get there. She wasn't sure if she had the nerve to fall into them any other way. She didn't know how to seduce a man. She'd never had to learn.

"Well, 'tis *your* death that I fear," she responded honestly, keeping pace with him.

He smiled. Now she knew they were mad. What an awful thing to smile about, yet here she was smiling with him.

"Knowin' that pleases me," he admitted with a teasing slant of his mouth.

"It does not please me," she told him. "I would absolutely hate it if you died because of me."

"Would ye weep?"

She tipped her gaze to him in the firelight. So, he had noticed. "I do not weep because it serves no purpose, save to make me feel worse."

He nodded and said nothing more until they reached the grand home of the late reeve, Osbert. Norman hadn't moved in yet. Not while Ivett was still alive.

Lily departed from Elias' side and watched him by his torchlight as he walked to Alan and Helen Carpenter's cottage.

Her heart yearned to go with him, to never leave his side again.

With resolve, she pulled up from her years of training, she turned away and stepped into Ivett's foyer and looked around. Where were the reeve's two servants, Millie and John? Had they fallen ill since an hour ago when she saw them at the vigil? Who then had kept the candles lit and put wood on the fire? She went to her friend's room with her tea, calling out for either of the servants. Had they abandoned Ivett because she was sick?

She stepped into Ivett's room and almost dropped her jug of tea when she saw Bertram lying on the bed next to Ivett and holding the edge of a blade to her throat.

"Dinna scream, Lily," he warned, "or I will speed this up." He glanced down at her sick friend.

Lily wanted to scream. She wanted to alert Elias. Oh, why hadn't she attached her knives to her legs? She was quickly learning how to use them but what good was it if she left her knives at home? She looked toward the window.

"Och, what the hell does it matter?" Bertram sneered. "She will be dead in a day or two anyway." He swiped his blade across Ivett's throat and blood flowed into the bed.

Lily screamed in her head. She screamed and screamed in silence, as she'd learned so well to do.

"Hmm." He slipped off the bed and went to her. "I see ye are still the same frosty bitch ye have always been."

"Not always, Bertram," she said, looking toward the window again. No one was there, but when Bertram turned to look, Lily pulled back her arms and swung her jug upward, directly at his face.

Thick clay smashed, along with a bone or two. Her precious tea spilled everywhere, especially in Bertram's face.

He went down like a lightning-blasted tree, and she took off, screaming for Elias as she went.

ELIAS SEARCHED EVERYWHERE for Bertram, even on top of the reeve's large house. He found Millie and John, dead from having their throats cut, as well.

He had to find the man. He and Lily were fighting to keep people alive and here Bertram was killing them for no other reason than his own sick desires. Elias had to stop him.

He left Lily with Father Benedict, who looked a bit stronger tonight, while he searched. He checked behind every bush and knocked on the door of everyone left alive in the village. He searched the shop and the empty homes of the dead, but Bertram was nowhere to be found. The bastard had once again eluded him.

When he returned to the priest's rooms behind the church, he wanted to smile at Lily and wash her in compliments. He wanted to tell her how delighted he was that she'd injured Bertram. But there was no time now.

They hurried home to make certain Simon and the children were safe, though Elias had no doubt Simon could take on the taller Scotsman. Like Eli, he'd been trained in the art of battle by the three MacPherson brothers and was quite deadly for a man of God.

He was surprised Lily had agreed to go on their promised walk, though they didn't go far and they didn't use their torches so as not to alert Bertram where they were if he returned.

"What passes through the mind of a hardened Highland warrior," Lily asked him under the moonlight, "that can soften his face and make him smile in the midst of a battle?"

He slipped his gaze to her and let his smile widen into a slow grin. "Ye watch me too closely, Woman."

"You are easy to read without your mask." She pulled down hers and smiled back at him. "Is it a lass? Someone from home?"

He laughed at her madness and looked up at the full moon. "Nae," he said, sobering a bit when he thought of home. "I was thinkin' of takin' Charlie home as my son and teachin' him how to fight."

Her expression went utterly soft and Elias watched as her defenses that she'd built long ago began to crumble.

"You mean to...make him your son?"

He couldn't help but gaze at her like a soldier seeing home after a long battle. She radiated, outshining the moon. "Aye, and Annabelle, too, of course."

She nodded and brought her palms to her belly as she walked. "Annabelle, of course."

"Lily." He took her hand and stopped walking, stopping her with him. He pulled her gently into his arms, afraid to squeeze too tight. But this woman, though she appeared as if she might shatter, never would. She never had. She stood bravely in the face of a devil and had never broken down.

He enveloped her as the treasured lass she was to him and let his lips steal slowly over hers. "And ye."

He kissed the breath from her, molding her mouth to his, sweeping his tongue across her lips and coaxing them open. He suddenly stopped and withdrew enough to look at her. "I'm goin' to put my tongue into yer mouth. Dinna bite it off."

"Your tongue?" she asked a bit nervously, tempting him to smile at her innocence.

"Ye will like it," he promised on a whisper and dipped his head to kiss her again. Her lips were soft, her mouth sultry and pliable. He parted her lips with his tongue and she opened to him and then stopped and withdrew.

"Why would you think I would bite off your tongue? Did Father Benedict tell you that I cut off Bertram's nether...sword?"

Elias stared at her for a moment and then stepped back, letting her go and bringing his hands to his groin. "Did ye say ye cut it off?"

She nodded, visibly upset that she had frightened him. But after a moment and a good, deep breath, he let his smile shine on her. Still, he was in too much disbelief to speak. This was Bertram they were talking about. She'd cut off his—how? When? He asked his questions numbly.

"I added a mixture of valerian and nightshade to his ale every night with his supper to make him sleep and keep him away from me. One night, when his men were on a mission doing I do not know what, he struck me and left me by the fire and made his own drink. I awoke later to find him atop me, trying to have his way. I snatched his dagger from his belt and reached between our bodies to grab hold of it in my hand. He did not know what I was about to do. I slipped my other hand between us and sliced it off with all my power."

Elias stared at her in the moonlight, marveling at her courage. "Ye are fierce, lass."

"I did not feel fierce. I still do not."

"'Tis instinctual to want to stay alive, stay safe. When that is taken away, some crumble under the weight, some stand up and even if they go down, they go down fightin'. To me, those are the lion hearts. That is who ye are, Lily. Ye have the heart of a lion. But why did ye not kill him with yer herbs?"

"'Tis not my place to take someone's life."

"Nae," he agreed. "'Tis mine."

She smiled and lowered her head. He put his index finger under her chin and lifted it. "Come and be my bairn's mother, the only woman who shares my bed, and my heart, and all that I have."

She wilted in his arms when he closed them around her, and opened her mouth to receive him. He smiled and dipped his head to take what she offered, knowing he was lost and not caring.

CHAPTER SIXTEEN

L ILY WOKE UP the next morning thinking about Elias. About his kiss, so passionate, so compelling. His lips had caressed her, his tongue explored her, leaving her weak and willing in his embrace. When she'd responded boldly by weaving her fingers through his dark waves and pulling his head closer to hers, his body grew hard and captivating beneath her fingers. She wanted to touch him everywhere, without the barrier of his clothes, but heavens, how would she ever get him to take his clothes off? She blushed thinking of it and sat up. By habit, she turned to look down at Cecily and saw Annabelle instead. She thought she might weep at the idea of Cecily not coming to Invergarry. Would any of them make it there? As long as people continued to die here, they couldn't...he wouldn't go.

She left her bed and peeked over the wooden railing to his and Simon's makeshift beds.

Elias was not in his.

She dressed in her chemise and a dark brown kirtle with full skirts, perfect for hiding a few daggers and a kitchen knife, and left the house quietly.

She looked around for Elias, unashamed for the first time, thanks to God and Brother Simon, for helping her understand that she was free. It had nothing to do with loving Richard. He was no longer here. *'Til death do us part*, had happened. They were parted.

She heard a sound farther down the path. Was it Elias? Bertram? She walked along slowly between her gardens, drawn by the sound of splashing water. Finally, she skimmed her gaze over Elias squatting off the narrow path between the house and the forest. He had a bucket of water from the well at his feet and scooped out some to wash his body. He splashed some on his face then dumped the bucket over his head and shook himself free of excess water.

He rose, tall and bare from the waist up. From *low* on his waist, for his leather belt was weighted by his heavy Scot's claymore, an axe, and two sheathed daggers. Water streamed down from his head, over his sculpted body.

He looked nothing like she'd imagined, for the only male bodies she'd ever seen were Bertram's, whose was layered in wiggly fat, and Richard's when she once stepped into his room without asking. It was nothing like this.

She could never have conjured up Elias' broad chest and the long, lean muscles of his torso. From the flare of his shoulders, down the tapered length of his chiseled belly, to the alluring curves below his navel, he looked like he might be made of steel...or carved from rock.

His arms, the arms that came around her last night in the moonlight, glistened with droplets falling from his hair as he turned in her direction, as if he sensed her there.

She remained still, like prey, though her heart thumped with the guilt of spying. What would she say? At least she would wait until he put on his léine and she could think straight.

She waited, slowing her breathing.

He smiled and came toward her. Was he happy to see her or was he smiling because she looked like a hapless fool?

She cleared her throat and backed away a little. Then stopped.

"My lady," he said with a voice draped in velvet—meant to seduce "'Tis nice to see ye so early."

She looked up into his eyes as he came closer. Her first error. Oh, what kind of magic was at work within him, reflecting in his eyes, making her breathless, helpless?

"Aye, and you." She felt her face go up in flames and laughed at herself. "Forgive me for stumbling upon you. I was looking for—" She stopped, hoping he didn't ask her...

"Who were ye lookin' fer?"

She blew out a huge breath and then reluctantly told him. "For you."

"Oh?" He didn't look curious. He looked infinitely happier. "What can I do fer ye, my lady?"

He could start by kissing her. She wanted to tell him but she didn't have the courage. She stepped closer instead, knowing by now that Elias adhered to stricter codes of behavior than most other men.

She didn't have to do much though. The instant he felt her move closer, the instant her breath mingled with his when she looked up at him, he swooped down, dragging her closer against all that rock. He held her, gazing into her eyes while she gazed into his and played with the hair slicked back at his temples.

He emboldened her. He made her ache for him, denying fear and embarrassment. "I want you to kiss me, sir," she whispered.

He bent to her and kissed her chin. "Here?"

"No," she giggled and then closed her eyes in sheer pleasure when he set a course with his teeth and lips gently down her throat. "Here?"

"Mmmm." She couldn't speak. She could barely breathe when he flicked his tongue across her neck then up to her earlobe. She felt his muscles tremble under her fingers and locked her arms around his neck. He kissed his way to her mouth and enveloped her like smoke.

His lips were firm and plump and delightfully sensual. His tongue was a hungry beast, tasting every inch of her and giving her tastes of him as well. His large, broad hands splayed down her back and drew her closer against his carved body.

He pulled back, as breathless as she and smiled at her. "This is a nice way to begin the day." The shards of silver in his eyes flashed like fire across the sky. "How shall we end it?"

She smiled, knowing instinctually what he wanted, for she wanted it, too. "By making me your wife in between."

He grinned at her and she could tell he was surprised at her boldness, and that he liked it.

"Ye would be my wife, Lily?"

"Aye, Elias, happily," she told him and he kissed her again.

They decided not to have a celebration. It felt wrong to have one in the midst of so much death. They would speak their vows in private with Brother Simon and the children.

But first, they had the sick to see to.

Still, they kissed a little longer amidst the scented flora and laughed at silly, inconsequential things like frogs and fairies. They strolled up the path and Lily pointed to herbs and told him what they helped with and how to prepare them. She was acutely aware of every inch of him on their way back to the house. She liked his dominating size and the scent of him, the sound of him, and the heat from him. She wanted to douse herself in it. "Do all the men in your family's stronghold look like you?" she asked with a teasing smile.

"Nae. They are handsome."

"Sir, *you* are handsome," she corrected with a flirtatious smile. "I would wager you are the most handsome of all."

He laughed and leaned in closer to her. "We dinna have to go there. We can live here."

She grew serious. "Do you mean it, Elias? Would you stay here? Oh no, I could not ask such a thing of you! You have a family! I do not. You—"

"Ye have a family, Lily," he corrected. "A father and three half-sisters. Ye never told me of yer mother. Did she die when ye were younger?"

She nodded. "At my birth. I never knew her. I was the daughter of my father's old age. The product of his new marriage after his first wife had died. He took care of me with the help of my older half-sisters. He loved me very much."

Elias pulled her into his arms. "We will find them."

She gleamed. She could feel happiness radiating off her. How did he do it? How did he always find a way to make her smile even in these dark days? "Do you think they still live? Our home was in Hastings."

"I do not know, but we still live and we will find them."

"Aye," she agreed, feeling better than she had any right to while others around her suffered.

They returned to the house and Elias helped her prepare her teas. Brother Simon was awake and cooking when Lily and Elias entered the kitchen. Charlie passed a secret smile to Elias, and Annabelle sat at the table playing with one of her dolls.

Elias made the announcement that they wanted to wed and everyone was delighted and excited for them. Brother Simon wept tears of joy.

After a quick morning meal of porridge with fresh cranberries that Brother Simon had picked yesterday, they left for Alan Carpenter's cottage. When they arrived, they discovered that the carpenter looked better. Was it her tea? Would it have helped Ivett? Thanks to Bertram she would never know.

They had to see to poor Ivett's fire today. Who else? Who was next?

They soon discovered that Norman the new reeve's daughter, Ava, had fallen ill. They went to her right away and tended to her. After spending time with her, they left to retrieve another mixture Lily had at the shop that would keep Ava's fever down. They returned to

Norman's and stayed with Ava and her family, feeding her sips of tea and keeping a cloth dipped in Lily's new mixture on her forehead and neck.

While they were preparing to leave, they reminded her parents to continue giving her the teas and to keep fresh cloths where they were now. And to keep their hands clean.

Before they left, Ava's sister, Emma, stepped forward and tugged on Lily's sleeve. "Did you go check on Clare and little Eddie?"

"Not yet," Lily answered. "We are going there now."

Emma shook her head. "I do not think they are at home."

When Elias bent to the girl, Lily's heart pumped a little faster. "Where do ye think they are, lass?"

"London I heard him say."

Lily's belly began to quake and she felt ill. "Him who? Who do you mean?"

"A man. There was blood on him. It frightened me to look at him."

At the look of horror on Lily's face, Emma began to cry harder.

"Nae, 'tis all right now, Emma," Elias promised her quietly. "I will bring them back."

He straightened and turned to Lily, "Stay—"

"No. I will not stay. I will go with you."

He shook his head. "Ye willna." He spoke with command and authority she hadn't heard before.

Still, she remained unmoved on her position.

Norman's wife, Hild, covered her mouth, frightened that they would fight right there over her child's bed.

Lily dipped her chin to her chest, ashamed of them both. She couldn't help but look surprised when Elias tugged on her arm, pulling her to the door.

"Lily, I—"

She slapped his hands away from her. "What do you mean by

dragging me away from my friends?"

"Ye would stay and bicker with me in their home?" he demanded with storm-colored eyes.

"No!" she argued. "You could have stopped pushing me about it. I want to go with you. You can use me against Bertram to get Clare and little Eddie back."

He gave her an incredulous look and began to walk away. "I willna *use ye* for anythin', Lily."

"But I am what he wants! We must save little Eddie," she demanded.

"I will find another way to save them!" he called back over his shoulder.

So he thought he'd be tough then, did he? She lifted her skirts over her ankles and marched to him. "How will you catch up with them? You have no horse."

"I will run."

"I can run, too."

He shook his head. "Ye will slow me down."

"She is my friend and I love that babe. Elias!" she shouted and he stopped and turned to her. "I cannot sit here and wait. He will kill them. I know what he wants."

"Ye," he said.

She shook her head. "He knows he will never have me. He wants to think he broke me."

Elias' face darkened and his hands balled into fists. "He willna get that. I will kill him."

"Elias, he has little Eddie," she argued. "What will you do while he holds him over your head?"

"What will *ye* do?" he countered.

"I will bargain with him." She put her hands on his arm and looked up into his eyes. "You must let me go with you. I will not sit around waiting."

He closed the distance between them in one giant step and took her in his arms. "Lily, if anythin' were to happen to ye—"

"Elias, I could wake up sick tomorrow...and you would not be here."

That seemed to shake him, as if it were he who was keeping the sickness away from them. She almost smiled at how little it actually took to turn him.

He pulled her close and inhaled her. "Our marriage will have to wait."

She closed her eyes, thinking how she was tempted to give up everything else to be married to him today.

"'Twill be worth the wait," she whispered to him.

A speckle of silver in his eyes caught the light and gleamed when he looked at her. "Come on then." He drew back and took her by the hand. "If ye are goin' with me, we should be off. We must stop at home and tell Simon."

Suddenly, he became a commander. "We need food and water fer the journey. I intend to find horses, but we will need to walk fer a while. Even run."

She nodded and followed him back to the house. Charlie wanted to go with them but Elias was firm with his no this time. Annabelle cried and Lily was tempted not to go. But she knew Bertram. She knew what would satisfy him. She could save Clare and little Eddie. Annabelle and Charlie were safe here...safe from the outside world that is. She had to go. She had to help.

"Elias assures me we shouldn't be gone longer than a sennight," she told Simon. "I have prepared more tea. For now, please see that Alan the carpenter and Ava, Norman the reeve's daughter, get a cup every four hours. If anyone else becomes ill while we are away, give them two cups to start and a cup every four hours. Do you have it?"

"Aye, I have it, gel," he said a bit curtly to her. "I have been doing it for days now. I think I should be the one goin—"

He disappeared in a blur when Elias shoved him out of the way and stepped into the brother's place. "Mayhap ye should stay."

"No. I'm going with you," she sang, wrapping the last of some extra herbs in a bag. She turned to kiss the children and waited for him.

He held up his hand for her to wait some more and pulled Brother Simon over again. "Marry us, please."

"What?" the brother asked and looked at her.

She nodded and smiled and took Elias' hand, showing the brother her consent—if that's what he was worrying about.

"Simon, come now," Elias huffed a bit more impatiently, and then pulled the children closer, as well. "We are wastin' valuable time. Marry us. I asked her and she agreed, did ye not, love?" He turned to glance down at her.

"Aye, I did."

Her consent didn't have the soothing effect on the brother that she'd hoped but, an instant or two later, he offered them a genuine grin. "'Twould be my honor—"

"Simon," Elias interrupted. "I want to get goin'."

"Do you want to be this lass' husband?" the brother asked acidly. "Then," he continued when Elias nodded, "let me finish. I will be quick. I am not a dolt."

Lily giggled into her hand and then tried to be serious when Brother Simon glared at her.

"Elias," he said as he finally turned to his friend, "do you vow before God to love, honor, and protect Lily, until you die?"

"Aye, I vow it."

Lily smiled at him and bit her lip. This was real and it was happening fast! She looked down at Charlie and Annabelle and felt dizzy with emotions.

"And you, Lily," Brother Simon said softly to her. "Do you vow before God to love, honor, and obey Elias until you die?"

"Aye, I vow it," she answered calmly, though she wanted to shout from the rooftops. *Aye!*

"Then go," Brother Simon whisked them away. "You are husband and wife in the eyes and in the Name of the Lord. And Eli, if you are not back here in a sennight, I will come looking for you."

Lily laughed with happiness and bent to kiss the children. She would be back soon. As she straightened, she was sure she heard Brother Simon say, "You are in *real* trouble now, Eli."

Was he insinuating that she was more dangerous than the plague? She was insulted. For a moment. And then she thought about what she wanted Elias to do to Bertram and thought the brother could be right.

She'd shown Bertram mercy for what he'd done to *her*. Now, it was different. Now, he'd killed and hurt the people she loved. She looked around as they left the village, decreased by almost half in number by the great pestilence. Bertram had done this.

For this, he would die.

But first, she thought, looking at the house and Elias leaving it, she would see to her husband.

CHAPTER SEVENTEEN

THEY TRAVELED NORTHEAST on foot for about three miles before coming to the natural beauty of the tiny village of Knockholt. The people there were friendly and quite helpful. They hadn't yet felt any of the effects of the pestilence. They let Elias and Lily in and claimed to have seen a man traveling with a younger woman and child. He said he was going to north to Downe.

Elias and Lily thanked them and were given two horses. They traveled onward, relieved to be off their feet. They could make it to Downe before nightfall.

The village of Downe was quiet. No one came outdoors to greet them. They stared from their windows. Lily dismounted and glanced at Elias watching her. She was going to find little Eddie and she wasn't going to let anyone stop her. Not even a village.

"I'm looking for a woman and her babe. They have been taken from my village in Sevenoaks by a terrible man. Have any of you seen them?"

Silence.

Lily waited another moment and then dug her heels in and shouted in a circle so everyone could hear. "You should all know that the man behind me is a cold, merciless beast much, *much* worse than the man who took my friend. If I do not hear from someone in the next few moments, I will unleash him on every house until no one is left but the ones we seek!"

"And what d'ye propose to do if no one comes oot?' Elias asked with an amused grin on his face.

She looked up at him. "Stop smiling and look mean."

When he obeyed, she had the urge to tremble and smile at the same time. She wasn't sure if he was more magnificent when he smiled or scowled.

"I will unleash him!" she shouted one more time.

"Aye," Elias muttered quietly behind her. "I believe ye will."

"Miss?" an older man called out from his opened door.

Lily saw that he wore a thick piece of wool around his nose and mouth. He didn't leave his doorstep and he held out his hand to stop her when she took a step toward him.

"The people you seek are not here," he called out, keeping his eyes on Elias. "As you can see, we do not open our doors to anyone. We did see who you are looking for but they did not stay. Now, do us the courtesy of leaving before you bring whatever disease you have to all of us."

"Tell me which way he went and if the woman and child looked well," Lily insisted.

"They seemed well but that was yesterday."

Lily felt relief wash over her and almost turned to smile at Elias.

"They went north," the man concluded and retreated back inside.

London. Emma had said London.

Lily prayed they did not end up in London. But for now, there was nothing to do but move forward.

"How is he moving so fast with Clare and little Eddie?"

When she heard what had just come from her lips, another possibility came to her. What if he no longer traveled with them? She looked at Elias and it appeared he had the same thought.

"We will find them," he assured her with a practiced smile.

She nodded, trying to remain as hopeful as him.

They reached the area of West Wickham by nightfall and were given a room at the inn, as there was only one room to be had.

Lily beamed when she looked up at the moon and a spray of twinkling stars from an open window on the slanted roof above the bed. One bed. She wondered if Elias would sleep on the floor. She didn't want him to. She wanted him to hold her tonight, just for a few hours while they rested. But she had no idea how to go about getting him in bed. She had no idea what to do about anything really. But she was not one to sit back silently and wait for things to happen. She would learn as she went.

Instead of telling him what she wanted, she asked him to turn away and then began untying the laces of her kirtle.

Letting her skirts fall to the floor, she looked over her shoulder at him, a bit shyly, for she had never thoughtfully seduced a man before.

He'd turned away but he couldn't keep his eyes off her. He seemed to grow bigger, more needful before her. He came to where she was standing with her back to him. His hands came around her slowly and, with exquisite thoroughness, cupped her waist through the worn linen of her chemise, clutching fistfuls of it across her belly, quickening her pulse with the thought of him tearing it from her body. But she knew that later, when she had only one chemise left, she'd regret it.

He didn't tear her clothes away. He ran his callused fingers over her erect nipples and tugged gently. He scooped her hair off her neck and kissed her pulse, slipping one hand down past her belly to between her legs. She gasped a little bit. She'd be content to die after this. No. She would want more.

She understood that they were here to find Bertram, but she couldn't help but find delight and amazement in her husband.

He stopped touching her and stepped away. Lily turned to see him closing his eyes and clenching his jaw.

"Elias? What is it?"

He shook his head. "I just…I hate the thought of losin' ye. It grows more…harrowin' every day."

Aye, she had thoughts of losing him, too. If they both felt it, it must be a common fear. What would she do without him? "I prefer not to think on it."

He sat on the bed with his back leaned up against the head frame and raked his fingers through his hair.

She sat next to him and took his hand. "Elias, are you afraid?"

"Of what?" His glorious smile returned. "My fears are not the truth and I willna live as if they are. We will both come oot of this unharmed in body. Our hearts will grieve, but we will live."

How could he be so certain that he could convince her? Of course, she wanted to believe him. Who wouldn't? Who would prefer spending what was possibly the end of the world with someone who was constantly terrified and talking about dying?

There was no one she wanted to spend these days with other than Elias. In fact, she wanted hundreds of thousands, if there were such an amount, more days with him. She trembled and closed her arms around herself.

"Lass." He sat up behind her and rested his hands on her shoulders. "Are *ye* afraid?"

"Not of you." She smiled to reassure him. "But this is so…like nothing I have ever felt before. When I think of you, my heart flutters and races. When I see you, I feel as if my breath has left me. Sometimes, I feel positively ill from the way my belly twists and flips when I am with you. I do not tell you because I do not want you to think I have the pestilence. I do not know what grips me."

"Simon would say 'tis love," he told her softly over her shoulder while he ran his hands down her arms. "He might be correct, fer I feel the same way."

She turned to cast her best smile on him. "Do you think you love me, Elias?"

"Aye, I do, my lady."

She leaned in and he caught her face in his hands. He kissed her and then gently withdrew and pulled her to sit between his legs and lean back against him.

While he held her, they spoke for a little while about Bertram and Lily's past. She told him her father named her Lily after the flowers, lilies of the valley. "He told me the flower is also called the May lily and means 'return to happiness'."

"Aye, 'tis what ye do, my lady. Ye bring happiness back," he told her, speaking into her ear while she nestled into his muscles. "Ye brought happiness back to me. Even in the midst of all this."

"Aye," she told him. "You have done the same for me. I feel like a silly fool sometimes, wondering how I can feel such happiness with all that is going on around me. But then I see you, or I hear your voice, and my heart sings."

She had never spoken things like this to any man. She was surprised to hear them coming from her now, but it was easy. Elias broke down her walls. She wasn't afraid to excite or entice him. After Bertram had tried to force himself on her and she had to do such a detestable thing to him, he never came back to her bed. Richard had never tried to be intimate with her, and he never asked her help with his impotency.

She was a widowed virgin. She thought she had more time to tell him. It was something he should have known before he married her. Would he forgive her?

"Elias? There is something I must tell you."

"What is it, my love?"

"When you hear it, you may wish you had not married me."

"Lily—"

"Though I was married for two years, I am a virgin. I—"

Elias sat up straighter, pushing her with him. She turned in his arms and gave him a worried look while he spoke...or tried to speak. "Ye are a—ye never—"

She shook her head. "No. Never. Poor Richard could not..."

His warm, intimate smile washed over her. "And yet ye remained faithful to him."

"I kept my promise."

"Aye, ye did." He leaned down and pressed his mouth to hers. He kissed her and breathed her. He caressed her as if she were adored. His mouth molded to hers as he turned her in his arms and held her, chest to chest. He sank down on his back, taking her along while his lips whispered how bonny she was to him.

Sprawled atop him, she almost finally wept at the freedom he brought her.

He held her face in his hands and leaned his head up to keep kissing her. Soon, she grew bold enough to pull her legs over his waist and straddle him.

She immediately felt him grow harder, bigger between her legs. Her head told her she should jump off him. Instinct told her to rub herself against him.

She moved herself over him. He groaned and told her how wonderful she was.

Oh, but he was large and his hardness felt so utterly delightful at her crux, she thought she might have smiled.

Elias seemed to think so, too, because he pulled her down to kiss her and cup one of her breasts in his hand.

She shuddered above him as her nipples grew into taut little buds at the work of his deft fingers. She didn't protest when he swept her over and lay on top of her. She trusted him.

He looked down, dominant, sheltering. "Ye tempt me beyond my limits, Lily. If ye knew the things I want to do to ye..."

He pulled himself up, off her, and ran a hand down her hip, down to her knee. He gathered some linen of her chemise and pulled it up slowly over her thighs.

When he exposed her, he caressed her with his hand. He kissed her neck and slid his tongue south to her breasts.

What was he doing to her that felt so scandalous yet gave her such pleasure?

Sucking her breasts and fondling a small nub that pulsed with what felt like a life of its own between her thighs.

Instinctually, she wanted more of him and tugged at his breeches.

He was out of them in an instant, boots flung to the floor nearby.

She marveled at his legs; his thighs, dusted with dark hair and thick with muscle. Her gaze was drawn to the large mound beneath his léine.

He ran his broad hand over himself and lifted his léine when he returned to the bed. She had her first look at it dangling over a silken pouch.

She'd seen others beside Bertram and Walter's, when he suffered from that terrible rash, or Osbert, last summer when a bee flew down his breeches and stung him. But none of those was so thick and springing with life as Elias'.

He climbed onto the bed and kneeled to peel away his léine.

Lily's breath grew short and she tugged on her chemise, pulling it up higher.

She knew she was mad not to be more afraid, but the beauty of his masterfully sculpted body, his contoured face, mesmerized her. He wouldn't hurt her. His hands were as tender as his words.

He came down, covering her. He rested his lengthening rod between her legs and stared into her eyes. "Dinna be afraid."

"I am not afraid," she declared. She wasn't. She would not let Bertram ruin her life.

She relaxed her body and enjoyed the feel of him on her. He was her husband now. She could do what she wanted with him.

She reached out boldly and ran her fingers over his muscles. She bent her knees and cradled him, moving under him to music that was both feral and silent.

He had to stop before he poured himself forth prematurely.

They laughed at how many times he asked her to cease moving. She teased him about his control, or lack of it. They kissed and whispered to each other and, slowly, he claimed her with a sweep of his hips. He broke through with patience and concentration.

She loved the power she wielded over him. She loved him for giving it to her. He rose up on his palms and she held his trembling arms, fighting to take him fully. Though she didn't have to fight for long. He stretched her and filled her. But still, he couldn't get enough of her, so he slipped his hands behind her and held her by her arse, pulling her closer, pushing himself deeper.

She muffled her cries in his shoulder. He slowed, apologizing for hurting her.

"No," she whispered through hollow breaths, "'twill hurt no matter which way you do it. I can do it."

Wanting him to fill her, she coiled her legs around his waist. He moved quickly over her, thrusting deep and holding her close until she flung back her head and cried out his name. Her eyes rolled back and, for an instant, she felt decadent and desirable. Every instant after that was filled with the zenith of pleasure, ecstasy that made her pant and cry out. She opened her eyes to see him while they climaxed together. His pewter eyes were like bolts of lightning shooting into her, tilting her world, her heart.

How was it possible that he could make her feel this way? Did all able husbands give their wives such pleasure? Oh, she'd never known! And she was glad. She was glad she had never felt this with anyone but Elias.

Spent, they collapsed together on the bed. He waited a moment and then rolled off her. He reached his hand out for hers and they basked in the aftermath of becoming one, in a joining more intimate than anything they shared with anyone else.

He moved with a grunt that stirred a little ember inside her and with a slip of his arm under her neck, he pulled her closer.

She nestled herself against him and ran her palm over the whip-cord-tight muscles in his belly. Her fingers played in the dark, springy curls on his chest and the thin trail leading to his...she closed her eyes. Should she touch it? What should she do with it?

"May I tell ye somethin' I love aboot ye?" he asked, awakening hundreds of butterflies inside her. "Ye dinna have to make up somethin' fer me in return. Just let me tell ye."

She leaned up on her elbow and looked down into his eyes. "Aye." She smiled. "You may tell me."

His gaze went soft on her and he lifted his knuckles to her cheek and chuckled softly, almost like a groan. "Ah, my lady, I was goin' to say somethin' else, but 'tis yer smile that I love most. It keeps me grounded. I havena taken a sip of chamomile tea since ye gave it to me. I have no need of it anymore. Ye are a light, sent to keep away the darkness of my past."

"And you," she said with her breath falling on his chest, "were sent to keep away the darkness of my present."

He smiled. "I said ye didna have to make up somethin' to respond. And ye did."

Her smile widened and she moved her leg up over him. "What do we need to do to make that happen again?"

He laughed. "Not much. And if ye continue to move around with yer body spread over half of me, even less."

She realized that she was rubbing her leg against his stiffening cock. Her tight-nippled breasts were pressed against his chest. The effect it was having on him made her want to shout in triumph and do more. She pulled up to kiss him on the chin. "I want you inside me again."

She needn't say anything more. She could feel his heavy arousal and flung her leg over him. She closed her eyes and smiled seductively then opened them again. "You are a raging whirlwind and I must settle you and keep you tame beneath my touch."

"D'ye think ye can, my lady?"

Her hooded gaze and the sight of her tongue dipping out to lick him, shattered his control.

He took hold of her and yanked her up and was about to impale her.

She escaped his hands and rose up on her knees and then watched him do the same. He smiled. So did she.

Without another warning, he grasped her wrist and hauled her close. When she reached him, he scooped her up by her bottom and tried to have her again. She pulled herself up and pushed him down on the backs of his thighs. His cock jutted upward like a flagpole to the stars. She wanted to sit on it but she wasn't so bold. She slinked over him instead, delighting in his tight, trembling muscles. Her mouth found his and her tongue delved deeply, exploring, tasting him. She was wet for him. She could feel it.

His head rolled back and when she raked her teeth over his exposed neck, she almost fell over the precipice of sanity.

He pushed her down on him. She felt the tip of him like a battering ram, ready to burst through her.

She wanted this. She sank down, taking him whole, through the pain, through the pleasure. His shaft felt never-ending.

She took hold of his neck and began to undulate her hips. She rode up and down, crying out at the size of him, the feel of him.

Pulling free of her, he stretched his legs free and sat with his erection glistening in the firelight, then pulled her back on.

He bent and kissed her mouth, her throat, while he held her hips and guided her over him, slowly, rubbing her nub against his chiseled belly until she found her sweet release.

Her gave her neck one last lick, like an animal marking its mate, and finally fell asleep.

Lily smiled in the soft light. She thought about what they'd done. She was his and he was hers. It thrilled her.

She felt different. Better.

She'd pulled everything from him and gave him everything in return.

Whatever tomorrow brought, they would face it together.

CHAPTER EIGHTEEN

E LIAS WOKE UP with Lily in his arms. She was actually stretched out on top of him, but one of his arms was flung around her.

From his position, he couldn't see her face without lifting his head and mayhap waking her. He didn't want to do that. He wanted to be with her like this a little longer.

Nothing in his life had been, or would ever be better than this.

He felt his heart quicken at the thought of her, the sound of her, the feel of her. Hell, he was going hard. No. It would not be enjoyable for her. She would be sore this morning without him jumping her.

"Elias? Are you awake?"

He gritted his teeth and felt his heart beat even faster. "Aye, love."

"I can feel your heart beating."

"'Tis beatin' fast."

She nodded and kissed his chest. "What is it?" she asked, lifting her head to look at him. "Does something alarm you?"

He looked into her sleepy eyes and saw everything he ever wanted. He moved a few stray strands of flaxen hair away from her nose. "I was just thinkin' aboot how good this moment was, with ye in my arms. My heart went fast on its own."

"Along with other parts of you," she whispered.

"Aye, but disregard that. I willna torture my wife fer my pleasure."

She gasped and covered her mouth then giggled. "Are we truly married, Elias? I mean Brother Simon is only a brother—"

"We didna pledge our lives as one to Simon, but to God," he reminded her with a loving grin. "There is no one higher than Him."

His smile went a bit darker an instant later. "And if anyone tries to disclaim it and take ye from me, I will kill them."

He kissed her forehead and pushed her off him when she tried to snuggle deeper into him. It would lead to no good. Besides, they needed to get moving if they were going to find Bertram and his prisoners before they reached London. That was the plan. Find them before they reached the large city.

They washed in the basin that had been set in the room, and then later again beneath a small waterfall between West Wickham and Beckenham.

He'd been correct; Lily's body was sore. Even if she hadn't told him at the waterfall, he would have known by the painful grin on her face while riding.

When they reached Beckenham toward the end of the evening, Elias caught her in his arms when she dismounted and carried her into an inn. Of course, the innkeeper eyed him as if Lily were a rotting corpse. Elias didn't give a damn.

She was as light as a veil. And the food was getting scarcer.

Elias paid the innkeeper for a hot bath for his wife while he went hunting for some fresh food. The innkeeper was happy to oblige—especially after Elias promised to take the man's head and the heads of everyone he loved if he tried to do anything foolish with his woman while he was away.

He caught two hares and wanted to get at least two more so that there would be more than enough food for everyone. He didn't know if there were other guests, but at least it would be enough for the innkeeper to store for food.

He came to the bend of a small river, where a moonlit shaft broke through the canopy. He thought of bringing Lily here in the morning.

He saw something moving in the stream and leaned in to take a closer look.

Bodies. There were bodies floating downstream.

He pulled up his mask and backed away slowly and returned to the inn. He wouldn't tell Lily what he'd seen, but he didn't want to go any farther than where they were. London, much more densely populated than the countryside, was going to be like walking into hell. They hadn't fallen ill yet. Did they chance it? Were they somehow immune? Or were they running out of time?

He only knew that every moment was precious, a gift. Any moment, the disease could strike. He wanted to return to Sevenoaks, but he knew Lily would not give up on little Eddie and his mother. Especially not when they were in the hands of Bertram Chisholm.

They would continue on for another day. If they hadn't found them by then, they would head back home to Simon and their children. Right now, he would bask in the glory of his wife. His wife! He could scarcely believe it. He, battle-hardened and weary, a man well-known among other soldiers as fearless, but at night, terrified of ghosts, *he*, he was now in love with a soft, perfect woman.

In the middle of the apocalypse.

He left the hares with the innkeeper's wife and she promised to make him some of her delicious rabbit stew.

"Go on," she shooed him toward the stairs. "See to your fortunate wife and I will call you down when the stew is ready."

"I will go," he called down as he went. "But 'tis I who am the fortunate one."

He was lovesick. He sounded like a fool. He didn't truly care how he sounded though. He was in love with Lily Be—MacPherson. He was in love with how she loved, how she looked, and sounded, and smelled, and smiled. There wasn't one thing he didn't love about her. It made him want to laugh as he reached the door to their room. He wanted a life with her, to have more children with her, to grow old with her.

He put his hand to the door then moved back quickly to the railing. "By the way," he called down to the innkeeper's wife. "How many guests are here besides my wife and me?"

"Just one man," she called back. "Do not fear. There will be plenty of food."

He laughed with her, feeling happier than he had since he was a child.

He entered the room and then stopped and listened to his heart faltering in his ears as his world ended in a single moment at the sight of Lily wiping her mouth with her bath cloth and covering the basin where she'd just thrown up. She was pale and—

She began to turn to look at him, and then something hit him hard on the head. The world went dark and Lily was gone.

"Do NOT HURT him, Bertram," Lily gasped out for breath. "For if you do, I will curse you."

He laughed, grabbing for her arm. "Ye will be dead in a few days. Exactly where ye wanted me."

"I will curse you from heaven. 'Twill be worse," she warned.

He must have believed she could do as she said because he left Elias alone and dragged her out of the inn, smiling as she coughed and pushing the innkeeper's wife out of his way when she tried to stop him.

"I shall enjoy watchin' ye suffer, Lily."

Lily ignored him and turned to look over her shoulder at the inn-keeper's wife. She winked and then returned her sickly gaze to her abductor.

She had seen him speaking with the innkeeper when she'd gone outside to use the privy. She'd hurried back to her room and tied her knives to various parts of her legs. She was glad he was here. The search was over. She thought it best to have him believe she was sick. He wouldn't be prepared for her fight when it came. She hadn't wanted Elias to see her and think...oh, she hoped the innkeeper's wife saw her wink and understood the sign and would tell Elias.

For now though, she had to find out about little Eddie and Clare.

"Where are Clare and little Eddie, Bertram?"

"Ye will see them soon enough," he promised, trying to be cryptic.

She hadn't wanted it to come to this. Would she finally have to kill him? She couldn't do anything until she knew. "Where are they?" she demanded then coughed again. She knew she was pale, waiting for his answer. "Are they alive?"

"Why do ye care fer them so, Lily?" he asked, turning to her while he pulled her to his waiting horse—waiting with the nervous-looking innkeeper. "They are nothin' but peasants." He took out his knife and stabbed the innkeeper in the belly.

Lily cried out, "No!" Then squeezed her eyes shut. Oh, how she wanted him dead.

"Why did ye choose them over me, eh?"

She pulled back, aghast as the innkeeper fell to the ground. "What? Do my ears deceive me? How can you ask me such a question? Do you think I would *ever* choose you over anyone else, Bertram?"

He pushed her the rest of the way and then hefted her into the saddle.

"Ye were happier with me before we went to Sevenoaks."

She could not believe what she was hearing. He was mad. He was vile. She should just pull out one of her daggers, but she had to know where Clare and little Eddie were. If they were still alive. Oh, please, let them be alive.

"I was not happy with you," she told him while he sat in the saddle behind her. "Not even once! I was docile and meek because it saved me from your whip. I had nothing to fight with you over. So I did not fight."

"Aye," he agreed after a moment of consideration, "ye always were a cold, defiant lass. Tell me, did ye weep when yer husband withered away before yer eyes? Or were yer eyes too busy on Elias MacPherson?"

She would not let him goad her. It was her emotions he wanted. "You made me this way, Bertram. I was a child when you took me from my father, my family, and then tried to have your way with me. 'Tis your fault that I am cold and defiant toward you. I despise you, you wretched fool."

He whacked her hard across her temple and cheekbone with his palm. She slumped forward. He grabbed her around the waist before she fell from the horse and laughed in her ear that he knew she wasn't truly sick.

But she didn't hear.

ELIAS OPENED HIS eyes and then closed them for another moment to decide if he ever wanted to open his eyes again. She was sick. Lily was sick. It had finally come to claim her. No. His muscles tensed. He tried to sit up and clutched his head. Who had hit him? Was it Bertram? The innkeeper? Hell.

He looked toward the stairs and called out. No one answered.

He sat up and then pulled himself to his feet with the help of the wall. His head spun and he swayed for a moment. "Lily?" Was that his voice that sounded so broken and hopeless…so on edge—as if he were afraid to scream? He wanted to disappear and hide the way he used to when he was a child. But he wasn't a child anymore. He'd learned how to face anything.

But this felt too big. If she was dead…he was afraid of losing her.

He hated this kind of fear and had fought his whole life to defy it. But here it was, staring him in the face; attached to the woman he loved more than his own life. He would give it. He would give it in exchange for hers.

"Lily!" he shouted. How long did she have? Had he been asleep for one day or three? He had no idea. It felt like a lifetime.

He had to find her. He had to find someone who could give him answers.

Was it Bertram? Had he found them? How? He had to have been around, somewhere close to have seen them. Was he the other guest? But if he was alone, then where were Clare and little Eddie?

He hurried down the steps and looked around for anyone. There was no one to be found. The innkeeper and his wife were either asleep, dead, or had run away. If they were asleep then they hadn't seen or heard anything, so there was no point in wasting time going back up and checking their beds. Whether or not Bertram was a guest didn't matter. Lily was sick and she was gone.

There was no time to ponder things. He lit a lantern, mounted his horse, and followed a fresh set of horse tracks out of the village.

He didn't sleep but kept on moving. Finally, when his lantern light faded into the darkness, he relented and stopped to rest against a tree until he could track the rider again.

The few hours it took were torturous for Elias. He hadn't wanted to leave her alone against the pestilence. That was why he'd taken her with him. But he'd left her. He'd left her and it came. Of course, it was Bertram who had taken her. He rode on the back of the plague.

Why hadn't he killed Elias? Why leave such an enemy alive? Had Lily somehow stopped him from doing it? She was sick. Why wasn't Bertram afraid of falling ill again?

He had time to think and he was driven mad with the thoughts digging into his head. She wouldn't be given any of her teas. Bertram would not take care of her and fight for her life. She would have to do it on her own. He knew she was clever and brave, but still, he wanted to be there with her, for her.

He said a dozen prayers for her, and for Simon and the children. They should not have left them. They had other responsibilities now. Simon was a good friend, but he wasn't a father and a mother and the village healer, along with everything else. It was wrong of them to heap so much on his scrawny shoulders.

He smiled thinking of his lifelong friend. Simon would forgive him—after a week or two of snappy retorts and making Elias suffer through his company.

He wished Simon were with him now, as he had been during so many sieges and battles. He was always there in the trenches with him, like a mother hen, scared and worn, and ready to give his life for Elias in a breath.

When Elias found Lily, he would get her well and take her home whether they found Clare and her babe or not.

He thought of other things, but not her death. Not that. He was too afraid of that.

Finally, the day broke. He stood up, able to see in the soft light. He found the tracks again and followed them.

It was another day for Lily. Was she sicker? Was she resting in a bed somewhere?

He stopped in the next village and his knees nearly betrayed him. West Wickham! He'd been here already! This was where he and Lily…he was going the wrong way! He was going south! Had he been going south for long? He didn't know which way to go now. Follow the tracks or admit that they were the wrong ones?

He looked south toward Sevenoaks and then north toward the city of London. He took a step north but stopped and kept going the way he was. But why would Bertram take Lily south?

He lost the tracks among the dozens in the area. There were four leading out, going farther south. Which one was theirs? He chose one and continued on. He went—without any food, for he would not stop until he found her.

She had to live. He couldn't allow himself to think otherwise or he would lose all hope. Lily. She drove him on. He would hold her again, kiss her, make love to her again. He would go mad if he didn't.

He arrived in Addington, a large settlement at the edge of south London.

The dead and diseased were everywhere. He pulled up his mask. Everyone around him was crying out in pain and despair, forgotten by society, looked upon with fear and disgust. There were piles of dead awaiting the fire. Some were moving in the piles. But barely.

He turned away, sickened to think Lily was in one of them. Should he go look? He knew he had to, so he did. He was relieved that she wasn't among them. Nor were Bertram, Clare, or little Eddie. It didn't mean much, but Elias held on to it.

He spotted a few men leaving a small church, and went to them. He questioned them about Bertram.

One man called Alex remembered someone who matched Bertram's description.

"Aye. Aye. When everyone is dead and dying around you, you see someone walking and you remember him."

His friends all smiled and agreed. Elias prompted Alex to continue.

"Right. Right. A big, angry-looking fellow with a cut up face. He said his name was Chisholm."

"Aye, that is him." Elias breathed a little. He wasn't sure if he was relieved to hear it or horrified to think of Bertram having her. Relieved only because Bertram was easier to find.

"He left and went north," Alex told him. His friends nodded.

He? Elias' heart slowed. Why did Alex speak as if Bertram had been alone? "And the woman with him?"

"Woman?" Alex knit his brow then shook his head.

Elias did not want to hear what the man was about to tell him. No! He couldn't bear the answer.

"He was alone, friend."

Alone. Elias' blood went cold. Then, she had died in the hands of the man she despised? It broke his heart too much to bear. For the first time in his life, Elias was too afraid to move. Too afraid of losing himself, his hope. Too afraid of death.

Her death.

His destruction.

CHAPTER NINETEEN

"**I**'M SO HAPPY to see that ye are not dyin' after all, Lily."
Bertram tried to catch her when she slid from his saddle. But she pushed herself left and slipped through his fingers.

She'd pretended and possibly led Elias to believe the worst for no reason.

"Why are we back here?" she asked, instead of arguing with him. She looked around at the village of West Wickham. They had been closer to London. Why had he come back here? She prayed the reason he still hadn't brought her to Clare and the babe was because they were here, and he would bring her to them now.

She hated asking him. She'd barely spoken to him since she woke up with a swollen head. He'd struck her. He'd done it before when she used to travel with him. But just as soon as she found Clare and little Eddie, she would make sure he never did it again.

She had hoped Elias would have found her by now. But why would he continue to look if he thought she was dying of the pestilence? What if the innkeeper's wife hadn't told him that she'd winked? What if the poor woman was so distraught over her husband that she didn't remember a silly wink? Even if he did search for her, he wouldn't go south. He would go toward London.

"Why did ye think I would let a plague get in my way?"

In his way of what? Surely it wasn't her he wanted. "Bertram." As much as she hated speaking to him, she wanted him to know. "If you killed Clare and little Eddie, I am going to kill you. I vow it."

"Well, well, somethin' does stir the princess." He laughed. He'd taken all her knives from under her skirts while she was knocked out. He may have tried to touch her but he hated how being aroused made him feel. He'd never gone near her or anyone else sexually again. She was more concerned about her knives, but then she saw that he hadn't disposed of them. Fool. He carried them with him.

All it took was one to kill him.

"Fear not. They live. At least they did when I left them. The mother will have to be left behind though."

"They live?" She dismounted and stood in front of him. "Where? Where are they? And what do you mean the mother will have to be left behind? I will not let you separate them."

He gave her a wilted look, and touched his fingers to a strand of her hair. "Then ye will have to be left behind as well."

"What are you saying, Bertram?" she demanded, moving out of his reach. "Do you think you will be separating the babe from his mother?"

"They will be separated whether I do it or not."

She had to kill him. "Where are they?"

"They are here in West Wickham," he told her. "My cousin's men will be here to collect him."

"To collect who? Little Eddie?" She had no idea what he was talking about. Why would his cousin—she assumed he was speaking of his cousin the bishop—want little Eddie?

A memory flashed across her thoughts. The bishop's name. Edmundson. The truth dawned on her when she remembered Clare telling her that the babe's father was an important man in England. Oh no, Clare. Lily's belly hit the ground. "Little Eddie is Bishop Edmundson's son."

When Bertram didn't deny it, she covered her face in her hands. "What does this mean? What does he intend to do?"

"He intends to finally put an end to all of this."

Her heart sank along with her belly. "He's going to have Clare killed? And the babe?"

"Hell, I have already told ye too much."

She looked around. Where was Elias? She had to do something. When the bishop's men arrived, it would be too late. She couldn't let them kill Clare and her son. "Which house are they in?"

"Do ye not want to know why I left them and went all the way to Beckenham to find ye?" he asked, ignoring her question.

She didn't want to know. She didn't care. "Why?" she asked just to appease him until she could get to Clare.

"Because I want ye back." He reached out and ran his fingers down her arm. "Now that Richard is dead, ye are free again. In time, ye will forget yer Highlander."

His touch repulsed her. "Where are Clare and her son?" She put her hand on his waist to push him away and slipped one of her knives that he had tucked into his belt into her palm and up her sleeve.

"First, Lily, pledge yer life to me."

She almost laughed right in his face. She wanted to shout that he was too late once again. She was already married to Elias. But she couldn't tell him. Not yet.

"What could you possibly want with me?" she asked him.

"I want to make yer life hell—just as ye have made mine."

"You are mad, Bertram. Mad and evil."

He laughed. "But I will have my way."

"Very well, Bertram, you have your wish. Now take me to them."

His lips curled into a thin, triumphant smile. "Follow me."

They passed the inn where she and Elias had made love. Where she'd spent the most magical night of her life. She followed Bertram past a cluster of houses north of the village, to the last small cottage near a wooded area.

The charcoal sky boded rain. She thought she heard a child crying. She ran toward the small cottage and pushed open the door.

There were a few small tables with various things atop them. A small alcove housed cold coals and a pot with nothing in it.

Against the western wall, Clare lay on a bed made of straw. Huddled on the floor at the foot of the bed was little Eddie. He was crying. He looked like he'd been crying for days. His eyes were puffy and red just like his little nose. His chin was wrinkled and his lower lip was sagging.

When he saw Lily, he scrambled to his feet and ran to her.

She bent and caught him in her arms with a smile. She had him. He was safe. Thank you, God.

Her elation soon faded and she lifted her face to the bed. Her heart felt as if it would fall out of her mouth if she opened it. She straightened and tucked little Eddie behind her.

"Clare?" she spoke on a soft breath, afraid to yell and confirm what she feared. "Clare!" a little louder.

Bertram startled her coming forward. He stood over the bed and gave her friend a shake. He looked at Lily and shook his head.

"Was she sick?" Lily asked, shaken and overcome with sadness. It was too much. It was all too much.

Bertram shrugged his broad shoulders. "She might have been. I canna recall. But the boy—"

The boy...

Lily remembered him talking about *the boy* the first night they had him in the shed when he had fallen into delirium. Was *the boy* little Eddie? He had said, *Always the boy*...did he mean they had gone to Sevenoaks in the first place because of little Eddie?

He turned his dark gaze on the babe. "He is well. Is it not a mystery that some become afflicted, and some dinna? Like ye." He didn't wait for her to answer but sat on the edge of the bed and patted his knee to receive the babe.

"It was always about him, was it not?" she asked, needing to hear it. "Us going to Sevenoaks?"

He laughed and nodded. "Ye dinna think I would have settled in such a dull, little village fer as long as I did, did ye? Louis wanted me to get rid of Clare and her bastard back then but I grew weary of doin' his dirty work and refused. He sent me back this time to see what had become of them, but I was struck with the pestilence before I arrived."

"And infected all my friends."

"Oh, do stop," he mocked her, "before I shed a tear. At least one of us would, eh, Lil?" His smile faded and he patted his knee again. "Now, let him come to me."

"I will not." She gritted her teeth and looked him square in the eyes. She knew where to cut a vital vein and kill him. There was no time for thinking about it now. She clenched her fingers around the edge of her sleeve, holding back her knife.

"Give him to me, Lily. 'Tis time this is done."

Her heart drummed like a war chant inside her. Her blood singed her veins. "No, Bertram. You will not have him. Now, get out."

She didn't think he'd go. But he started for the door. Passing her, he stopped and pushed her out of his way. He was upon little Eddie in no time.

She was about to take a step, but she stopped and cast him a horrified look.

She had to keep a clear head. Eddie's life depended on it. She couldn't let her emotions rule her.

She looked at her target, remembering her lessons with Elias. She took a step forward, arriving at the correct distance for the blade to fall into him. She wanted to do the most damage and aimed for his thigh.

But little Eddie was too close to fling the weapon so low. She'd have to get close to the savage. Aye, the villagers were correct to call Bertram that.

"Do not kill him!" she cried out.

Bertram's face lit up. "Ah, finally, some true passion!"

This was what he wanted. What he'd always wanted—for her to weep and show fear.

She had told Elias to use her in this way to get back Clare and her babe. She knew what he wanted. "Please, Bertram! I will do as you ask, only let me hold him." She wiped her eyes, though there were no tears there.

He smiled triumphantly again and pushed little Eddie toward her.

She caught the boy and picked him up to hold him close to her. She whispered low in his ear. "Get ready to jump and run. Ready?"

He nodded. She turned him away and released her knife at the same time. Her heartbeat slowed, along with his movements.

She flung her blade and missed.

Bertram stared at the hilt of the blade sticking out of the wall just to the right of him, and then he turned to her. "Ye bitch."

"Eddie, run!" She pushed the boy toward the door and began to turn back to Bertram.

But the savage reached her first. He took her by her hair and forced her to her knees. "Now, ye get no more mercy from me." He dragged her to the door. "I willna fall fer yer bewitchin' schemes again. No! Now, ye will be the one to call the boy to ye! Do it! Call him!"

"No!" she said through her clenched jaw. "I will not call him!"

He tried to pull her up to her feet, but she kicked him and clawed at his arms. She tried to pull another one of her blades from his belt but he raised his hand to strike her.

Little Eddie called out her name from outside.

She resumed her wild kicking. Bertram let her go and took a step toward the door to fetch the babe.

Lily ran to the wall where her first knife had landed. She yanked the blade free and aimed at the back of Bertram's hip. This time, the blade met it's mark. Blood gushed from him and he collapsed to the floor.

Run. She turned and shot off like an arrow from a taut bow. She ran outside, quickly caught up with little Eddie, and scooped him up in her arms. She ran back to Bertram's horse, mounted with the babe and took off.

South. She wanted to find Elias and bring little Eddie home. His mother had been struck down by the pestilence. Was the babe going to fall ill as well?

No. She would look after him, Annabelle, and Charlie, and anyone else who needed her.

And right now, little Eddie needed food. She made a quick search for the market, found it and bought a few apples, two loaves of fresh bread, and some of water.

From the way he was bleeding, Bertram would die from his wound. If he didn't, and if he ever came near her or the children again, she would kill him without hesitation. And the bishop? What would be done about him? Lily would kill the bishop, too, if she had to.

She had little Eddie! Oh, but poor Clare. Her victory was bittersweet. Her heart was heavy. She missed Elias and his eyes always on her. She missed Richard, and Joan, and all her friends.

She couldn't break down now. The boy needed her. How long had he sat on the floor crying for his mother who could no longer answer him? Oh, she couldn't think of it.

They reached the road just as the rains began—and Bishop Edmundson's men arrived.

ELIAS SAW THE last of the bishop's soldiers entering the village and wondered what the hell they were doing here. Hadn't Lily told him that Bertram was the bishop's cousin?

He followed them, staying far behind, clearing the rain from his eyes so he could keep them open.

He'd found hope that Lily wasn't dead when, while leaving Addington, it came to him that he'd been so forlorn over her that he hadn't realized Alex had told him Bertram had gone *north*. He also wasn't aware of what day it was. Alex had said Chisholm had gone north, alone. But after Bertram had taken Lily in Beckenham, he'd gone south, hadn't he? Either Elias was traveling the wrong road or Alex had seen Bertram going north *to* Beckenham a few days ago *before* he'd kidnapped Lily, not after. It didn't mean for certain that she was still alive. But it was a thread of hope—and he took it.

He'd turned his horse around, back to West Wickham, where he'd lost Bertram's horse's tracks. He would find her. He didn't allow himself to doubt it. Just as he hadn't let himself doubt he would get her through the pestilence alive. Until he saw her pale and vomiting and then woke up alone. He'd faltered and allowed fear to show its ugly head.

He swiped the rain from his eyes again. Or were they tears? The bastard Bertram had to be here. Lily had to be with him. Alive. He felt ill with worry over her. He'd left her...no! He shook his head, defying fear. If she lived then the fear was useless. If she did not live, fear would come anyway. Why let it come now? It had been how he entered every battle. If he thought about it for days before, fearing the battle, all it did was eat away at his confidence. When he lived through a battle, which he always did, fear was proven worthless. Aye, the sickness was strong but Charlie had recovered, as well as Father Benedict and others. It was possible. She could do it.

The soldiers broke off into groups. Elias followed a handful of them into the inn and listened from a secure place, cloaked in shadows while they questioned the innkeeper about a man fitting Bertram's description traveling with a child. A boy.

Little Eddie? But what about Lily and Clare?

The innkeeper hadn't seen a man with a child and sent them away, complaining that they likely brought with them the pestilence. The soldiers threatened to take him outside and beat him senseless, but the innkeeper didn't care and swatted his broom at them.

When the soldiers, six in all, began pushing the innkeeper back and forth between them, Elias stepped forward. He didn't try to say anything but dragged his claymore out of its sheath and cut four down before the other two realized there was only one of him.

He moved with unleashed power, speed, and sublime precision, getting the task done quickly and efficiently.

He swung his bloody sword across one of the remaining men's necks while the man was in mid-swing, his blade pointed at Elias' chest.

Elias backed up a step and then turned to the last man standing, his comrades' blood splattered across his face.

"Why are ye here?" Elias demanded and then followed the soldier's eyes, down the hall to where little Eddie stood. "For him. The bishop wants him dead."

"And ye came here to see the duty done, aye? To a wee boy." He didn't give the soldier a chance to answer but swung his heavy blade. The last soldier tried to block but he wasn't quick or strong enough, and he ending up losing his head.

After a moment he heard her voice.

"Elias?"

He missed it. Was it real? His throat and his eyes burned as he turned to see her, to lay his eyes on her again.

"Lily," he breathed her name as if it were a prayer.

She didn't look ill. She looked breathtaking and beautiful to him. She held little Eddie close in her arms, holding his head away from the carnage.

Was he dreaming?

"Is any of that your blood?" she asked as if she feared she were dreaming, too. She came closer, looking at his face, his clothes.

He shook his head. "Nae, my lady," he answered softly, afraid to move lest she disappear, "'Tis not my blood. Are ye well?"

She nodded. "Forgive me."

Were those tears in her eyes?

"I tried to fool Bertram. I was never sick."

Elias felt so relieved...his knees buckled beneath him. What the—his stomach twisted into a tight knot. He felt his blood begin to burn just before he hit the floor. He saw little Eddie's tiny face, his deep blue gaze staring down at him.

And then he saw only red.

CHAPTER TWENTY

L ILY WASN'T GOING to lose him. Not him.

Once he saw Elias and realized he had the plague, the inn-keeper would not help her get him to her horse.

At least the rains had stopped.

"Elias," she said as she gave his cheek a few small smacks. "There are soldiers around. I need you to stand up!"

Thankfully, her beloved came to enough to make his own way to one of the six soldier's horses, and then motioned for her and the babe to take another and leave Bertram's horse behind.

They traveled south to a small village outside of Downe. But Elias refused to stay there and continued on toward Sevenoaks.

He needed rest. Twice, she feared he would fall from his horse, but he managed to hold on and even take command over his mount.

He was a man with a strong will. It would help him.

"Stay with me, Husband," she commanded softly, keeping her horse at an even pace with his. "Did you think to even see me again?" She hated bringing it up, but if it produced an emotion in him to distract him from the sickness, then so be it.

"At first...I didna." He looked away and up at the sun. His eyes gleamed in vivid hues of deeper blue against bloodshot red. "The thought of ye dyin' with Bertram at yer bedside made me suffer madness."

Nothing in her life since being taken from her family affected her this way. She felt a wave of emotions battering outside the doors to the innermost chasm of her heart. "Forgive me, Elias."

"I do, my love," he assured her with a smile that convinced her. "I'm happy to be with ye again, thankful that ye are well."

"As you will be," she told him. "Aye, Elias?" Her words only mattered if he believed them.

"I will be well."

She smiled at him and he swayed in his saddle. She realized then and there exactly how much this man loved and cherished her. He'd stayed in her village before the pestilence struck. He could have outrun it, but he hadn't moved away from her. He said and did things to make her forget the world falling apart around her. He'd waited until she was free to take her to his bed, to even kiss her. She believed he would have waited years. He'd dug his boots into the ground around her and nothing could move him.

"Elias, just a little while longer," she promised and kept urging him on.

When they finally reached their village. Simon and Father Benedict were there to meet them.

When he saw Elias, Simon immediately began praying while he helped Father Benedict haul him to the house with the red roof.

They managed to get Elias into Lily's bed while she went to work on mixing herbs and boiling most. Her hands shook while she strained the contents of the pot into a cup.

Her friends came by to welcome her home and offer their aid. They mourned the loss of Clare, and the beautiful little Lizbeth. Alfred the merchant had also perished in the few days she'd been gone. Still, thank God, Ava, Norman's daughter, had lived. The disease came and went in a whirlwind, taking or leaving its victim swiftly.

She felt faint with a rush of fear. *Please*, she begged God, *not him. Not him.*

Her friends and neighbors went outside to gather the herbs she needed.

Charlie would not leave Elias' side and Annabelle helped look after little Eddie.

Brother Simon stayed behind to help her in the kitchen and hurry up making whatever Elias needed.

"Do you feel ill, lass?" His voice was stained with worry.

"No," she assured him. "I am afraid to lose Elias. My heart faints at the thought of it."

Brother Simon actually smiled and continued cleaning the herbs and roots and then cut them up for her.

"I am thankful he has found you," he told her. "From the very first moment he saw you, you captured his heart. He disagreed with me about you not being divine." He smiled and Lily blushed and stirred her herbs.

When she told him to go rest, he refused. "Doing these small tasks helps me keep my thoughts fixed on the Lord and not on Elias being sick. I cannot continually pray in fear."

She nodded. "I understand." Then she asked, "Would you mash some peas for supper?"

"Aye, and we have plenty of salmon." He grinned and Lily realized that she hadn't noticed his scars since the first day he came here. Brother Simon was a sweet, stern man and a loyal friend and soldier to Elias—and to her. And the children loved him.

She prepared Elias' cup and rested her hand on his dearest friend's shoulder.

Lily didn't leave Elias' side again until she left him to prepare supper. She cooled his head with vinegar and water. She fed him her remedies, and she prayed.

Elias cried out in his feverish sleep more than once. Lily was there to comfort him. She applied more salve and cooling rags to the swollen lumps on his neck, under his arms, and on his groin, then covered him again.

She ate her supper with the children while Brother Simon stayed above stairs with Elias, who had not grown worse. She didn't visit anyone nor was anyone in the village sick.

All in all, it was a good day.

At night, she tucked the children into the bed that had been Richard's and brought Brother Simon a cup of warm chamomile tea to help him sleep. He looked a bit gaunt, but he promised that he was just weary. He needed sleep. She nodded then bid him goodnight and thanked him for all he had done.

She climbed the stairs, praying for Elias and that God would help her not to weep and fall apart. She was afraid she would not be able to be put back together. Not if she lost Elias. What man was like him? She'd had the opportunity to meet many of them and none, not one, was like him.

She stripped down to her chemise and climbed into her bed with her husband. She moved close, wanting to hold him. He'd cooled down, thanks to her herbs, and she was able to hold him in her arms.

"Elias," she whispered with her lips tilted to his ear, though he hadn't responded much since they put him into bed. "If you can hear me, my one true love, listen to what I say. You came into my world and shook the earth and the heavy rubble that had gathered over me.

"I have never spoken of it before but...my childhood was a mixture of many different things. My father was very kind and doting. He took me everywhere with him and had been teaching me everything he knew when Bertram took me from him. It has been too long since I have seen him. I often..." she sobbed out her next breath and closed her eyes. She didn't know one could weep without tears. She had been holding back so desperately all these years. "I have never let myself hope to see him again.

"Bertram brought me into a life too grown up for the likes of me, and I had to quickly learn how to do the worst to save my life." She thought of little Eddie on the other side of the curtain. Or someone else's life.

"Your love is like no other's. Not even Richard's, whom I love and hold to a high measure. Your smiles have cleared away the stones. Your face, revealed in the light is, oh so glorious to behold. How could my spirit, my body not want to be free of the world? In the blackest days, you brought me hope and laughter. You faced this thing without fear and did not care about your life when it came to mine." She paused to close her eyes and tried to continue. "Thank you, Elias, but I do not want you to give your life. I want more nights with you like the last one we shared. Please, my love. You showed me what a lion heart means, for you are as gallant as the knights of old that my father used to tell me about. Fight this for me. Please, Elias."

She wept. For the first time in nine years. It wasn't the unbridled emotion she'd been feeling rising to the surface, but it was something. She muffled her cries against him so that the children wouldn't hear. She almost didn't feel Elias' arms close around her until she relaxed into them and opened her eyes. She drew in a deep sniff and then kissed his chest and smiled. "I love you, Elias."

"I love ye, too, my lady."

He would fight. He would fight.

Content in knowing that if he fought, he would win—for he'd killed six English soldiers and she saw him kill three of them. She closed her eyes and slept for an hour before little Eddie's cries woke her.

She went to his bed and remembered what he'd seen. Poor babe probably had a nightmare. Charlie left the bed and slept on the floor beside it.

She held little Eddie and kissed his golden curls until his cries ceased and his breathing became regular and deep.

Like her own.

IT TOOK ELIAS almost an hour to get out of bed. He swore in his head, for it sapped too much of his strength to speak.

He'd heard her. Her voice, so distressed, telling him her life and what he meant to her, had seeped into his thoughts and pulled him from his deep slumber. His fever had gone but he didn't know for how long. His thoughts were still jumbled.

A child's cry had pulled her from the bed. Elias wanted her back.

When he finally reached the draped curtain, he had to lean against the wall to remain standing. He looked into Richard's room at the bed and Lily holding little Eddie in her arms, with Annabelle sleeping beside her, her small hand on Lily's.

His wife looked peaceful, content, and happy. It was what he wanted for her. He could die happy.

But he wasn't about to. She'd asked him to fight this for her. He didn't intend to lose. But he would admit the battle was a difficult one. Still, not as difficult as thinking her dead.

He watched her sleep. He was tempted to go inside the room and wake her, ask her to come back to him. For he was weary. Too weary, in fact, to go get her.

He forced himself to walk, holding onto a chair and a table for support. He finally reached his bed and fell into it.

His neck and groin were still swollen and sore. His head pounded in his skull and he felt like hell all over. But he remembered her in his arms, in his bed at the inn. He remembered how she felt, so tight around him. He thought of groaning then wondered if it was wise that he should work himself up in such a way. But the scent of her covered him from being in her bed, in her arms. The memory of her smile, her kisses, her voice as she cried out his name made him feel hot again. He wouldn't die. He wouldn't leave her.

He fell into a deep slumber and didn't hear Simon waking up and moving about downstairs. He didn't see Lily leave her spot next to little Eddie in the middle of the night to prepare some tea for his dearest friend.

CHAPTER TWENTY-ONE

L ILY STAYED AWAKE all night with Brother Simon, feeding him her blends, and wiping his forehead with vinegar and water as she had done with Elias.

Strangely, Pip spent the night beside the brother. At first, Brother Simon reacted with fear but Pip purred and the sound seemed to calm him. After an hour, they became friends, with Brother Simon giving in quickly, mostly because he had no choice. Petting the feline seemed to calm his breathing as well. But not enough.

Morning came quickly. Lily didn't want it to—for with every hour, her dearest friend, Brother Simon grew worse.

She didn't know why it had waited so long to attack him, or why so viciously? Was it a stronger strain coming from Elias?

"Do you think the children no longer need you?" Lily asked at his feet. She'd done her best trying to make him comfortable, sitting him in an oversized chair with his feet up on a cushioned stool Lily had sewn herself. "Do you think your duty to Elias is over?"

He shrugged his scrawny shoulders under his robes. "Elias has you. I have not seen him so lost to anything—anyone, the way he is lost to you." He closed his eyes and shivered and coughed beneath his blankets. Pip crawled into his lap and snuggled closer to him. He took a moment to gather himself again. He reached for her hand with a trembling one of his own. "My heart is glad for him," he reassured her. "I knew he would be well for I saw him struggle to walk to the pulled curtain where you slept. It took him a long time and my heart roared for him in silence. For he is a strong, determined man and one I am very proud of."

She wanted to be glad Elias had felt better enough to get out of bed but she couldn't feel happy with Brother Simon so sick.

Oh, how she hated this sickness. How randomly it chose its victims. How quickly it devoured them.

"Brother Simon?"

"Aye, lass?"

"You do realize that you are petting a cat, do you not?"

He smiled and looked down at Pip. "She is soft and not so bad, after all." He stroked the cat between the ears and was quiet for a moment.

Then he told her, "Beneath all the confidence and bravado, he is still the boy who hid under the bed."

Lily didn't think her heart could break for Elias anymore than it already had.

But no time to think on that now. She heard footsteps and looked up at the children coming closer, staring in horror at Brother Simon.

He spoke to them, assuring them that he would watch over them from heaven, but they all wept.

Lily looked up to the second landing. Was Elias awake? How would she tell him about his friend?

She asked Charlie to sit with the brother while she went upstairs to check on her husband. She would make them something to eat when she returned.

She had to stop once before she reached the top. She felt overwhelmed, on the brink of hysterics at any moment. She didn't want to tell him, but what if he was well enough to come belowstairs and see and speak to his friend for the last time?

She continued up and went to her bed. She was hoping to see his eyes opened, him smiling, everything all right.

"Elias, my love." She leaned down and touched his face. He was burning up with fever. No! She put her hands to her temples. She wanted to scream and cry and never stop. Did he make himself worse by getting out of bed during the night?

"Elias?" She gave him a little shake but he did not stir.

Panicked, she hurried down the stairs to prepare his tea and something for his fever. She'd had hope for him. He was a fighter. He held her last night. He fired her hope, but today...oh, today...they might lose Brother Simon. She couldn't lose Elias, too. She prayed and did her best to reassure the children that everything would be all right, but she didn't believe it. How could it be? Richard was gone. A future without him in it frightened her. She'd lost all her friends, Alice, Joan, Deirdre, Agnes, Ivett, and Clare. And the poor children, Cecily and Lizbeth. Who would be next?

"Are they both going to die, Lily?" Charlie asked her quietly. "Because if they do..." he paused again, his dark hair falling over bloodshot eyes. "I will take care of you and Annabelle, and little Eddie."

"Charlie," she managed, though she wasn't sure how she did without a tear. She had to be strong for them. "That is not your concern. I have the shop and, well, they will not both die."

He gave her a look like she was only saying it for his benefit, like she didn't truly believe it.

Because she didn't.

"Here," she said, handing him a cup. "Go and feed this tea to Brother Simon. Annabelle," she called, beckoning the girl to her. "Dab this cloth on Brother Simon's head."

"It smells!" Annabelle scrunched up her face and held the cloth away from herself as she went to her task.

Lily finished preparing Elias' tea and then carried it up to him.

Wiping a rogue tear from her eye, she set down the tea on a nearby table, then lifted his head and shoulders and put them in her lap as she sat behind him on the bed.

"Elias, my love," she said softly, then a bit more firmly. She gave him a little shake until he opened his eyes. "There now, Husband. Drink this. Careful, 'tis hot."

She reached for the cup and held it to his lips. "Drink a little, Elias. Your fever needs to come down. Drink, my love."

He sipped some. She coaxed him to drink more, holding him in one arm, her head bent to his. "I will not let you go, Elias MacPherson. Not until you return to me."

"ELI?"

Elias turned to Simon and smiled. He didn't look around at his surroundings. He didn't care where he was. Simon was here and his friend had something to tell him. Something important.

He put is hands on Elias' forearms and looked up into his eyes. "Eli, I have to go."

He had never left. He had been in Elias' life for as long as Eli could remember. He would always be there. Would he not? "When are ye comin' back?"

Simon shook his head. His soulful gaze warmed. "'Tis time for me to go on home."

"I will go with ye, as ye always went with me," Elias told him and took a step forward.

"Lily is a fine wife. You chose well. She is very much in love with you."

Elias turned and looked behind him. "Lily," he said in a soft whisper. His heart pulled him back. He wanted more time with her. More nights, more mornings with her. He wanted to be with her to help her get through this life.

But Simon.

"Eli," his best friend said, his voice, so good and familiar to Elias' ears. He didn't want to stop hearing it. "Tell Lily that tears are water for her roots and will make her stronger, not weaker.

"As for you, I have loved you like a little brother and a son and I like to think I had some good in how well you turned out."

"Mayhap a wee bit. Half the time I was only pretendin' to ignore ye. The rest of the time I was listenin'."

They both smiled and wiped their eyes.

"Your father saved my life," Simon told him. "I went from being a slave to being one of Nicholas MacPherson's closest friends. I would have done anything for him. I vowed to look after you when you were little Eddie's age. I have kept my word to your father. You are Lily's now. You have little ones of your own to care for."

Elias pulled him into his arms...but his faithful companion was gone.

He opened his eyes.

"Simon!" he grasped at the air.

"Lily!" He heard Charlie call her name. She was there with Elias, sitting behind him on the bed. She moved him gently from her lap and then bolted to her feet.

"Brother Simon," she whispered and then hurried down the stairs.

Elias knew his old friend was gone. He left the bed slowly, but with more strength than he had last eve. He padded to the stairs and looked down at his family, his wife and his adopted bairns crying around Simon. He thought he might collapse, not from exhaustion or sickness, but from sorrow.

LILY LOOKED UP from Brother Simon's left side and thrilled at seeing Elias standing at the top of the stairs. He lived. He'd fought a monster and he lived. She wanted to go to him but she felt rooted to her spot, kneeling beside Brother Simon, trying to remain steady and steadfast.

Her gaze followed him as he came closer and reached for her hand to steady him. She stood up and let him take it. Feeling the weakness in his arm, she rushed beneath him and aided his next few steps.

"Where is Chisholm?"

"Dead," she told him beneath her breath.

He stood over Brother Simon with tears falling over his cheeks and onto the brother's hand. "Any man or woman would be blessed to have a friend like Brother Simon."

Lily and Charlie agreed, and then so did Annabelle, not wanting to be left out.

They bid him their farewells in waves of tears. Most of them.

"I dinna want his body burned. I want him buried," Elias declared.

"Who will dig, Elias?" Lily asked him, hoping he didn't think he was strong enough to do it himself. "Certainly not you! You are just out of bed!"

"Tomorrow. I will bury him tomorrow," he said as if it were now carved in stone.

Lily wanted to demand that he stay in bed for at least three days. She knew he wouldn't.

She looked down at Brother Simon. His body would remain here all day and all night, and until his grave was ready. They could lay him in the shed or in the back of the shop, but who would carry him there?

"I wish to take the children to Eleanor's. They should not—"

"Aye," he agreed. "They shouldna."

She went to him and touched her fingers to his face. He was cool.

"I will make you some tea first."

He shook his head. "Nae, love. Ye will go now fer I wish to have a wee bit of time with Simon."

She took little Eddie from Annabelle and turned for the door. She stopped and turned back around. "Charlie, come with me, please."

The lad shook his head. "I want to stay with—"

"Go with her," Elias told him. "Go on."

Charlie left the house and went the other way.

Lily said nothing and walked toward the village, to Eleanor's and asked her to keep the children with her and Terrick for the night.

She felt on the edge of a mountain-moving breakdown of her senses, her joints, her control, as if her weeping last night was just the beginning. She didn't want the children about when or if it happened. She was close though. She could feel the bubbling rumble in her belly.

She returned to the house alone and discovered Brother Simon covered with Elias' long plaid. She looked up to the second landing and prayed Elias was still in bed.

She was so happy to see him asleep but alive. She wished they hadn't had to bid farewell to Brother Simon on the same day Elias recovered.

She prepared some salmon from the night before and boiled him some tea, then carried it to him.

She stood by the bed gazing at him, half-covered by a thin blanket. It reached a little below his belly and draped his strong, shapely legs. His arms were cut from stone. One of them was slung over his head. The other was curled around his waist.

She wanted to go to him and fall into his arms, but he was fighting his own demons.

She set down her tray and touched her fingers to his face.

His eyes opened. He turned them on her.

"I came to feed you and check you for fever."

He nodded and closed his eyes. He grieved his friend. What could she do?

He opened his eyes again and looked at her. "Where are the children?"

"Eleanor agreed to take them for the night. Charlie walked off—"

The sounds of men's voices outside stopped her from saying anything else.

Had the bishop and his men discovered Bertram's body and come to take her to prison?

Lily bolted toward the window and spotted Alan and Father Benedict. They carried shovels with them.

Someone knocked on the front door, and then it opened and Charlie entered. "Lily?" he called. She moved to call back, but scolded Elias for swinging his legs over the bed.

"Morning, Lily," Alan called up to her. "Elias, you are looking well."

"I am well, thank the Lord," Elias said, coming to stand beside her with his blanket wrapped around his waist.

"We have come to bury poor Brother Simon." Alan bowed his head and crossed himself.

Lily's heart nearly burst with thankfulness and love for her neighbors. Now Elias could re—

"I will be oot to join ye in a moment."

What? She spun around to face him. "No! 'Tis too soon."

"Lily, I must! I am able. I will let the others do most of the diggin', but I will be there. I willna be moved on this."

He turned away to dress. She wanted to kick him. His pride and stubbornness would get him killed.

Charlie called up to her. "Was I wrong to tell them that Brother Simon had perished? They all liked him. They *love you* and would do almost anything for you. I knew they would help, as you have always helped them."

Her throat burned. She smiled through it. "No, you were not wrong. Thank you for thinking clearly when we," she paused and glanced back at Elias, "apparently, cannot."

"I will keep an eye on him when he comes out," he promised with a smile and left the house. She was glad she could be here for Charlie, and Charlie could be here for her, though it was Elias the boy clearly loved and wished to help.

She turned back to Elias. "What if you fall ill again? What will Charlie—?"

"My love, I must be there." The tears in his eyes gleamed in the candlelight. "D'ye not understand? The only time he ever left my side fer longer than a sennight was when we were livin' at the stronghold. Then, Simon stayed by my father. He was a loyal and steadfast brother to me. I will be there to see him off."

She nodded, understanding, but not being happy about it. "I will help you down the stairs when you are ready." She sat on her bed and watched him pull his thin, woolen léine over his head and shoulders and then let it fall down his chest and his flat belly. His long, strong legs were already covered in thick, black hose he'd pulled on while she spoke with Charlie.

He sat beside her on the bed and turned to smile at her. But she noticed his breathing was a bit labored. He pulled on his boots and ran his fingers through his hair.

"Is there a shovel in the small shed?" he asked her, rising from the bed.

"Elias, you are not well enough for this," she tried one last time.

He stepped close to her and kissed the concern from her lips.

"Come ootdoors and stay with me," he offered, withdrawing and leaving her without breath, "and ye will see how much I do, aye? I willna have ye worry."

She nodded and followed him to the stairs. He went down slowly, leaning on her when he had to.

"Ye are surprisingly strong fer one so slight," he remarked when they reached the bottom. He was silent when they passed his friend's body in the chair covered in his plaid.

They left the house together, slowly.

CHAPTER TWENTY-TWO

FOUR HOURS LATER, with the help of Lily, Father Benedict, Charlie, Norman, and Alan, Elias dug his best friend's grave close to Lily's garden. He didn't want Brother Simon burned as everyone else had been. No one challenged him.

Father Benedict presided over the burial. Everyone who was left was there. The children stood by Elias and Lily. Charlie patted Annabelle's shoulder when she cried.

When it was over, everyone returned to their homes for the afternoon. Since the brother's body was gone from the house, the children didn't need to be gone all night. Lily bid them to come home, but they asked to stay with Terrick for the afternoon. Elias and Lily agreed.

They returned to the house with Elias leaning on her with his right arm on her shoulders.

"How are you feeling?" she asked him. He'd kept his word and did not do much digging, but even a little was much for him.

"Just tired," he admitted.

"Come," she said as she took him by the hand. "Let me put you to bed and get you some tea."

"I grow weary of tea," he complained playfully. "I am hungry."

"That does not matter to me," she scolded. "You will drink what I give you. The salmon has spoiled. The villagers will bring food later and then you can eat."

She led him to bed and sat him in it then helped him out of his clothes. She did her best to see him as a patient and nothing more right now. The man needed rest from burying his best friend and recovering from the plague a day ago! How could tugging off his boots arouse her? Was he breathing harder? Faster? "Elias, are you feeling worse?"

"Nae," he promised softly and pulled his léine over his head. Her eyes drank in the glory of his sculpted shoulders and muscular arms as he undressed. She remembered the last time they were together. The pain, and the pleasure of his body…she thought she was a monster for having such intimate thoughts about him when they had just finished burying his best friend. But then he was a monster, too. Or just a soul in terrible need of comfort.

She leaned in and pressed her lips to his shoulder.

He groaned and her bones felt like dry tinder, her blood, pure flame.

Emboldened by his groan, she kissed his collarbone. If he wanted to stop, she would without question. But he pulled her wrists around his neck. She melted against his chest and tilted her face up to his when his hungry mouth sought her.

His lips burned hotter than her blood.

He dragged her over his lap to straddle him, she went with only a moan of her own. She landed atop a hard mound between his legs—a mound he adjusted with a sensual stroke of his hand under his hose.

It felt like a stroke to her when his knuckles touched her *there*. She sucked in on her lower lip when he flipped his hand over beneath his hose and slid his palm over her heat. His touch sparked another flame between her thighs. When he pulled his hand free, she closed her eyes at the stiff erection pushing against his hose, as if to get to her.

She pulled up her skirts and rubbed herself over the length of it and then waited anxiously for him when he lifted up his hips and pulled at his hose, releasing himself, hot and hard enough to lift her.

She glided over it one more time, taking in its fullness, and then set herself down on the head. Pain shot through her like a lance, but it didn't last. It couldn't last against the pure pleasure of impaling herself on him to the hilt and watching the rapture of his release, just before her own.

It was quick and filled with passion. Elias wanted more but soon fell asleep.

Lily washed and changed into her long-sleeved, indigo kirtle. The skirts were one layer and straight and the belted overcoat reached her hips.

She looked at him sleeping and felt the threat of a whole new army of tears gathering with the rest. She loved him and was thankful she could comfort him in the most intimate way.

She still hadn't told him about Bertram and the bishop wanting little Eddie dead. To keep the bishop's name unaffected by scandal, no doubt. She was still afraid that the bishop's men would find her once they figured out she had the babe and she had been the one who stabbed Bertram. She would have to tell Elias soon.

She heard a sound at her door and braided her hair behind her head, but when she hurried down the stairs to greet Estrid, entering the house, most of it had come loose. She wished she had thick hair like Clare—

She stopped as the memory of her pretty friend's smile swept across her thoughts.

She greeted Estrid and the two women embraced and held each other for a long time. They greeted Father Benedict and Norman and his wife, Hild, along with Emma and Ava, their daughters. Alan returned with his wife, Helen. Everyone, including Estrid, brought a pot of some dish or another and some brought fresh bread or dessert. Even Eleanor managed to prepare two of her delicious chicken pies with four children running around her skirts. When everyone arrived, they sat outside and ate together and spoke quietly about their lives and the loved ones they'd lost.

Lily wasn't surprised to look through her window and see her beloved descending the stairs inside. She barely heard what Father Benedict was saying to her and Eleanor about the children running around in the church earlier. She nodded. Aye, she would scold them, of course. "Pardon me, Father. I see Elias coming. I will go aid him."

Father Benedict bent to look inside and shook his head. "He does not look like he needs any help."

But Lily was already gone.

"My love, are you well enough?" she asked, rushing to him.

"To eat? Aye, I'm starvin'." He threw his heavy arm around her shoulders and kissed her then let her help him out.

Father Benedict intercepted them before they had a chance to get Elias any food.

"Young man, did I just see you both kiss? You understand she is—"

"My wife," Elias interrupted. "Brother Simon married us."

The priest looked taken aback. "He did not tell me."

Elias smiled at him, looking far too handsome for a man who'd had the plague. "He probably thought 'twas our decision when to tell everyone."

Father Benedict smiled. "Aye, of course. 'Tis good to see you up, Eli. Of course, we will have a ceremony in the church."

"Aye," Elias agreed then waited patiently while Father Benedict complained to him about Charlie, Annabelle, and little Eddie—and of course, Terrick the Terrible.

Finally, they were able to escape him, only to run into Norman, and then Eleanor and Estrid. Lily smiled, looking up at her husband while he reassured everyone who was concerned about him, loving him more than the last time she thought about how much she loved him. Especially after she heard his belly grumbling.

"You will excuse us while I show Elias to all your special dishes. He is quite hungry."

Everyone made way, eager to get him fed.

"You are part of the family," she told him, fixing him a bowl of Estrid's rabbit stew. "We must tell them about our marriage before my good name is ruined."

He chuckled softly, the sound coming from someplace low in his throat and traveling down her spine.

"Everyone!" he called out, taking the bowl she offered. "Brother Simon married me and Lily before we left. The children were present."

Charlie and Annabelle nodded. Elias smiled and winked at them and spooned some stew into his mouth.

He ate while everyone cheered. In fact, he ate three times while everyone came over to wish them well and ask them questions. When they had answered every one, Elias took little Eddie in his arms and walked him to Brother Simon's grave. He exchanged smiles with the boy and spoke to the mound before him.

A little while later, he called his two older children and Terrick to where he was.

Lily...and Father Benedict watched him speaking to them, listening to them, and then speaking again. They all nodded, including little Eddie and ran off once again to play.

He returned to the priest. "They will be a trouble to ye no longer." He reached for Lily and took her hand passing Father Benedict.

"What did you say to them?" Lily asked, a bit breathless at the way he had just whisked her away.

He led them to the other side of the house, where it was quiet and dark. When they reached the east wall, he stopped and pulled them into the shadows, against the house. "I told them the church is God's house and if they dishonored it again, they would shovel the cattle manure every day fer a month."

"A month!"

He nodded. "Aye."

"They are not fool enough to disobey," she remarked, and then giggled when he coiled his arm around her and dipped his mouth to her throat as he drew her in.

"I have been thinkin' aboot ye since I woke up alone in our bed."

"It was the middle of the day, sir," she told him with teasing indignation. "Was I supposed to lie around in bed all day with you?"

"Aye. I would like that." He dove for her throat and raked his teeth over her pulsebeat. "Send everyone away."

"And the children?"

He left her neck and breathed against her face. She couldn't see him, but she could hear him.

"I thought they were stayin' with Terrick?"

"They want to come home, remember?"

He shrugged his shoulders beneath her palms. "We will be silent."

He covered her giggle with his mouth. He drank her in. He tasted her, and explored her, and she showed him what she liked. Just a slight parting of her lips, enough to slip in and out of her mouth, soft strokes across her tongue. If she wanted more, she could suck him in deeper.

She thought about lifting her skirts and letting him take her here, but it was disrespectful to their friends who had cooked all day for them, after they'd buried Brother Simon.

He must have been thinking the same, for he withdrew from their kiss as well.

"Forgive me fer my peach-faced eagerness to be with ye?" he asked her with his head bent.

She smiled and took his head in her hands to turn his face up. "I am eager for you as well, Elias," she assured him.

"We must wait," he groaned.

"Aye," she agreed miserably.

They walked back to the western side of the house, and spent more time with their friends and their children, and each other. She told him what happened with Bertram in West Wickham just before the bishop's men had arrived, and she told him what the bishop meant to do to little Eddie. As she suspected, Elias was angry and swore to kill the bishop for trying to kill his wee babe.

Oh, how could her heart be so deeply, so madly in love with him in a fortnight? After a while of anxious fidgeting, Lily managed to gracefully announce that it was late and time for bed. She thanked everyone for all they had done and embraced each one as they began to leave.

She caught Elias' furtive wink and blushed.

She wanted to be with him again, but her passions ran high. Perhaps too high. He would surely bring her to the edge of the precipice again. What would happen if she fell?

They tucked Annabelle into bed with little Eddie. Charlie slept beside them on the floor, in a cozy nest of blankets and cushions. They sat with the children for a while talking softly about things until little Eddie and Annabelle, and even Charlie fell asleep. Then they stepped through the curtained doorway and Lily let the curtain fall loose, cutting off their rooms and giving them privacy. Still, Elias vowed to build a wall separating their rooms within the sennight.

She wanted to clean up a little in the kitchen. She kissed Elias and promised to come to bed in a short bit.

She felt on edge, like she had earlier today. She'd had all day to think about things. She couldn't relax or think right. She didn't want to know what tomorrow would bring. It wasn't over. Brother Simon was proof.

Finally, she climbed the stairs and entered their room without looking at him. She began tidying things up, stalling for time.

Her life had never been secure from the age of twelve on. Every day could have been her last. But it had been nothing like this. This involved others. People she loved. The man she'd fallen in love with.

She was afraid of teetering on the edge of madness. If she'd lost him...if she'd lost him to this...

He was quiet watching her then reached out for her from the bed. "Come, let us lay together. There is somethin' I wish to tell ye."

CHAPTER TWENTY-THREE

L ILY STRIPPED DOWN to her chemise and went to him. He pulled her onto the bed and into his arms. They lay under the blanket in a tangle of arms and legs, their faces close so they could speak softly and hear each other without waking the children.

"We have lost much in the last fortnight. 'Tis difficult to think of movin' forward," he said.

"I'm so sorry about Brother Simon." She wasn't sure if she'd told him in all the bustle of the day.

"Lily," he breathed hesitantly, as if he weren't sure he should say what he was going to say. "I saw him. I spoke to Simon. He came to bid me farewell."

She felt the wetness of his tears in her hair. She pulled him closer, trying to comfort him. She believed his words for she had seen him reach for his friend just as Charlie had called out to her.

"Lily?"

"Aye, my love?"

"He wanted me to tell ye that yer tears are water fer yer roots and will make ye even stronger than ye already are, and believe me, lass, ye are strong."

The bubbling was rising, climbing higher. Water for her roots. She felt like giggling but when she smiled, her eyes filled up with tears. Let them fall, she heard in her heart. Let them really fall. Oh, she couldn't. She was afraid. "I do not feel strong," she let out but even as she spoke, her throat felt as if it were closing up. She'd wept a little last night and she was able to stop. And today, over Brother Simon. But this was all of it. This was the storm, and panic engulfed her. What if she never stopped crying?

"My love," he said, gazing down at her. "Nothin' will hurt ye again."

Pressed against him, she closed her eyes. "What if I can never stop my tears once I let them fall?"

"Ye will stop. I will help ye."

She knew he could. He always helped her feel better. She looked at him and he smiled. She ran her palm down his cheek. "You were worth whatever I had to endure. If I knew you were at the end of every journey, I would go on each one." She could feel her nose turning red. Her voice quavered. She wanted to let it come and there was no one she wanted to shed her tears over more than for Brother Simon. She asked Elias to tell her about his closest friend.

"I think he was proud of me."

"He was," she pushed out. "He…he told me he was proud of the man you had become."

The bubbling spring finally erupted. She held on to him like an anchor in the storm as she wept for all her friends and their children, for Elias, for her father, for Richard, for Brother Simon, and for the strong little girl Bertram had tried to destroy. She cried for all of them and for every day she spent away from her father, her half-sisters. She told Elias through sobs and hiccups about the destitute, broken women she'd met while traveling with Bertram. She wiped her eyes but it was a heedless endeavor.

He held her and listened to her and soothed her while she sobbed out stories about Joan and Agnes, all the women she'd called friends for the last two years. She'd lost so much, but she'd gained Elias and a new precious family in the other room. "I want to go to Invergarry. I want to meet your kin."

"Yers now, as well."

She wept again at the thought of gaining another family.

After a quarter of an hour passed with her still weeping, she wiped her eyes and kissed his arm that was slung around her neck and made her feel safe. "Elias," she said with a sniffle, "are we keeping the three children?"

"Aye, and any more we find along the way. My home in Invergarry is modest but I can add to it and there is more than enough land fer many children. Not includin' the ones we have together," he added with a hopeful smile that made her laugh. "If we remain here, I shall add more rooms to this house and make it even bigger than Norman's."

It started as a giggle and grew into breathless laughter she muffled in his arm.

He held her and watched her, amused by what he saw. He kissed her smiling lips then he kissed her tear-stained cheeks. When he rolled on top of her, she didn't protest but coiled her legs around his to keep him close. She wanted this...she needed this intimacy with him.

He moved gently, slowly, running his palms over every curve he exposed while he pulled her chemise over her thighs, and her soft, ticklish belly.

He lifted himself up onto his elbows and stared into her eyes. "I love ye, my lady."

"Umm," she purred like a cat, feeling his strength atop her. "I love you, sir."

He found her wet and waiting and broke through like a husband home from a long absence and eager to see the love of his life.

They made love quietly though the sound of their breathing

boomed through their ears. Short, ragged gasps as he sank deeper, moved with more purpose, filling her with every inch and then retreating again. She dug her fingers into his back and gripped his hard, tight buns while he pushed her to the brink of ecstasy. She held on as he dove over the precipice with her, thrusting slow and deep until she almost cried out. He covered her mouth with his hand and then she did the same to his an instant later as they found their releases moments apart.

They slept, first, wrapped together and then apart, each back to their own usual sleeping position.

Lily didn't remember little Eddie crying in the night. Had he been too tired to wake? Or had she?

When she finally did rise the next morning, it was to find herself alone in the house. She washed and dressed quickly and dashed outside to find them. Silence met her ears.

"Elias?" she called out. "Charlie?" They wouldn't just leave her.

She didn't panic, knowing that Elias would die before he left her. And he wasn't dead. He'd fought off the deadly pestilence. He wasn't going to go down easily. She wasn't worried about Charlie either. He was very much like his new father. He'd fought the same illness and lived.

They must have gone to the village. But what was so important that Elias would wake the children and take them there?

She decided to find out.

She didn't get far when she saw Father Benedict outside, trimming the bushes around the church. "Father, 'tis good to see you well this morning," she greeted happily. "Have you by any chance seen Elias and the children?"

He smiled like he knew something she didn't and beckoned her forward. "Come, child."

"Come where?" She laughed softly, not understanding what he was up to.

She followed him to the church and entered the small, front foyer behind him.

He snapped his fingers and Annabelle sprang from her stool. Lily smiled at her and was about to ask where the others were when her friend's child, now her daughter, asked Lily to bring her head closer. She held in her hands a circlet of rosemary and pine interwoven with tiny white lilies and placed it over Lily's brow.

"Elias made it for you." The little girl smiled at her and then took her hand and led her inside. "Come," she beckoned Lily onward.

They turned the bend and Lily stopped to gasp and take in what was happening. She gazed upon dozens of candlelit faces, all turned toward the entrance, toward her.

She saw Estrid and Eleanor, Alan and his wife, everyone left in the village...and woven amongst them, she saw Joan and Clare, Agnes, Walter and Brother Simon. She saw them all, smiling at her.

She looked up the aisle and saw Elias waiting there for her, especially handsome in his Highland plaid, his tousled waves, and his fearless, confident smile. Charlie stood at his side with little Eddie in his arms.

Lily wasn't sure she could make it to the altar without the floodgates bursting open once again. This time with thankfulness for the man before her.

Annabelle led her to them then giggled with laughter and clung to his neck when Elias lifted her into his arms.

Father Benedict cleared his throat and Lily looked into Elias' eyes. In the deepest pools of silvery-blue, she saw what she meant to him, what the children meant to him.

He told her in his vows to her and before God, but she already knew. He would go to the ends of the world for her. Surrounded by their children, he promised to love and cherish her and them until the day death took him. (Which wouldn't be anytime soon if Lily could help it).

"I adore you and cherish you, Elias MacPherson," she told him. "I promise before God and these witnesses to be for you and never against you and to be a good mother to all your bairns."

Her heart pounded in her ears. Look what he had done for her! She could not wait to leave church and kiss him.

Father Benedict said a few more things, but it was the last thing he said that made Lily's heart go even faster. "You may kiss her."

She blinked. Richard hadn't kissed her.

She blushed and felt her blood swooshing through her as Elias bent, with Annabelle in one arm, and drew her in. His kiss was quick but filled with both possession and passion.

When he let her go, the villagers cheered and she blushed even more.

Elias led her and the children to the church dining hall, which was decorated with sprigs of flowering rosemary in neat bunches on the two tables pushed together and covered in undyed linen.

"What is all this?" she looked up and asked her husband. "When was there time to—"

He shrugged his draped shoulders. "I had told the priest my plan last eve at supper and he enlisted the help of the others. I was awake most of the night, restless to do this fer ye. I even prepared dinner."

She stopped and stared at him. "For all of us?"

"I cooked in the army, remember? Some nights, I cooked fer forty men. This is far less."

He led her and the children to the table and then disappeared again with Estrid and Eleanor.

They returned with ale and then with herring, boiled eggs and melted cheese, roasted chicken and brown bread.

Everything was cooked to perfection and Lily thought that watching Elias eat and laugh with her friends was one of the best parts of the day, besides marrying him again, of course.

"Oh, Elias," she breathed, sitting close to him. "This is all so thoughtful. I do not know how to thank you."

"Thank me later," he said on a deep-throated purr, raising his cup and the corner of his mouth to her.

She blushed and looked around at the faces smiling back at her. They knew! They had to know! Anyone could see the hunger in his smoldering gaze. Or did she alone see it?

He loved her. He'd gone through the worst days of her life with her and he made her smile. He went out of his way to make her smile. "Have I told you how much I love you, sir?"

He turned to her again and nodded, beaming at her. "I believe ye have, my lady, but ye will never hear me grumble aboot it."

"I better not," she warned playfully and sipped her ale.

After they ate, Elias left the table again and disappeared with Alan and the promise of a surprise for the children. He'd arranged to somehow get Norman to play his lute and Father Benedict, of all people, to play a psaltery. The mood was peaceful and pleasant. Lily laughed with Eleanor at the way Annabelle and Terrick constantly bickered. Some things hadn't changed.

Some things had, like Estrid admitting that she was glad Elias had come here—even if he and Brother Simon hadn't stayed at her inn.

Lily kept in mind that her friend Helen had lost her child, but she was glad to see her smiling and enjoying the day. This was what they all needed to heal. Rest and companionship.

She was no longer willing to permanently leave any of them—not even to go to Invergarry.

The sound of banging outside drew them all to their feet. They hurried outside and found Elias and Alan. The men had set up a small wooden stage with pinecones and flowers attached to the top. They both disappeared behind the three-foot wall, both men having to crouch low so their heads were not seen over the makeshift stage.

Everyone waited a few moments. Not a sound was heard. Then, from behind the wall, a doll appeared and then another. They were crafted of fabric and acorns and pieces of wood and they moved to and fro over the stage thanks to Elias' and Alan's hands under the fabric of the dolls.

The children all moved closer and laughed at the faces Alan had carved. Two had huge noses and pointy chins and strips of cloth for hair, the other two were left bald and had no noses, but protruding chins.

Annabelle squealed with excitement when Elias poked his head out the side and asked the children to all sit. They did, and Elias and Alan proceeded to act out stories they made up as they went.

The children...and the adults laughed at the dolls' antics and sat mesmerized, forgetting everything else but the dolls Annabelle affectionately called Big Nose, Baldy, No Nose, and Pinky (thanks to its pink "clothes").

When the performance was over, the children took turns behind the wall, handling the dolls and making up their own stories.

Lily went to her husband and let him pull her under his arm. "Thank you for this. For everything."

"The children seem to like it," he said then kissed the top of her head.

"I think 'tis masterful! Where did you first see such a thing?"

He shrugged and the movement pulled her even deeper into him. "France, mayhap Italy. I dinna remember. 'Tis as if nothin' before this mattered, and yet I know that it did. If I hadna fought, I would likely not have ever come here fer a remedy fer what ailed my heart. Everythin' brought me right here to ye." He smiled and raised his brow as if he were surprised and stunned by it all.

He awakened butterflies in her belly and she lifted her hand to her mouth and giggled.

"'Tis the truth," she agreed, sobering. "Bertram brought me here. 'Tis one thing he did good for me."

"Aye, Bertram. Ye said he was dead, aye?"

She nodded under his arm as they walked away.

"How d'ye know he is dead?" he asked.

"Because I killed him."

CHAPTER TWENTY-FOUR

ERTRAM CHISHOLM AWOKE in the bedchamber of a lavish manor house in Bromley. He looked around and then tried to sit up. He cried out from the pain in his hip and thigh and fell back on the bed. That bitch! The first time she missed, he was sure she was aiming for his balls. The second time she sent her blade flying into the back of his hip! Did she mean to hit him between his bones? It was the same kind of blow that Lion Heart had used on his arm. Bertram was still recovering from it and was sure he would never be able to use his sword again. Now this! His leg! He was going to find her and, this time, he would show her no mercy. He would kill her the way he should have years ago. Why hadn't he done it already? He'd wanted to make her life hell. He'd even gone back to Sevenoaks when he was sick hoping to spread the disease to her and her friends, and if Louis' bastard son were infected, so be it. Bertram wouldn't have to put his knife to the boy. He'd rather not have such a grievous sin on his soul as killing a child. But Lily hadn't become infected. She lost her husband and that made way for her stallion lover. She always came up out the dregs smelling like the morning mist.

"Who is there?" he shouted at the door. Who had carried him

away dying in a pool of blood? It had to be his cousin's men. Where was he? He demanded answers and shouted again and again until the door to his bedchamber opened. He narrowed his eyes, waiting to see who entered.

An older soldier, perhaps a little over two score years, came inside with two of his men behind him and another larger man at the rear of the two. He spoke calmly and with a chilling smile. His eyes were almost black, like his hair that was slicked back into a queue at his nape. His skin was tanned and weathered. Beneath his red uniform and muddy boots, he moved with elegance and authority.

"Mr. Chisholm, we meet again."

It was Commander Roger Parrock, his cousin's right-hand man. They had met once before in a castle in Winchester, when Bertram returned to Louis to tell him that his whore, Clare, had had a boy.

What should Bertram tell him now? That a veil of a woman had almost killed him and thwarted his mission?

"I was sent to retrieve a small boy called Edward. Where is he?"

"I had him but…he is with a woman—a slave of mine."

"You let a slave woman injure you and take the boy?" the commander asked without so much as a hint of amusement or mockery on his face.

The man behind him on his left smirked at him, as did the bigger brute at the rear.

"Aye," Bertram admitted, not caring what any of them thought of him. "She is a hellcat." He thought about her slicing off his—"If I had my way now, I would make her wish she never crossed me.'"

"Well, you do not have your way now," the commander told him with authority, making his voice louder. "The bishop wants the boy dealt with by this time tomorrow. Now, I must tell him that you failed yet again. Do you think he will be surprised?"

"I dinna give a shyte what he is." Bertram belched and scratched his head. "I dinna care what ye do with the boy. I am killin' the bitch."

The soldier to the commander's left mumbled under his breath, "I wonder why the bishop cares about what happens to a boy from some village."

Commander Parrock turned his dark gaze on him.

The soldier stared straight into his eyes with defiance in his gaze.

Parrock released his sword and pierced the soldier through with his blade and then pulled it out and watched the soldier collapse to the ground.

He looked at the soldier unmoved on his right. "Do *you* wonder anything?"

"Nothing at all."

"Good," Parrock said with a slight smile. "I would not want to kill one as pretty as you just yet. You will do as I say if you want to live. You will help me and I will make things easier for you. Aye? Good. Let us get ready to leave this place. Mustel," he said to the last man in the back.

Had Parrock just called the man Muscle, Bertram wondered? It would be fitting for he possessed many enormous ones.

"Help this miscreant stand and walk. You," he pointed to the man on the right, "stay with him and meet me at the table later." He turned to Bertram, who took little insult in being called exactly what he was. "Do you know where this slave took him?"

"Aye," Bertram answered. "She likely took him to where he lived."

"And where is that?" Parrock asked, his patience at an end.

Bertram had a feeling that Parrock wouldn't hesitate to kill him if he didn't need him anymore. He wouldn't tell him exactly where to find the boy. It would keep him alive until he thought of something else. "South of here."

Parrock moved closer, his dark, merciless gaze on him. "Where?" he growled.

A lesser man would have shyte his breeches, but not Bertram. What could any man do to him that was worse than what Lily had done?

"I dinna know the name of the place or if it even has a name at all," he said. "I need to show ye where it is."

"Very well. Be outside in an hour or I will cut out your tongue, since you do not need it to speak." He turned for the door and stepped over the first soldier.

The second soldier waited while the commander left and then he produced a blade that flashed in Bertram's eyes so that he almost missed the soldier's lightning fast movements. The man shoved the blade into Muscle's guts and then turned around to stand face to face with his dying victim as he twisted his dagger. "That is fer pushin' me."

Bertram watched, stunned as Muscle went down with a thump. "Ye there!" he called out in his loudest voice. "Help me! I am the bishop's cousin!"

The man turned around and aimed his striking green eyes on him. "I know who ye are."

"And ye?" Bertram asked him. The stranger was a Scot. That was for certain. Would Parrock hire soldiers from Scotland? They were known to be particularly violent people. "Are ye one of Parrock's soldiers?" He glanced down at Muscle, dead on the floor. "Or somethin' else."

"Somethin' else. Now move yer arse or stay here and die." He came near and gave Bertram his hand.

With the light from the hearth behind him and the crown of raven curls around his face, the man appeared radiant, like a dark prince come to aid Bertram in his ways.

Bertram took his hand and the man pulled him to his feet. Howling ensued. He would have a permanent limp from this. He may even have to walk with a cane! How would he ever fight again? What if Lily's friend, the Lion Heart was there at Sevenoaks?

"If ye shout—"

"I need more time to heal!" Bertram cried out, cutting him off.

"Time isna mine to give ye."

"I canna go yet! If she is there, she will remain there. 'Tis where she lived, too. Tell him. Tell Parrock that I need a few more days, just a few. My wound is deep."

"I'm not Parrock's man," the killer told him. "But I know he wants ye dead. He thinks quite poorly of ye, so I am savin' yer life. Now get movin'. He has more men with him and will return. I will be gone. Where will ye be?"

Bertram believed him about the commander. Parrock walked on the edge, like him, crossing over from life to death and back again. If he didn't fear the bishop, as everyone else did, he would kill Bertram. Bertram was surprised he hadn't already. He'd been clever not to give the commander the information he needed. Should he go with this ruffian?

"Verra well. Help me."

With aid, Bertram dressed quickly. His breeches had not been replaced and the blood had dried around the hole. Bertram looked through it, and then at the soldier. "She is a hellcat," he warned on a low voice, "and though she seems afraid, watch oot for her blade."

The Scot studied him. "Ye say she was yer slave."

"Eh, that is correct," he said with a grunt as he fastened his belt. "She was mine and then she turned on me and wed an old man to be free of me."

The man smiled and Bertram was tempted to look away and keep this stranger from looking clear through him.

"Ye were particularly abhorrent in her estimation, I would wager," the man remarked, his smile deepened into a smirk with a touch of something dark behind it. "So much that she would prefer the bed of an old man over sharin' one with ye."

"Particularly, aye," Bertram grinned back, exposing three missing teeth.

The Scot laughed then led Bertram out of the manor house. He killed four of Parrock's men on the way and set fire to the manor house.

Bertram watched the outlaw in awe, happy to be traveling with him. He wanted to get away from Parrock. He had never trusted the English commander. He figured this was his best chance of escape. The outlaw knew how to fight, that much was obvious. Why, he'd killed four men with ease, not including Muscle, speed and precision. It was like watching a masterful dance. Bertram needed him to fight for him. He would pay him anything.

The Scot put Bertram's arm around his neck, pulling the shorter man up a bit, and they hurried out through a back exit. The soldier disappeared around to the front of the house for a moment and then returned with a horse a few moments later.

Smoke was beginning to make Bertram's eyes sting. It was too painful for him to sit astride the large stallion, but bearable if he sat sidesaddle—like a woman. If he shifted his weight to one side, his wound wasn't so agonizing. Still, twice, he thought of going back and letting Parrock kill him.

"Scot," he said, trying not to sound too affected and mortified when the man leaped up into the saddle behind him. Sitting between the killer's legs was bad enough. Sitting between them sidesaddle was the worst embarrassment Bertram had ever suffered. But he owed this man his life.

"What is yer name and yer offense? Mayhap I will ask my cousin and he will grant ye a pardon."

The killer laughed but there was no humor in his gaze, only a detached iciness that Bertram had seen somewhere before.

"I am Tristan. Tristan MacPherson, and my offense is that I'm goin' to kill the bishop, and now, ye are goin' to help me do it."

Bertram's eyes opened wide staring at the Highlander. MacPherson? Bertram narrowed his eyes on him. Where had he—MacPherson.

Elias MacPherson! No! This murderous mercenary couldn't be kin to Lion Heart. His heart fainted within. Bertram would die before admitting it, but Elias MacPherson frightened him. Never had he seen anyone move so quickly once his knife was in the air—until he saw Elias MacPherson. But this one. Tristan, he said he was called. He moved even faster. His aim was to cause carnage and chaos, as the burning house and shouting men proved. He wanted to kill the bishop so killing a man of God didn't bother him. Had Bertram been a fool to go with him? This MacPherson would never fight for him as long as his relative was alive. What were they, brothers? Cousins? Oh, was this the end of him? Bertram lamented. The pestilence didn't kill him, would a mere man?

"Why do ye want to kill the bishop?" Bertram asked him.

"Why does the bishop want to kill a babe?"

"'Tis his son."

Tristan shook his head and stared at him. "And ye ask me why I want to kill him? No more questions. We are goin' to Oxford to see yer cousin. Ye will help me get inside his castle if ye want to live."

This could work to his advantage. Bertram didn't care about his cousin, Louis, all that much anymore. They had been close as children, but Louis had become a pompous ass who thought he shyte gold. Bertram wanted Lily. He wanted to drag her through her precious village by her throat. First, he had to get to Sevenoaks.

"I know a MacPherson," Bertram told him. "Elias. We call him Lion Heart."

"My cousin." Tristan took a good look at him and gave him a doubtful smirk. "Ye are friends with Elias?"

"Aye, he is a friend," Bertram told him confidently. "I am a bit concerned that he might be in trouble."

"Why?" Tristan's brows dipped low over his eyes, making them appear darker, like roiling storms gathering in the distance. "Where is he?"

"In the middle of the plague."

The killer pulled another dagger from somewhere on his person and held it to Bertram's throat. "Ye are goin' to show me where he is.'

Bertram pointed south and then thought of different ways to kill Lily as MacPherson set their horse toward Sevenoaks.

ANOTHER DAY AND no one woke up ill. Could it be over? Was it possible that they were both truly going to come out of this alive? They and the children? Elias would have laughed at her. Of course he'd never doubted it for a moment.

"You gave me hope, even when you were ill," Lily whispered across his chest. They had made love in a quiet house—thanks to Eleanor asking to keep the children for their wedding night.

"Ye have more courage than I, lass," he replied, running his fingers over her bare back. "When I thought ye were infected, I didna think I could go on."

"But you would have." She nestled closer into him.

He nodded and spoke in a quiet tone. "I had to face what I didna even understand was such a terrible fear for me until I thought ye were dead. I had to stand against it as I had done with so many other fears. I couldna run and hide, though I wanted to. Anythin' was better than goin' back to Sevenoaks without ye. But ye lived and I was spared."

She lifted her head and gazed at him. "And now you will be cherished and adored beyond measure by your wife and your children."

He smiled at her and leaned down to kiss her. "Then I shall need nothin' more."

"You are terrifying, Elias," she told him and licked his taste from her lips. "I have never seen a man fight that way you fought the bishop's soldiers at the inn. I can see why you were a commander."

"That is a part of me that will never come against ye, my lady. With ye, I am the gentleman knight ye deserve."

She giggled and gave his nipple a little tweak.

He yelped out and sat up, folding her shoulders and head between his chest and thighs.

She squealed with laughter and leaped from the bed. She turned for the stairs and made a step to run but his arm shot out and took hold of her. He yanked her back to the bed and climbed on top of her.

He looked into her eyes while he pushed her thighs apart with his knees and then sank deep inside her. She cried out. He scraped his teeth along her neck and moved his hips, withdrawing and thrusting, tightening his buttocks on reentry. She held them and guided him with gentle squeezes and salacious little slaps.

"Ye are bold, lass," he groaned and then erupted inside her, surging against her.

She watched and then rolled them over and took him from on top in the last moments of his rapture.

Aye, she was bold, and unafraid, and adventurous with his body. She worked her hips, undulating and pushing, impaling herself on him. She spread her body over his much bigger, much harder one, and trembled when he closed his arms around her, holding her waist in his hands.

He pushed her up, almost off him, then pulled her back down. He stayed hard enough to take her to the edge of passion and satisfaction and then leaped over the side of the precipice with her in his embrace.

They both slept until the middle of the night when Elias woke up hungry and padded down to the kitchen. He was quiet, but after only a few moments of sleeping in an empty bed, Lily woke up and followed him down.

They baked bread together and Elias took her from behind while they kneaded the dough. He moved slowly, naked against her backside. She cried out his name and sapped the last of his seed when she straightened and lifted her arms around his neck.

Later, they ate the bread, slathered in butter and washed it down with ale.

"I thought the last night we were together was the best night of my life," Lily told him, sitting next to him at the table, "but I was wrong. Tonight was even better than today."

He smiled, looking so handsome, disheveled and weary. "I like hearin' that, lass."

He popped another piece of buttered bread into his mouth and groaned with delight. "'Tis so warm. Like ye."

She blushed and let him chase her back to the bed.

Morning came too quickly. Lily wanted to stay in bed and sleep for another twelve hours. But the children were coming home and she missed them!

They washed and dressed then Elias left the house to fetch the children while she stayed behind and prepared them something to eat. She left the house to go to the field for fresh milk.

Strolling along in the morning sun, she thought about how happy she was. She saw Hild leaving the field and the two women waved and greeted each other. "Is everything well with you and Norman and the girls?"

"Aye, and you and Elias and the children?"

Lily explained that Elias had gone to bring the children home but, aye, she and Elias were well. She had a hard time not blushing and finally excused herself and hurried off.

She continued walking, feeling like a woman, sore from her husband and ridiculously happy about it. She brought her hair to her nose and inhaled. She could smell him on her. She liked it. She wanted to bring him back to bed, or behind the shed. She didn't care where, as long as she had him. And she did have him. She was his wife, she was adored, and she was certain she would be carrying his bairn in her belly soon enough.

She was finished living in her past with Bertram waiting to break her. Hatred hadn't done it. Love had. She needed to be broken in order to be put back together again, the right way.

When she saw her children running toward her a few moments later, laughing and calling to her, she waved and felt a ray of hope that the pestilence was over.

At last, it seemed as if the tragedies were finally over.

She welcomed her children in her arms and smiled at her husband coming toward her.

None of them were aware of the men watching from the trees.

CHAPTER TWENTY-FIVE

L ILY STOOD BEHIND her table in the shop and sliced off some sprigs of potted lavender. It was three hours after they ate and no one had turned up sick. She closed her eyes and said another prayer of thanks that it seemed to be over.

Still, almost everyone who lived had trouble getting to sleep at night. She knew of a good remedy that included lavender and chamomile and a few other things.

"Lily?"

She heard the dulcet voice of Annabelle and smiled, turning to look at the little girl walking in fanciful little circles into the shop.

"Aye, my love?"

"May I go play with Terrick?"

"I thought you did not like Terrick's company."

The petite girl looked at the herbs, not her. "I do not like him. But he is sometimes humorous and, that, I do like."

Lily did nothing to hide her smile at the six-year-old girl. "Aye. Humor is important."

She grinned and then stopped when Annabelle gave her a curious look. "Have you finished all your duties?"

"Aye."

"All right, then. Find Charlie. He is likely with Elias and little Eddie at church. Father Benedict needed your fath—Elias to help him move some things."

Annabelle smiled. "'Tis all right to call him that. I have never had a father."

Lily's heart swelled. "Very well, then. I will come get you before dark."

"Bring Father."

Now Lily did smile at the child's back. Annabelle loved Elias. They all did.

She examined several more stems and snipped more cuttings of lavender before she became aware of the silence from outside.

She dropped her cuttings into a basket on the table and, stepping around the table, she walked to the open door and looked outside for Elias and little Eddie. How long had it been now?

She looked around again. Everything was too quiet. The birds, the bugs. Even the wind had stopped. An uneasy feeling washed over her. She left the doorway of the shop and began walking toward Eleanor's house—where her children were. She felt the need to be near them, to protect them. She passed the church and kept going, quickening her steps until she reached Eleanor's door. She knocked and stepped inside.

"Annabelle?"

"Aye," the little girl came hurrying to her. "Here I am."

Lily breathed a sigh of relief. "Sweeting, where is Charlie?"

Annabelle shrugged. "He and little Eddie left already."

Lily frowned and went to the window. How come she didn't see them on the way here? She told Eleanor she'd be back soon for Annabelle and then left the house and headed for the church.

She was being foolish. Of course it was quiet. There weren't many people left in the village. It didn't mean something nefarious was going on.

She hurried into the church and called out for Elias. She didn't care if Father Benedict grew angry with her for it. "Elias!"

"I WANT TO hang it in the hall before the sanctuary." Father Benedict led Elias to the west wall where a very large painting of heavenly beings floating in the clouds was leaning against the wall.

They were in the basement. Father Benedict wanted him to bring the painting above stairs. "Mayhap with Alan's help—"

"Elias!"

He heard Lily's voice above stairs and ran toward it.

"Here!" he called back hurrying to her. She sounded alarmed.

"Elias, are Charlie and little Eddie with you?"

"No," he called back, on his way up. "Annabelle came lookin' fer Charlie. They went with her. Why?" He reached her, taking three stairs at a time. "What is it?"

"I do not know." She felt like a fool for alarming him. Charlie probably took the babe home for some food. "They left Eleanor's but they never passed me. And have you been outside? 'Tis too quiet and—"

He was gone in the next breath. Out of her arms and into the beginning of a storm.

The skies had changed to charcoal gray and rumbled with thunder, as if from within the earth, for Lily felt the vibration in her feet and in her legs as she left the church and stood behind Elias. She looked around and had the urge to scream for Charlie.

"Should we head home?" she asked Elias as the wind picked up and blew her hair around her face.

He listened for a moment and, twice, Lily thought she heard a babe crying. Little Eddie was the only babe in the village. She moved to run but Elias stopped her. "'Tis the wind."

She listened again and disappointment filled her. He was correct. The sound came from every direction.

She started for home, but Elias stopped her again. He moved in close so she could hear him. "If they are home, they are safe. If they are somewhere else, I intend to find them. If 'tis the bishop's men, we will find their horses first, so keep yer eyes open."

Aye, horses...unless they took Charlie and little Eddie and left!

Oh, she couldn't think it. She couldn't take another threat to her family. She felt for her knives hidden beneath her skirts and the ones secured to the belt at her waist. If she saw any strangers, she would throw her knives at them and question them after that.

After taking a quick look into the few homes leading to the largest one in the village, they came to Norman's house. They didn't request entry from their friend or walk right in. They listened through the shuttered windows for any sounds of their children and were about to move around to the other side of the house when they both heard a muffled cry.

They decided it was enough of a reason to enter, ready for battle. Elias asked her to stay at the church with Father Benedict, but she wouldn't hear of it. He didn't argue too long for he knew her and he loved this part of her. "Stay close to me then, Lily."

She agreed to that and entered the house quietly, blades drawn.

She knew the layout of the house better than Elias, so she led him to the different rooms.

When they came upon the large room where Norman held meetings with appointed officials—who were mostly dead, they heard a man's voice through the closed doors. Elias held his ear to the cool wood.

"When the hell will he be back?" one male voice complained.

"I do not know, James," said another. "Do I look like his nurse-maid?"

"We have not figured out yet what you look like, Gilbert," said another male voice. More laughter rang out.

"Do any of us look like nursemaids?" James roared. "I did not join the bishop's forces to look after children!"

He'd heard enough. Elias pulled back his leg and then kicked the doors in.

The room was quite large, more like a hall, with a long, wooden table and wooden chairs set around it. There was an enormous hearth with a blazing fire for warmth and more chairs, these cushioned, spread about the room.

Charlie and little Eddie sat in one of them. Charlie was doing his best to keep the babe from crying. Norman and his wife and daughters were there as well. Terrified but quiet.

Lily counted five men sitting around the table. They all bolted to their feet when the door cracked and split. She grabbed one knife by the handle and flung it at one of them. The blade settled nicely into his belly. It wasn't likely enough to kill him but Elias leaped onto the table and hacked at the man's throat, finishing him. He killed three more, while Lily threw her knife at the last man and hit him in the chest. He went down quickly, proving she'd hit him in the heart.

She ran to the children while Elias checked behind more doors and curtains.

They were alone.

Lily thanked God that the children were unharmed. According to Norman, these men had been waiting for someone to arrive, keeping little Eddie alive until he got there.

"He is the Bishop of Oxford, Louis Edmundson's child," Lily explained to the others.

Elias vowed to kill the bishop and the man the soldiers had been waiting for. But who was he? Charlie had only heard a name. Parrock.

They weren't going to sit around and wait for him to show up. They had to go now! They raced for Eleanor's house and gathered Annabelle and Terrick and his mother. Then they stopped at Alan's and after that, Estrid's. Nine of them were gone. Fourteen were left, not including Brother Simon and Elias. Either way, they beat the odds. Reports had come in to Norman about how sixty percent, possibly more of the people in London were dead. Lily wanted to weep for every one of them, but now was not the time. Now it was time to move. Where would they go?

Elias was leading them back to the church. One by one, he made certain everyone entered. He directed them to the basement with Father Benedict, then he shut the door and stayed above stairs with Lily, Alan, and Norman. Lily filled the others in on what they knew. The bishop wanted his son, little Eddie, dead. While many kings fathered illegitimate children, most bishops did not.

"We will protect him with our lives," Alan swore.

"Let us hope it doesna come to that," Elias said.

He stationed them near a window on every side to look out for any movement. There shouldn't be any, for no one else was left.

Lily stared out of a window on the west wall. Elias covered the south. It was closest to her but still far enough away that they could not speak without shouting.

What kind of monster was this Parrock that he could do the bidding of another even when asked to kill a child? Oh, she hoped Elias got his hands on that one. She wondered how they had found her and suffered the horrible notion that Bertram hadn't died after all—again. No. She had seen all the blood. He had been bleeding out on the floor.

But what if he hadn't died?

She turned, wanting to go to Elias for reassurance. Her one hope remained that Charlie and Norman hadn't heard mention of Bertram, nor had they seen him. Then how had Parrock's men found little Eddie?

The rush of horses' hooves outside her window snatched her breath clean out of her body. It was them! How many? They passed her window! She jumped up and ran to the next window in their path. It was the one Norman was guarding. She looked out. Three riders. She ran to Elias with Norman behind her.

He was already on his way to them. "Three. There are three of them," she told her husband. He nodded and they all ran to Alan's window to look out at Norman's house.

The three men dismounted slowly, cautiously. One of them called out. No one answered. That was because his men were dead.

"They are goin' to start searchin' the cottages," Elias told them. "Then they will come here. I want ye all to go down—"

"No!" Lily was the first and the loudest to refuse. Alan and Norman were not far behind.

"There are only three of them," Elias argued. "I will have no trouble with them. Ye will do I say in this," he said to all of them but stared at Lily. "The children need their mother, my love."

"They need their father, as well."

"They will have him," he promised with a tender smile. "I will be well. Now go."

She went, rather than have it appear as if he had a wife who defied him at every turn.

In truth, she was happy to get back to the children. They looked terrified. They had been through so much, each one of them. "There are only three men," she said, reassuring Charlie when he insisted on going above stairs to help Elias. "I have seen him fight. He will return to us."

Still, Charlie climbed the stairs and sat at the top, by the door. He pressed his ear to the wood and closed his eyes.

Lily wiped hers and went to Father Benedict and asked him to lead them in prayer.

BERTRAM HUNKERED DOWN on the other side of a slight ridge to the west of Alan and Helen's cottage and watched everything. When he saw Parrock arrive, his blood went cold. How could the commander's men have arrived before him? Granted, it had taken him and Tristan a little longer to arrive because of his condition. He could not help from slipping out of the saddle. The pain of bouncing was unbearable. A few times, MacPherson had threatened to throw him from the saddle and continue on without him. But Bertram knew that he was now a pawn in the hands of a proficient killer for hire. For that's what the Highlander did to earn coin. He killed and, according to him, many prominent Scottish barons wanted Louis killed and had hired Mac-Pherson to do it.

"Why do they want Louis dead?" Bertram had asked him before they got here.

"Because he is a madman. He should never have been given the honor of his title but Edward needed a man in the church as cruel and as devious as he was."

Bertram looked at Tristan now, lying on his back in the grass, knocked out cold by a rock to his head. What was he supposed to do? Tristan was never going to let him kill Lily *or* the boy. He only wanted to make certain Lion Heart was alive and well and then he was going to go after Louis.

Bertram didn't kill the Highlander. If it weren't for him, Bertram would have died at Parrock's hands. But he hoped his good deed didn't come back to bite his arse. It was only the second one he'd done in his lifetime. The first was when he let the babe, called little Eddie after his father, live.

He would have liked to use MacPherson's bow and arrow but he feared the man would awaken. He could have killed Tristan but all he had was the rock and hitting the Highlander hard enough to knock him out had taken every bit of strength Bertram had.

He had to move. He took his time, holding on to trees. He needed to rest after a moment or two, but Tristan would not sleep all day and Bertram wanted Lily dead, so he kept moving. He didn't care about escaping. She had taken everything from him and then tried to take even more. If he died, so be it. He was taking her to hell with him.

He made his way toward the church at about the same time as Parrock's men did.

CHAPTER TWENTY-SIX

ELIAS KICKED OPEN the heavy, wooden church door. He waited with his axe in one hand and his sword in the other. He didn't step outside. He had the advantage over the soldiers since they had to come at him through a doorway. The first man in received a chop to the throat with Elias' axe. He left it where it landed and blocked the heavy blade of the second man with two hands. He rolled his wrist around and made his blade dance through the air. It sliced across the second soldier's face, neck, chest, and belly. All in a matter of seconds. The man dropped to the floor bleeding from everywhere.

Elias didn't think either man was Parrock. No, the commander waited outside for him.

With one last look at the basement door, Elias left the church. His eyes were like that of a hawk's on its prey. Patient and merciless. Where was Parrock hiding? He would come out soon enough. He was alone, and he should be afraid.

Elias made his way to Eleanor's cottage carefully, and then to Joan and Clare's empty houses. "What kind of fearful boys does the bishop send to fight me?" he called out.

He heard a movement in Clare's cottage and went closer to it.

"Come now, Parrock. Surely everythin' ye heard aboot me isna true. What matter is it that I killed eight of yer men? It only means ye hired unskilled peasants. Come oot and fight me and let us see who stands at the end."

Elias could almost hear Simon admonishing him for being so reckless.

He caught a movement at the end of the path to Clare's cottage. He turned to see a man coming toward him.

He readied his sword.

The man held his own blade in his hands but he did not hurry his steps.

His eyes were dark, matching his slicked back hair. He looked to be living in his late thirties or early forties. His skin was weathered and rough looking, like leather.

"I have heard nothing about you stranger," he corrected Elias' earlier presumption.

Elias quirked his mouth to one side. "Perfect. 'Tis more merciful that way. Ye dinna know what is aboot to befall ye."

"Where is the boy?"

Elias offered a fake pout as they reached each other. "I was hopin' ye wouldna ask that." He swung his sword high over his head then brought it down hard above Parrock. The commander blocked and then parried, driving Elias back on his feet.

"I have no quarrel with you." He changed position and took a step back.

"The boy is my son," Elias told him.

"No, he is the bishop's son."

"The bishop has no more right to him. He lost it all when I adopted the boy and discovered the bishop wanted him dead. Imagine how I will protect him now that he is mine. I will no longer sleep if I must. I will kill ye, and I will kill yer bishop." He swung and swiped and slammed his sword down hard, again and again on Parrock's arm. The commander might be experienced, but the wear on his arm was now showing.

One more colossal chop and Parrock's sword fell.

Elias held his blade across the commander's throat and closed his eyes. He didn't want to kill this man. He'd seen enough needless death, including the villagers and their children dying of the pestilence. Enough!

He stepped away. Then leaped back when an arrow came flying and landed in Parrock's throat.

What now?

Elias picked up Parrock and used him as a shield as he ran for cover around the side of Clare's cottage.

He heard footsteps running and readied his sword. He was ready to swing when he saw his cousin. His cousin? What the hell was Tristan doing here?

"Eli! Are ye well?" Tristan grabbed him by the front of his plaid.

"What the hell are ye doin' here, Tristan?"

"I'm after the bishop. I hadna planned on killin' Parrock—and that bastard cousin of his hit me in the—"

"Cousin? D'ye mean Bertram Chisholm?"

"Aye," Tristan answered, "yer friend, accordin' to him."

"He is no friend of mine," Elias told him. Damn it to hell, the bastard was still alive. "Ye said ye had him, Cousin. Where? Where is Chisholm?"

"I dinna know," Tristan told him, his expression going darker at the horror on Elias' face while he spoke. "He smashed me over the head with a rock. What? What is it?"

Elias didn't answer but ran for the church.

"Who is the woman he wants to kill?" his cousin asked, racing on foot to catch up.

"My wife," Elias told him and sprinted forward. He reached the church door first. He ran inside and looked at the door at the bottom of the stairs. It was open. Bertram stood against the wall with Charlie under his arm and his knife at the lad's throat. Elias was going to kill him.

Seeing him and his cousin, Bertram moved with Charlie along the wall. The lad saw him and made a move to fight his captor. Elias held him still with a subtle shake of his head. As long as that knife was against his throat, any kind of heroics could cost Charlie his life.

"Bertram, I will do whatever you want from this moment forward if you let the boy go unharmed," Lily told him. "If not, I will set his father free upon you to rip you to pieces and beat you to death. He is barely restrained right now." She pointed to Elias.

What was she doing? Did she think he, her beloved husband, would use her as a pawn?

"Swear it to me before God," Bertram demanded, knowing her. Knowing, as Elias did, that she would not go back on such a vow.

But Elias also knew, thanks to Simon's constant teaching while he hovered about him, much about God's laws. Since Elias was her husband, he could reject her vow and God would forgive her.

He rejected it.

He waited for her to agree to Bertram's demand. When she did, Bertram set Charlie free, pushing him toward her. Elias kept one eye on Bertram and one on his son arriving safely into the arms of his wife.

One of her hands slipped under her skirts. When it came back out, it held the blade of a knife.

She pushed Charlie away and pointed the handle at Bertram. "Do not tempt me." Her voice shook on a low warning. "Do not."

"Lass! I'm Tristan MacPherson. I need this bastard alive to get to the bishop."

Elias didn't want his son, Eddie, growing up in a world with the bishop. If Tristan could get close to him, then he was for it. Even if it meant letting Bertram live. *Yet again.*

She lowered her knife and turned to them. "Tristan *MacPherson?*"

"Aye, lass," his most handsome of cousins said, smiling at her.

While they became acquainted, and the others broke apart from the huddling mass they were—behind Norman, Alan, and Father Benedict, Elias went to Bertram and yanked his arms behind his back. He ignored Bertram's howls about the pain in his arm and a few of them, like Estrid, told Elias to pull his arm harder.

"I'm goin' to come back fer her. I'm goin' to heal and raise an army and—"

"Who wants to cut oot this man's tongue?" Elias called out. All the men, including Tristan and Charlie, held up their hands to be seen.

"See it done," Elias ordered, waving his hand. He set his gaze on Bertram and smiled. "Let us see what kind of army ye will raise without the use of yer words."

He watched as the men carried him away. Soon, no one would have to listen to him.

"I trust he can show ye the way to the bishop without his tongue," Elias said to his cousin, standing beside him.

"'Tis how I found this place," his cousin murmured, watching them take him away. "He didna want to tell me what the village was called, only that everyone here suffered the plague. Includin' ye."

"That much is true," Elias told him. "I have recovered. Many didna."

Tristan stared at him and shook his head. "Any advice to avoid gettin' it?"

"Wash yer hands often and eat the rind of a lemon every day," Lily told him. She was still smiling.

"Stay away from people who have it." Elias told him, not smiling.

When his wife giggled, his heart went soft and he smiled at her. He put his hand to her flat belly and swept it around to her back. He encircled her waist with his fingers and laid claim to her with a kiss to her neck, just below her earlobe.

She blushed and slapped him away, then hurried to the children.

"Ye wed the hellcat," Tristan remarked with a wide, understanding eye. "She is bonny. And surrounded by the love of the village children, she appears more like a dove."

Elias nodded, fastening his gaze to her. She was fast and fearless, and she had enough passion against Bertram in her to kill him. She was brave, giving herself up for Charlie. She was merciful, doing as Tristan asked and letting her former master live.

When she looked at him over her shoulder, he winked and she smiled.

TRISTAN STAYED FOR supper and to help bury the fallen soldiers and Parrock—without his head—that part was put into a sack filled with herbs and leaves that Lily had supplied. They would keep it fresh for a few days, and tied to Bertram's horse.

As much as it sickened Lily, she accepted that it had been best to kill at least one of them...and render the other almost completely helpless.

With Bertram tied up in the shed, a rag stuffed into his tongueless mouth, Tristan stood over Brother Simon's grave and prayed, and then they ate and shared stories beneath the setting sun.

"Did ye cultivate this abundant garden?" Tristan asked Lily after a supper of tasty turnip and cabbage stew.

She nodded and then shook her head. How was any woman who didn't have someone in their life like Elias supposed to resist Tristan's emerald eyes and curious smile?

"He is pretty, my love, but 'tis the sight of you, the scent of you that intoxicates me," she told Elias later that night while she straddled him and took him fully.

She looked into his eyes and revealed all she was to him—and then took in everything he was. The good and the bad. She would take him any way he came.

"You are everything to me," she whispered against his neck, grinding up and down. "You are my hope. You become my hope more each day. You stand utterly immovable against everything that comes against you." She pushed down to his hilt then rose up like an empress awakening from her nap "There is just one thing—"

"What is that?" he asked skeptically and gave her a push until she sat up, impaled on him. He slipped his hands behind her and gave her bottom a sharp little slap. He took her by her bottom and by her nape and thrust himself deep inside her over and over until her untamed passion spent itself upon him.

She was mortified by the sounds she made in her ecstasy, high-pitched, and grunts, and unintelligible words that should not pass from any lady's lips. Though Elias seemed to like it.

After, she pulled him to the brink of complete surrender, when he emptied his seed into her with a few sounds of his own.

"You do not believe in how much I love and adore you," she whispered, holding him. "That no one could ever have my heart after you have had it. 'Tis yours, Elias."

For a moment, she thought he might have fallen asleep. But then he spoke, "Forgive me fer not appreciatin' what I have been given. I never thought I would have this. I never thought I needed it. Fer a long time, I thought I would never recover from the ghosts of war," he said softly, quietly, trusting her with everything, every part of who he was. "But then I met ye, lass, and the more my mind becomes filled with ye, the less filled it is with those ghosts. I find myself well in the midst of darkness and death. I find the me who once was, better because of who I have become, and excited again to see who I will be.

"Ye are…" He paused to let his dusky blue gaze stare into her eyes. "Ye are the most beautiful lass my eyes have ever seen."

"Elias," she laughed, blushing. "No."

"Aye." He pulled her close. "My eyes will never stray from ye, my lady. My heart is yers. Always."

She finally felt safe and fell into a deep, restful sleep.

And so did Elias.

CHAPTER TWENTY-SEVEN

The village of Sevenoaks, England
Late Spring
The Year of Our Lord 1349

"GOOD MORNING, LILY," Father Benedict greeted her merrily when she strolled by him on her way to the shop with a basket piled with herbs looped through one arm. She waved at him with the other.

"Good morning to you, as well, Father."

"'Tis cold, child," the priest admonished. "You should wear your cloak. I know you have that fur-lined mantle Richard purchased for you last winter."

"Father, 'tis a perfect day. The sun is shining and warm—but I shall wear it tomorrow if it gets colder," she promised when his scowl grew darker, and then she kept walking.

She didn't mind the crisp air. It awakened her body...and she needed it. She was exhausted every single day no matter what time it was and also sick to her stomach. Eleanor, Hild, and Helen assured her that all was well. Lily was heavy with child, due in just a month. The last stages were difficult, according to her older, more experienced friends, because everything in the body was stretched to its limit, preparing for the birth. That kind of talk didn't make Lily feel any better.

Lily knew a few remedies for nausea but she didn't take them. She didn't mind being ill with Elias' babe. She wanted to enjoy every moment of it. She was alive. Elias was alive. Charlie, Annabelle, and Eddie were alive. And now she and Elias were bringing another life into the world. It truly amazed her and as she had heard Elias and dear Brother Simon do, she gave thanks to God.

As she neared the shop, she saw Annabelle and Terrick playing together in front of Eleanor's house. She didn't remember them being such close friends before the pestilence came. Tragedy brings people together. They'd gone through terrible days. Just like her and Elias.

She waved at the children and at Charlie, carrying sacks of seed to the shed.

Elias had awakened the children early, as he had every morning to let her sleep more. The children didn't mind. They loved doing things with or for him.

She tried to pick up her steps to get to the shop faster, but the babe kicked in response and made her feel ill, so she slowed.

She finally reached the shop and stepped inside. Elias was behind the table speaking with Alan on the other side. Eddie sat on top of the table, swinging his legs over the side.

When he saw Lily, he leaped off and was caught in mid-air by Elias' quick hands. He set him down and the boy ran on chubby legs to her. "Mama!"

She bent with a wide smile to pick him up in her arms. She loved Clare and she promised her every night that she would love Eddie with all her heart. And she did. She planted kisses on his face and laughed with him.

"Oh!" She opened her eyes wide on Elias and placed her hand on her huge belly.

Elias ran around the table to her. "What is it? Is it time?" he asked with a frantic note in his tone. "Ye are early—"

"The babe kicked me very hard," she told him. "He or she must be jealous of my little darling Eddie." She kissed him again and again the babe kicked her. She grabbed Elias' hand and set his palm on her belly, in the place where the kicks were happening.

She kissed Eddie and he squealed with laughter, so she did it again and again.

With his hand on her belly, Elias looked amazed and laughed. "This one has a temper!"

The babe kicked against his hand and then stretched its leg and pressed its tiny foot to Lily's belly. She told Elias what his bairn was doing and he chased Alan out, pulled her and Eddie to the back room, and lifted her skirts over her belly to see the outline of the babe's foot.

Elias made a small sound in the back of his throat and then fell before her on his knees. He placed his hands on her bare belly, on the foot, and let her skirts fall back down over his arms.

"Good mornin', babe," he whispered close. "'Tis I, yer father."

Eddie squirmed in Lily's arms and reached down, almost hanging upside-down, to touch her belly, too.

They fussed over both of their children and then continued on with the day.

No one had fallen ill with the pestilence again after Brother Simon had died. It was over. For them.

Elias' cousin, Tristan, had returned a few months back and let them know that the plague was still rampaging through some cities. He'd killed the bishop, but Bertram had escaped him.

Tristan had vowed to hunt him down and kill him, and Elias promised to kill him the instant he showed his face here.

But he hadn't shown up. Perhaps he had finally given up trying to ruin her life. She didn't know, but she always carried her knives with her.

Elias straightened and dipped his head to kiss her. "Did ye sleep well, my love?"

"I would have if our babe had slept," she told him with a little laugh.

"Good morning," Eleanor called out from the front of the shop.

Lily hurried around to see her and they spoke about the children and about food, and sewing. Elias smiled every once in awhile when he caught her eyes.

He finished mashing up some coriander and put it into a square piece of cloth, then wrapped it up with twine. "Alan wanted this and I forgot to give it to him after my bairn interrupted me. I will go take it to him."

Lily nodded and continued talking to Eleanor for another quarter of an hour. She didn't see two mounted riders passing the other houses and coming toward the shop.

When she did, she grabbed Eddie and ran outside for Annabelle and Terrick.

"Pardon us," said the first rider, an old man beneath a dark brown hood. He sat upon an older mare. The rider behind him also wore a hooded mantle but Lily could see a hint of a chestnut braid falling over a delicate shoulder.

"What do you want?" Lily didn't care about being polite. She'd been through too much to trust anyone she didn't know.

"We are looking for the village of Sevenoaks," said the old man. "We received a letter several months ago claiming my daughter, Lily, lived here. I have not seen her in nine years. Please, Miss, if you know of her, tell me where I might find her. We have been traveling for a while now and I hope we are finally in the right place."

Lily's knees shook beneath her. Was it...? She drew in a deep gasp and took a step forward. She held her hand up to her brow for shade against the sun and gave the old man a more careful looking over. It was her father. Was it possible?

"Aye. You have the right place, Papa."

The woman with him pulled back her hood and leaped from her saddle. "Lily?"

Her half-sister. "Sarah?"

They both began to cry but Lily reached for her father as he dismounted. She never dared to dream of seeing him again.

"Lily?" his weak voice called out as he pushed back his hood. "Is that you, my sweet Lily of the valley?"

"Papa, you are alive. 'Tis you. 'Tis you!" She fell into his arms and wept into his shoulder.

Then she stepped back and drew her half-sister in for a long, tearful embrace.

When she withdrew, she saw that Eleanor had been joined by Father Benedict, Norman and Hild. They had all come out of their homes to see who the riders were.

"Look everyone!" she called out to them in tears. "'Tis my father and my half-sister, Sarah!" She looked at her. "Where are Mary and Eva?"

"They did not survive the pestilence," Sarah told her, dabbing her eyes. "Nor did anyone in their families. They lived in London. Most there died. It was not so bad in Hastings where father and I remained."

Everyone was quiet for a few moments in respect of the dead. Then Lily went back to her father. She couldn't keep from staring at him. "Papa, from whom did you receive such a letter?"

She saw Elias coming from the path to Alan's house with Charlie and wanted to call out to him. Her father! Her father had found her!

"'Twas from a man called Elias MacPherson."

Her father's words sank deep. From Elias. She wasn't surprised that he had done such a thoughtful thing for her. But she would never stop loving him more for each thing he did. But this...when had he...how had he...?

"Is he here, Lily?" her father asked her. "Is he here so that I may thank him for bringing back my dear babe to me and doubly so since you will soon give me a grandchild?"

"He is here, Papa," she told him. "He is my husband."

"Elias!" She went to him and set her teary, loving gaze on him. "'Tis my father. How did you find him?"

"I didna. I sent my letter to a friend of mine, the Earl of Pembroke, Baron Hastings, and asked him to look into findin' them. I wasna certain he could."

He greeted his new "kin" with open arms and well wishes and announced to everyone that there would be a celebration tonight in his great hall—the one he built onto the house with the red roof, down the hall from the three bedchambers for his children, separate from the bedchamber he shared with Lily above stairs.

Norman invited her father and half-sister to stay in Sevenoaks if they wished. They had two cottages that were still empty. Alice's and Clare's.

Two hours later, plans for the celebration were halted while Lily labored with her child. She was a month early and everyone was afraid it was too soon. But the newest MacPherson was coming whether they were ready or not.

Cecily Lizbeth MacPherson was very small, but she came into the world screaming, only to be quieted at her mother's breast.

Elias had never left Lily's side, holding her hand and feeding her tea, prescribed by her father. He was the first one to hold his baby daughter in his arms. The second was her grandfather, and then her siblings.

"I am goin' to miss yer belly," Elias said, lying down with her and the babe later that night and running his hand over her considerably smaller stomach.

She giggled and leaned into him, sleeping Cecily between them. "Is everyone eating?"

"Aye," he told her. "The lasses have taken care of the birthin' bed and everyone has gone to Norman and Hild's house so ye could rest quietly with the babe."

She smiled, loving them all so much, thankful for those she had left. She wouldn't leave them. She would visit Invergarry, but she would live here with her family, with her father and Sarah. She could scarcely believe it was real. She had Elias to thank for all of it. She would never stop thanking him. She would never stop loving him in life or in death.

Her smile grew looking at him. "I am happy."

"I am happy, too." His smile was just as bright.

She giggled at them both, and then yawned. "Are you going to Norman's? I am hungry. And bring my father back with you," she added, calling out before he left.

She lay in bed for a little while staring at her new daughter.

She was fair, like Lily, and she was already strong-willed, like both her parents.

Lily wiped her eyes and leaned down to kiss Cecily's head. She looked up to see Charlie standing in the doorway.

"May I come in?"

"Of course, my love," Lily replied, her joy overflowing as he stepped inside and came close to the bed.

"How is my sister?" he asked, gleaming down at her.

"She is well."

"Thank you for calling her Cecily. I love her already."

She was about to reply when she caught a movement out of the corner of her eyes coming up the stairs.

Lily didn't move at the sight of Bertram standing at the doorway. Charlie was just as still, his back to the man who had taken her childhood from her.

He would take no more.

She sat up and shielded her babe from him, then reached under the blanket for her knife. She knew he'd come back one day. She'd been prepared.

Bertram tried to speak but was unable and growled at her instead.

Lily pulled the knife free at the same time Charlie turned his body and flung a knife of his own at him. The two blades hit their mark in Bertram's throat.

They watched him fall to the floor.

Lily was quite stunned. She'd known Elias wanted to teach Charlie to throw, but goodness, he was good at it.

"Charlie—"

He turned and smiled at her over his shoulder. "I have been practicing, Mother."

"You saved us," she said tenderly.

"We both saved us," he replied smiling. He threw his arms around her and told her he loved her and Elias, Eddie, Annabelle, and now Cecily.

They both scowled at Elias when he shouted from the doorway with Bertram at his feet, "What the hell is this?" loud enough to shake the walls and wake the babe.

"'Tis Bertram!" Lily told him happily then watched him hand over the tray of food he had for her to her father and then drag the body away.

Elias was still shaken though they were unharmed and came into the room. "Charlie, is that yer knife in his throat with yer mother's?"

When the boy nodded, Elias' glittering gaze met his son's. "Come here to me."

When Charlie went, Elias cupped the boy's face in his hands. "'Tis a serious thing to take a life. We will speak of this later."

"This is another thing I'm thankful to be here to see," Lily's father said, looking down at Bertram. "The death of the man who took my child from me."

Elias, still pale, went to his wife and took her in his arms.

"Do not be hard on Charlie, my love," she whispered into his dark, glossy locks. "He is growing up."

He nodded then kissed her head. "He will be a good man."

She heard the sound of her soon-to-be three year old running down the hall to her room. He squealed with laughter at Annabelle chasing him.

"May I hold my new granddaughter?" Lily's father asked. "And perhaps later you will tell me of your life."

"The past no longer matters, Papa," she said, handing the babe to him. "This, right here, is what matters." She wiped her eyes but the tears did not stop.

She didn't mind them anymore. They were there to water her roots and make her stronger.

She had everything she had ever wanted, and she had Elias Mac-Pherson to thank.

The End

About the Author

Paula Quinn is a New York Times bestselling author and a sappy romantic moved by music, beautiful words, and the sight of a really nice pen. She lives in New York with her three beautiful children, six over-protective chihuahuas, and three adorable parrots. She loves to read romance and science fiction and has been writing since she was eleven. She's a faithful believer in God and thanks Him daily for all the blessings in her life. She loves all things medieval, but it is her love for Scotland that pulls at her heartstrings.

To date, four of her books have garnered Starred reviews from Publishers Weekly. She has been nominated as Historical Storyteller of the Year by RT Book Reviews, and all the books in her MacGregor and Children of the Mist series have received Top Picks from RT Book Reviews. Her work has also been honored as Amazons Best of the Year in Romance, and in 2008 she won the Gayle Wilson Award of Excellence for Historical Romance.

Website:
pa0854.wixsite.com/paulaquinn

Printed in Great Britain
by Amazon